Postcards from Garda

Mother Mary Agnes

Postcards From Garda

Rosaleen Orr

Kennedy & Boyd

Kennedy & Boyd
an imprint of
Zeticula Ltd
Unit 13
196 Rose Street
Edinburgh
EH2 4AT
Scotland

http://www.kennedyandboyd.co.uk
admin@kennedyandboyd.co.uk

First published in 2015
Text and illustrations Copyright © Rosaleen Orr 2015

Cover design Copyright © Rosaleen Orr 2015

ISBN 978-1-84921-150-5

to my loving husband, Robert Mulhern

Contents

Introduction

Good Luck and Blessings

Lena Wallace had fallen on her feet when she fell pregnant, a little late in life. Her maternity benefit had enabled her to escape from the hell-hole that was her art classroom in rowdy Saint Jude's school. And when he was born, rather precipitately, during the school show, her cute baby boy had continued to bring her nothing but good luck and blessings.

First of all, the holy Sisters of the Convent of the Bleeding Heart had taken her in as their first unmarried mother, when their supply of 'orphans' dried up following the tragic murder of poor Sister Philomena on the convent premises. The good nuns had given her the nicest bedroom in the east wing, which the little kitchen maid Imelda had occupied before she eloped. It had been re-decorated with new Victorian wallpaper, although Lena couldn't help noticing a few rust-coloured stains here and there on the oak panelling.

Anyway, Lena had been able to give up her studio flat in the West End of Glasgow (just one enormous room with four little plywood cubicles cut out, one halfway through a window, and another seeming to saw a marble fireplace in half). Lena's room in the convent was perfectly proportioned, and, as well as an en-suite, there was a box-room attached where bonny baby Joel slept. Most of the time he slept. And then Lena was able to keep her suite of little rooms as neat as three new pins. The trouble was when Joel woke up, and, developing his motor skills, started crawling round at speed and upsetting everything. Back at Saint Jude's, her art rooms would have been lovely, if the school kids had all been kidnapped, and not allowed to roar in and disrupt all her nice arrangements. So sometimes Lena would collapse in tears, as she had done at Saint Jude's, where she had hidden pathetically in the messy art store. The difference at the convent was that help was always at hand, and the tender-hearted nuns always listened out for her fits of sobbing, and would rush in to rescue her, whizzing Joel off in his buggy for fun and games in the convent grounds. Sometimes they didn't wait for Lena or Joel to sob. Lena had even caught big Mother Agnes waking the baby up so that he could come and see a new little foal that had been born in the stable block. Lena had had the sense to bite her lip and not protest, and she had been rewarded when Mother Agnes made over a corner of the tack room for Lena's private use, and helped her set up her easel and oil paints there. And Sister Mary of the Angels, herself a published poet, had examined a small volume Lena had had privately printed, and said it wasn't too bad. From a nun whose vows had meant she was committed to telling the truth, Lena knew that was praise indeed.

It happened that Lena's lover, Joel's daddy, Sammy, was himself a poet (they had met at a reading in the Tartan Arms, a scabby pub up Roystonhill, which none the less was a well-known poets' tavern). And apart from doting on baby Joel, he loved visiting the Convent of the Bleeding Heart. He said its austerity gave him inspiration. Lena couldn't work out what he meant by austerity, because the convent was very well appointed, with state-of-the-art central heating, and comfortable furniture. Only a few of the older nuns' cells (that is, their bedrooms) were bleak, and that was because, Lena knew, those Sisters had chosen to keep them that way out of badness, to show the other nuns up. The only places that were austere were the outbuildings where Mother Agnes quartered her rescued animals and looked after any tramp who happened by. Maybe that was what Sammy liked, Lena surmised. The animal sanctuary was certainly popular with film-makers and TV documentary makers, whom Sister Mary of the Angels charged a huge whack to film there, which, it seemed, they were eager to pay.

Sam Plaister had grown so pleased with Lena that he had even asked her to lunch at his club, the Scriveners and Limners, in Glasgow, a very snooty place for poets and artists where he had never taken her before. Lena didn't blame him, since his wife was also a member there. And Sammy had always shown respect for his wife, even when rolling about Lena's queen size bed in her studio flat. He said he would never leave his spouse, never could. They had been through too much together, both artistically and emotionally, so Lena was forced to respect his attitude, and give up all hopes of marriage.

In return, Sammy Plaister had dedicated his latest poem to Lena. Although she wasn't sure if the subject matter was totally appropriate for a sweetheart and nurturer, she all the same understood the honour that had been done to her by his inscription, "To L.W., My Ewe Lamb".

"Fellow Feeling" was the title.

Think of the poor bloody magpie
What a bad press he gets
A hero unsung has his neck rung
For scoffing blackbirds' yolks
By sentimental folks

Who lay out maggots for tits
It's a fact the magpie commits
To the survival of the fittest
Gorgeous but with a hard heart
His counterpart would be
Not you my lamb but me."

Sister Mary of the Angels, Angel to her friends, and Sister Mary of Perpetual Succour, Peppy to hers, both nodded understandingly as Lena quoted the poem to them. Then, deciding to take her mind off things poetical, they crowded into Lena's small en-suite bathroom. They were determined to sort out Lena's unkempt appearance and began to give her a home perm to prepare her for her posh lunch at her sweetheart's club. They were anxious in case Lena got upset and left the creamy mixture on her hair too long. The chic effect Peppy was trying to create was a *Coupe Sauvage*, where the curls were relaxed and wild.

They hadn't managed to get her to go on a diet, and lose some weight. But Lena had said thanks anyway, but her lover liked his women plump. And that had shut the pair of holy nuns up right away, Lena registered, as her head was dunked again under a running rather hot tap.

The perm turned out all right, though not exactly as Peppy had envisioned it. Not so much wild as domestic, like a lamb's coat. Joel liked it anyway, running his little fists through it, as he was lowered into Lena's taxi by Peppy for a last farewell to his escaping Mamma.

Peppy made Joel wave goodbye from the convent's front steps. Lena felt rather grand as she waved back and the taxi took off.

"The Scriveners and Limners Club, Beechwood Square." She directed in a posh voice.

Now Read On.

1

Scriveners and Limners

The clubhouse of the Ancient Society of Scriveners and Limners stood a snooty step back from Beechwood Square. It had retreated further back than the townhouses on either side, guarded by its own small front garden. Offended as a duchess on being told a rude joke. Because the Square had become a haunt of whores. Turf wars had even broken out among pimps over the central gardens, and lady members, if ultra-fashionably dressed, ran the risk of being taken for sex workers.

Lena Wallace, arriving by taxi at the club entrance, hesitated for a minute as another cab drew up and decanted two ladies. One, the plump red haired one, staggered, obviously tipsy. She wore horribly wounded tights, possibly the result of an earlier stumble. Her companion, severely dressed in chic black, dived quickly through the swing doors without a backwards glance at her.

Lena decided to avoid them by taking a walk round the central gardens, where rusted gateways hung off their hinges, giving bright glimpses of romantic dereliction beyond.

From the far end of the square, the clubhouse premises looked even more imposing. The Ancient

Society of Scriveners and Limners was one of the best kept secrets in Glasgow. One secret its hallowed halls kept was that they were not truly ancient. The quaint stone building had been built at the turn of the twentieth century, and for an entirely different purpose from the encouragement of art and poetry, its later noble remit. The antiquity referred to was that of members' favoured eras in art (limning), and in writing (scrivening), the Renaissance, and well before. The building as it had existed had been a luxurious love-nest for a wealthy Glasgow businessman and aristocrat. He had built it in the gap site between two mansions in Beechwood Square, giving it an unobtrusive entrance, by which he could slip discreetly in and out. And there was room in the drive in front of it to turn a carriage, or indeed, the odd noisy motorcar, without infringing on the neighbouring respectable purlieus.

The Ancient Society club rooms had one advantage that the Glasgow Art Club just round the corner did not have. A truly delightful back garden (almost a set of gardens) which took up the feus that had been abandoned when the builders of the neighbouring mansions had gone bust, and that the love-sick aristocrat had snapped up. He had envisioned it as a palatial formal garden with fountains, where his opera *diva inamorata* could stroll to cool off, after her fans had taken her horses from the shafts, and dragged her carriage up Sauchiehall Street from the Theatre Royal. Unluckily for him, his lover's style of *bel' canto* had quickly gone out of fashion ('wee chookie birdie' unkind punters called it), and the lady had retired to the shores of Lake Garda, where for many years she exerted a powerful attraction to passing tourists from the club. And she left behind a beautiful Bechstein Grand in the music room.

So the gardens had never realised their original potential, and had become rather run down, the arches of wisteria growing over the stained and chipped mock classical statuary. The wooden benches, named after artists' loved ones, were mantled by ivy and had not received a lick of varnish in living memory. The stone alcoves containing busts of poets were screened by rampant honeysuckle and rambling roses.

And all the more charming for that, the members thought. It lent privacy to assignations that might have seemed too crude if they had taken place indoors (the club had many nooks and crannies not overlooked by its CCTV system, such as the sub-basement, and the rear upper attics). There were also semi-public rooms, such as the library, which were lockable, for 'special projects'. The club housekeeper, showing distinguished visitors around, could be embarrassed to find the leather sofa cushions still arranged lasciviously on the floor. No-one, though, ever owned up to her blushing accusations.

The club had come to be called the Gardens, or the Sally Gardens (reflecting the initials S and L, from its long-winded title.) And the gardens boasted large willows at the back (sauchies, or sallys in Scots tongue), which gave a lot of cover to romantic couples.

If you think that 'Sally Gardens' is a name a shade too romantic for a highbrow club, the antique society had strayed so far from its original concept that many of its activities were lowbrow, louche, and even criminal (money laundering for one) instead of ultra-genteel. Money laundering was considered easy-peasy by the shadier elements. Since paintings by members were always on sale, it was easy to pay for a work in cash, take it home, and find it didn't match the curtains, when your money would be returned in a cheque from the club. Backhanders persuaded the artists to connive, although some naive ones were constantly being disappointed, without liking to complain.

But the newly appointed honorary treasurer, a smart young guy, always immaculately dressed, had started paying the tricksters back with their own rolls of cash, which he had got his mammy to run through her machine on a 'delicates' programme.

"There it is!" he would say, "All freshly laundered!"

The rumour was that the young guy was an undercover cop. That wasn't true. He wasn't undercover, but up front, in fact recently promoted to Detective Inspector, at a phenomenally young age. He had owned up to his occupation on his application as an artist member. He had had some poetry published, and he had also rather a nice touch on the violin.

But over-riding these dealings, the club's main object was romance, perhaps true love.

Lena Wallace, as she walked up and down outside the 'Gardens', had just the vague hope in her heart that she might find both. Her fortunes had taken a turn for the better recently. She had chanced to get pregnant by a striking-looking poet she'd met at a poetry reading. All the luckier since the poet was usually regarded as being gay, though happily married. He'd said she reminded him of his first wee girlfriend when he was a tiny laddie. A plump wee lassie, with frizzy fair hair just like hers. But the poet, who was a member of the Sally Gardens club, had never taken her there before, although the Sally Gardens had an upper suite of rooms (bookable by members a fortnight in advance, so as not to encourage them to yield to sudden desires for venal encounters). The poet had truly admired Lena's work, her poems, that is. She was also a painter. She'd been an art teacher, too, but had got out of that hole when she got pregnant, and never gone back in it. She'd claimed mental instability, although she had used every ounce of her intelligence and knowledge of body language to persuade the medical boards that her depression was post-partum. She had done this by calling up a vision of her probable life if she was forced to go back to teaching. Then she could cry uncontrollably for hours. Only one member of the panel who last examined her had voiced the Catch 22 suspicion; anyone sensible enough to want out of teaching cannot be quite mad.

So she had a small occupational pension, and a small allowance from the poet, whose wife had always wanted a child. In return, she had granted him joint custody of Joel, her cute little boy. At one year old he was so sweet that the poet had, in gratitude, put her up for membership in her own right. Since she was one of only a few who had ever applied as a poet and a painter, and as her poet was the vice-president of the club, he told her that she would have no trouble getting elected. At that moment she was waiting for her poet, Sammy, to appear, to conduct her into the club. And he was late as usual.

Lena didn't much mind. She was quite good natured, and it was a nice day.

Samuel Plaister, Lena's poet, had offered to put her up for membership of the Scriveners and Limners because he really liked her work, and also because the club would be nice for her to bring Joel to, on Saturdays when children were allowed. Also because some of the bedrooms where the staff slept could sometimes be leased from them for illicit liaisons, colloquially known as ' wee lie downs'. His wife Emilia, herself a member, had agreed to second her, but didn't like the idea. She was up to all Sammy's dodges. Lena Wallace, then, had been told she'd walk it, but it wasn't at all certain if she'd be elected. It was Emilia's idea that Lena should apply both as a painter and as a poet. Which actually gave her two chances to fail. It was a trick often used to deny an applicant membership. But silly Lena had been thrilled to get together the best of her figurative colourist work for the committees to consider, as well as her little poetry pamphlets and the few anthologies she'd got into.

And she didn't know how traumatic the election procedure was. The applicants had to sit on the platform in the gallery, with the application committee, and listen to the opinions expressed by members, for and against. After all her problems getting out of teaching and on the dole, Lena wasn't very good with committees. If she'd known what was in store for her, she'd have run away or burst into tears. And although Sammy had been eloquent, chinning his chums about her, Emilia had been more eloquent, giving the low down to their wives, who wasted no time in nipping the ears of their spouses. They reminded them of secret peccadilloes and threatened them with what would happen if they voted for Sammy's light of love.

So Lena, fat in her finery, her new curly perm brushed up around her head, was like a large ewe lamb, ready for the slaughter, all on her lonesome. She decided to take another turn round the central gardens of the square, where lilac, clematis, jasmine and wisteria peeped over the close cut beech hedges just coming into leaf, bringing delicious aromas to her on the early summer air. When she got back to the club's decorative semi-concealed entrance, she slowed her pace. Being rather statuesque (and, as she admitted, never having been able to shed the baby pounds) she was beginning to feel a little weary.

At the top of a shallow flight of curved steps, within the alcove that hid the main carved doors, a dainty figure was lurking, a sweet little dark haired lady, trying to make up her mind. Dame Georgie brushed her stylishly urchin cut dark hair from her forehead in perplexity. She could see that the poor large lady hovering about the door was exhausted, perhaps in a state of collapse. Who could know what kind of life these

Lena Wallace

poor women led? This one must have been so desperate she was actually parading about at noon. And she was so bizarrely dressed, she must be on her uppers. (Lena would have been outraged. Her costume had been carefully put together from a retro chic boutique and an ethnic wear shop. And having gone to Edinburgh School of Art, she thought that the Sally Gardens was located in a similarly respectable square to Charlotte Square, where the Edinburgh Arts Club stood sedately. Otherwise, even she would not have strolled up and down so languidly.)

Dame Georgie made up her mind to do the charitable thing, and dashed forward.

"Dear!" she said to Lena, "My dear, do come in for just a moment, and rest. It's far too hot out there, to ... do business!" Dame Georgie tried to pull her inside.

Lena resisted, as courteously as she could.

"I'm just waiting for someone to turn up."

"Of course you are, dear, but it will be quite alright if you wait inside. We're all very broad-minded here."

Lena blushed. She must be referring to her single mother status. Who had told her?

"Well, I should think so too. I'm not the first."

"No, dear, and you won't be the last! But do come in." Georgie's huge dark eyes glowed.

Lena allowed herself to be conducted through the swing doors and into a small vestibule.

"This lady is with me! She is my guest!" Dame Georgie said imperiously to the bored young girl behind the desk there, who couldn't possibly have cared less.

"Look here!" Lena drew herself to her full height, and pulled in her stomach. "I think you have the wrong idea. I'd arranged to meet a gentleman friend here. We had an appointment."

Georgie contented herself with giving Lena a glance full of sympathy. Then she led her to a tall lady already seated at a table near the French windows that led to the gardens. Tall and ridiculously good-looking, Lena noted. She'd seen her getting out of a taxi.

"Dolores! This is a new friend of mine. We met outside, in the square!" Georgie made a face. "She was walking about in the heat!" Georgie gave a peculiar emphasis to the words, then, seeing that Dolores didn't twig, she expanded. "Walking about! Up and Down!"

Dolores raised her well plucked and pencilled eyebrows. Rising to her feet, she set her gaze down her delicate aquiline nose, assuming Georgie meant the newcomer was a social climber. People were always trying to scrape acquaintance with Dame Georgie, honoured for her services to opera (especially *bel' canto*). Her husband was Professor Donald McDonald Donald, the architectural historian and archivist of the Scriveners and Limners.

"Elena Luisa." Lena used the fancy names on her passport, trying to impress.

"How do you do?" Dolores asked, not looking towards her, however. "Can't stop! Just waiting for Sammy! I've got some stuff I'd like him to print in this issue of *Willow Leaves*."

Dolores sniffed. Dame Georgie needn't think she would unload the creature on her!

As Dolores expected, Georgie scurried off, towards the bar.

"I'll just get us all a cool drink!" she called, over her shoulder, as she rang for the barman.

"Sammy! That's funny! That's who I'm waiting for!" Lena blurted out.

The two women looked at each other from head to toe and back again in puzzlement, just as Sammy, Lena's poet himself, came blustering through the door.

"There you are, dear!" he shouted to Lena. "I see you've found a friend already!"

And that wasn't the end of the misunderstandings. Later, Georgie took the distraction of the luncheon gong sounding to hiss in Sammy's ear. "Street walker! I mean sex worker! You know! One of the tarts."

"No, I don't believe I'll have one of the tarts after all. Quiches, aren't they? And real men don't eat them." Sammy joked to the room at large, his beady dark eyes twinkling.

In spite of wanting to shake off Lena, Dolores placed herself opposite to her at a table for four, with Sammy in the middle. She kept up a sparkling conversation with Sammy, way over Lena's head, abstruse and intellectual. And Lena found the lady's pronounced Oxford accent intimidating, though terribly cool. Lena struggled to keep up.

Then Dolores gathered from something Sammy said that Lena was a poet. Her eyes lit up with amusement, as she looked over at Dame Georgie, who was obviously, because of the heart rent expression on her face, telling her husband the sad story. Occasionally Georgie smiled over at Sammy, nodding, as if congratulating him on his quixotic action of taking the woman to lunch.

Lena tried again bravely to get into the conversation, about sonnets, oddly enough.

"Are you fond of Donne? Sorry, I should have pronounced it Dunn! Are you fond of him?"

"Can't say!" Dolores answered curtly, not taking her eyes from Sammy's face.

"Oh my god!" Lena gasped, "You can't be. You can't be 'Kant!' Dolores Kant! Oh! I do so love your work! Any relation to Emmanuel? I so love his work too!"

Dolores Kant finished chewing a tiny frond of lettuce daintily. Then began to torture a minute piece of lamb chop. Finally she looked up, and glanced towards the door. She was hoping she'd catch another of the magazine's editors. "Thank you. And no." she said frostily, then lowering her voice, she hissed to Sam, "God, what a Diva that Dame Georgie was being!"

Leaving the bright flower bedecked dining room for the dim gallery, with its dusty cupola, Lena found herself alone. Dolores had cut Sammy out, and cornered him as she delved in her large handbag for the poems she wished to show him.

The red-haired lady she had seen arriving in the cab bounced off when she saw Lena approach. Lena felt her throat tighten, and looked around for a way out. She had made it to the exit at the far end of the gallery, when Dame Georgie confronted her, and took her by the arm.

Georgie had been surprised at Sammy taking the woman into lunch, rather trumping the glass of fizzy water she herself had ordered. She determined not to be outdone.

"Come and see the pictures!" she coaxed sweetly. "They're all the work of members here, and I'll introduce you to the artists, and the poets. Don't be nervous, dear. They're exactly the same as everyone else. I used to be nervous of them too! Do you like painting? How about poetry? Do you like that? You're not shy with me, are you? Do I seem bossy?"

"No, you've been so kind. I think you're one hell of a nice dame! Not at all a diva!"

"Now never mind the Dame! Call me Georgie! And forget the Diva, too!"

So Dame Georgie led her large new friend round the tightly twined little groups, which opened like flowers to receive her. When they heard Lena call her Georgie, they stretched out their tendrils to her too.

When the time came for the election, Georgie drew Lena up onto the platform beside her. First Sammy spoke on her behalf, quite jolly, asking the members, as a special favour, to elect his little friend. He smiled round over his horn rimmed specks, urbanely conspiratorial.

"And her work's not bad either!" he ended as the wives cast fierce looks at their husbands.

Then Dolores, to Lena's surprise gave a very terse but positive appraisal. (Dolores was hoping for a grant from the club's trust fund, disbursed by Professor Donald.)

Others popped up eagerly to be more effusive. No-one had a bad word to say of her. The wives started to give their husbands countermanding looks, which were meant to convey the reverse of what they had commanded them before. Some husbands didn't 'get' it, and swithered, half rising from their seats to condemn Lena for femininity, vacuousness, and lastly, and worst, sensuality. They were pulled down again. There was a pause.

Into this lacuna, the youngish cop boldly dived.

He brought out a shining appreciation of Lena's work. He thought her poems were like the New Symbolists and her paintings were like the New Expressionists. Lena was amazed. She had always just dashed off her work in a state of exhaustion from her day job, with hardly any rhyme or reason whatever. She saw nothing wrong with that method, anyway.

"Thank you, Mr. Childers!" the President intoned. "I take it there are no votes contra! Then I can say the applicant is elected by acclamation!"

So Lena was elected by acclamation, an honour very rarely given to an unknown. Some members did not know they should be flinging their voting papers and caps in the air. The old poets and artists in the know, not then wearing academic caps, rattled the now unsullied, built into the card tables, silver Art Nouveau ash trays, which was the current correct procedure.

Dame Georgie took the opportunity to whisper in Lena's ear.

"Clever young lady that! I wonder where she's sitting! She should be up here with us."

It was a pity Dame Georgie missed the bit where Lena got up and stood shyly at the mike reciting the best of her poems. But she had already arranged to take Lena for lunch the next week, by the time her huge husband Donnie Donald nudged her, insisting on whisking her off to declare open an abattoir.

"It would be lovely, dear!" Dame Georgie had whispered, fixing her with a tender gaze, "If you could become truly interested in the arts. You might give up your former way of life!"

"But I have already, Georgie!" Lena gasped. "How on earth did you know? Today was my last day under contract. My life from now on is an open book. A fresh slate! *Tabula rasa!*"

Lena was referring to her teaching contract, which came to an end that day, after her maternity leave of absence and her ensuing depression sickness leave.

Dame Georgie was dumbstruck. Did the pimps put the hookers under contract now? She'd heard of erotic contracts, which whores made, too. She blushed to have thought of her new friend in such crude terminology. She must be watching too much television. And the girl had hidden depths. She must look up *tabula rasa*. She hoped the term wasn't obscene.

Sammy Plaister swaggered round the gallery, checking out which works had sold. He was dressed all in black. Black to match his eyebrows, and the remaining streaks in his white mop of hair, and to contrast with his luxuriant white beard. Broad shouldered and spindle shanked, he looked like a magpie, as, cocking his head to the side, he surveyed the room, as if on the lookout for a juicy worm, or a fledgling to devour, with no hard feelings.

He strolled into the library, where his eye lit on Pascal Stone. Pascal, an elderly poet of saintly reputation, who was an artist member of long standing.

Sammy Plaister

The usually parchment tones of Pascal's venerable face were flushed with anxiety, as he rummaged among the lower book shelves. He looked up warily as he heard someone enter and started to gabble some excuse. But Sam Plaister, putting an arm about him, led him gently out and over to the bar. Pascal smiled, as Sammy whispered reassuringly in his ear.

"Two Glenmorangies!" Sam instructed the barman, winking at him over Pascal's head, "For old time's sake!"

2

Bleeding Hearts

The Convent of the Bleeding Heart became an unusually silent demesne when Sister Mary of Perpetual Succour (Peppy to her friends) was no longer around. She had been redeployed to a single-end unconverted convent flat in the Gallowgate district of Glasgow, where dereliction and yuppie kit houses lent the enclave a glamour which all the young nuns thought their mansion house premises lacked.

Sister Mary of the Angels envied her. She would have loved to go. But, despite her heartfelt pleas, Mother Benigna, the deceptively mild and soft spoken Mother Superior, had insisted that her academic studies had to be put first.

"Stick in at your Renaissance studies, like a good girl." Mother Benigna had coaxed, "The poor we have always with us."

But Mother Benigna was beginning to worry about Sister Angel, as she was known in the house. She was beginning to stoop from being hunched over her computer all day, administering the convent's web site business, when she was not scrubbing out the kitchen, or writing her treatises for Glasgow University fine arts department.

Angel's face had become pale and not quite as pretty as usual. She missed the daft carry on she'd had setting up practical jokes with Peppy. The last one had been a good laugh. Peppy had phoned up Mother Mary Agnes, the estate manager of the parklands and fields surrounding the house with its far flung outhouses and stables. Peppy had put on a brilliant Middle Eastern voice. She said she was acting for a sheikh who was looking for a place to build a summer palace for his harem, and offered four million pounds sight unseen. It looked as if Mother Agnes had fallen for it too, when she accepted eagerly. Till she had suggested throwing in all the nuns, too, as extra concubines. Although she pointed out that not all of the nuns were what you'd call pretty!

Sister Mary of the Angels was exactly what you'd call pretty. Even, or perhaps especially, in the white traditional habit that the nuns, by special agreement with the Holy See, were allowed to wear. The convent used to be dedicated to Saint Philomena, but when Philomena was declared a non-saint it had been renamed 'The Convent of the Bleeding Heart' and had a dedicated website, run by Sister Mary of the Angels. She found that pictures of the nuns in old world habits drew in more subscriptions to the charities than pictures of them dressed in the smart Marks and Spencer's gear a few of the Sisters still opted to wear.

Mother Mary Agnes, who looked after rescued animals in the outbuildings, and also took in a few derelict humans too, sometimes unofficially, was not quite herself these days either, Mother Benigna noticed. She had had something on her mind ever since the tragic death of her best friend Sister Philomena. She seemed to blame herself for it somehow. None of the other Sisters could understand why.

Agnes had begun to do special acts of penitence, and some of the young nuns were beginning to follow her example, which Benigna did not approve of. For instance, they had stopped sending out for fish and chips on Fridays, a traditional treat which had been such fun, eaten straight from their plastic trays and brown paper wrappings. Now Fridays had become a little bit grim, which was not Mother Superior's idea of a pious atmosphere. Benigna had considered sending both of them on retreat, but she thought that might just be pandering to their hysterical desire for sack cloth and ashes.

By that morning's post she had received, in Sister Angel's name, an invitation from The Ancient Society of Scriveners and Limners, for Angel to take up an honorary membership.

Angel had published a treatise on 'Erotic Sculpture and Painting in Garda Palazzi'. The Society had been impressed by her erudition (picturing a Sister Wendy type), and had wondered if the lady would consider joining the society's summer trip to Lake Garda. All expenses would be paid, in return for just a few lectures. They regretted she would have to provide her own spending money for shopping, and any meals taken outwith the allotted hotels. There was a hand-written postscript explaining that the society were making a series of videos on the club's activities, and would Sister Mary of the Angels agree to appear? It was thought the traditional white habit they'd seen on the convent's website looked very cinematographically interesting. This was signed 'Guy Byron Everard' in large curlicued calligraphy.

Mother Benigna sent for Mother Mary Agnes, her second-in-command, to show her the letter, on parchment, with fancy scroll work surrounding the august name at the top. Agnes came in still wearing her muddy dungarees, just with her brown cape draped over them. She tried wiping her boots on the doormat, and finally kicked them off. Benigna had a nice pot of strong coffee ready, and Sister Evangeline's newly-baked croissants. She raised one hand, to defy Mother Agnes to refuse them.

"It is my disagreeable duty, Mother Agnes." she began, "to remind you of your vows of obedience to the order, and to myself."

Agnes didn't beat about the bush. She'd already been established at the convent, in full habit, when Mother Benigna was a young postulant called Sister Betty, whom very many of the Sisters had not been at all sure of. And Agnes could have been appointed Mother Superior before, if she had agreed to give up her outdoor duties.

"You mean the fish and chips, don't you, Benigna?"

"Not just the fish and chips. Although that was an obvious break with tradition."

"What, then?"

"Well, to be honest, Agnes, you're becoming a real pain! A pain in the neck, as they say. You're just no fun any more. I hear you're starving yourself. You're never out of the chapel, at all hours of the day and night. That privilege was given you to accommodate your care of the animals. You are abusing it, for your selfish ends. What are you up to, Agnes? Come clean! If you have something on your conscience you don't want to discuss with me, I can send for a Father Confessor from another parish."

"He'd only say what everyone says. Sister Philomena's death was not my fault. But I promised her mother all those years ago I'd look after her. And where was I when she was struck down in the night?"

"Where we all were, Mother Agnes. Tucked up in our beds. Where else would we be? And you know the police thought she'd let in her assailant herself. Her mind was wandering. You know that. We would have had some hard decisions to make about her care."

Mother Agnes got up from her seat as if about to leave. Benigna rose to stop her.

"Sit down please, Mother Agnes. We all have secrets, even here. You may keep yours. But about the fasting, Mother Agnes! God made you the good build you are!"

"Fasting? Nothing of the kind, Mother. It's simply Sister Peppy's latest diet. She put me on her silly grapefruit diet, before she left. I promised I'd try it. But I'm sick of it! My face is quite yellow! Look! I'm turning into a grapefruit!"

Agnes wasn't kidding, Mother Benigna saw; her face was rather sallow.

Mother Benigna refilled their cups. "Now to another matter. I want your advice about our little Sister Mary of the Angels. I don't know if you agree, but I don't like the look of her."

"I know what you mean. Stooping. And pale and miserable. Too much art history, do you think? Or not enough? Is she suited to the convent life?"

"In a nutshell, Mother Agnes! You have summed up the problem in your usual astute way. Now what do you make of this?" Mother Benigna passed the letter across the table to Agnes. "Shall I let her go? And if so, shall I let her go on her own? Unchaperoned, I mean!"

"Sure, let her go! But I can't see whom you can spare from here, to go with her. We'll get someone in, I suppose. Pity Sister Mary of Perpetual Succour has so much on her hands now, with all those winos and jaikies, sorry, substance abusers."

"There's only Sister Evangeline, but she's become so interested in the care of the animals, and in the Travellers' encampment. She wouldn't like to be taken away."

"Yes, that's true, Mother. I can't turn round but she's cleaning out the stables. Makes me feel quite useless sometimes."

Mother Agnes stopped suddenly. She saw the trap Benigna had laid for her, but not before she'd dived headfirst into it.

"You mean me. You mean I should go. Is that an order?"

Tears had sprung up in Agnes's sorrowful amber eyes.

"Excuse me, Mother! But I didn't expect this! You want rid of me, don't you? I'm a drag!"

"No, Mother Agnes! It is I who am the drag."

Mother Benigna took her hands from within the wide sleeves of her habit: she stretched out a hand and put it over Agnes's large work stained paw. Benigna's hand was shaking slightly.

"That 'wee turn' I had, last month, Agnes, I may get more of them. I'll need you then. My poor old heart's a bit dodgy, they say, on top of everything else that's wrong with me. I should have taken more exercise, right, as you always told me."

The two women stood in the doorway, grasping each other's hands, in the cover of the wide flapping sleeves of their habits.

"I knew I could rely on you, Agnes. Try and see the trip as a holiday to strengthen you for the task ahead. Not that it will be any picnic looking after one of the young ones. They've got their own ideas. And we're old fogeys. Would you send Angel to me? I'd better get it over with. She'll be giving me a lot of blarney. She wants to go to the Gallowgate."

When Sister Mary of the Angels dutifully turned up, Benigna explained the situation frankly to her. She explained that Agnes was having a hard time recovering from poor Philomena's death. She was at her wits' end, she said, trying to get her to leave the convent for a while, perhaps take a little holiday. And didn't Sister Angel think Agnes was looking just a bit yellow, in spite of all her work out of doors?

"I think her heart may be breaking" said Mother Benigna. "Old hearts break, too, as well as young ones, you know. More so. Our hearts are more brittle, like our bones!"

Benigna passed the letter to Sister Angel.

"It seems that this learned society is offering you honorary membership because of your last published work. They wish you to take part in an art appreciation trip to Lake Garda. I would have no objection to this, of course. But it may be difficult to furnish you with a Sister Companion, as required by the rules of the order. That is, one who would be acceptable to you, on the grounds of intelligence and temperament. I'd hate the trip to be a penance. Now, if you have any bright ideas about that, please let me know. I hope I haven't disturbed your work on the website."

"But Mother Benigna, don't you see? Agnes would be perfect, and it would give her a break. And I'll look after her, don't worry. You can leave it all to me. And my trip won't cost us anything. Except for pocket money. And there's Saint Philomena's miraculous, sort of, medals, that I sell loads of, will pay for that."

"Good Heavens, Child! What a wonderful idea! Our order has a couple of houses round Lake Garda. We could send her on a pilgrimage from one to the other. If you wouldn't mind accompanying her.

And by the way, Sister Angel, congratulations on the signal honour bestowed on you. I'll expect a full account of it on the website. No hiding your light under a bushel!"

As Sister Mary of the Angels left the Mother Superior's room, she didn't know what had hit her. She would have liked to join Sister Peppy in the flat in the Gallowgate. But if Benigna had asked her to give that up for Lake Garda, she must remember her vows of obedience. Cheerful obedience, too. Angel smiled as she sat down at her computer.

She was humming 'o Sole Mio' as she clicked on.

Later that evening, Sister Angel slid her dainty fingers through the plastic files in Saint Philomena's 'miraculous medals' filing cabinet. (Nobody really believed in them, but it didn't stop people buying them to take on long car trips, or to leave by their baby's cot if it had a sudden illness.) From the top drawer, she slid out a file and took out the folder it contained, marked 'Messages from Bleeding Hearts, Poems by Sister Mary of the Angels.'

She had noticed, on the letter from the Ancient Society of Scriveners and Limners, that there would be a poetry reading on the evening she had been invited to come and accept her honorary membership at a champagne reception. Her heart beat faster. Would they let her read her poems too? Maybe she'd meet real poets! She loved poets!

The only problem was, she also loved winos and jaikies, the politically incorrect gallus way that she and Sister Mary of Perpetual Succour, Peppy to her pals, referred to the clientele of the little urban convent in Gallowgate. Down Crimea Pass, over an odd ramped bridge tethered by cast iron railings. Sister Mary of the Angels had enjoyed one blissful night in the kitchen hole-in-the-wall bed recess, to keep Peppy company on her first night there. Peppy had been bundled up on the other side of the wall in an identical bed recess, the spaces left being used for storage. (It had all kinds of rubbish still in it). The Tenants' Association had put in a shower and toilet, but the rest of the one bedroom flat was a conserved property. They had been able to rap through to each other, when the noises reverberating round the tiled close outside began to become ferocious.

After a while, during which the young nuns had pulled the patchwork quilts over their heads, the screams and roars died away, and the sound of a guitar being strummed had been heard from the close mouth. That would be the young guitarist who had claimed Crimea Pass as his. The tourists who came off buses to see the Single End flats retained there gave him a nice livelihood, and enough to pay for Protection, Peppy had told Angel. Not that he looked as if he needed protection, Peppy had remarked. A fit young guy like that.

Angel herself had not, on that first visit, managed to get a view of him, and she longed to do so. But on the doormat, the next morning, Peppy had found a *Welcome to Crimea Pass* hand-made card, with an old-fashioned glass bottle of milk from the conserved Dairy round the corner, and a plain loaf you had to cut with a breadknife.

Angel loved plain loaves. She also adored guitarists, like the unknown one.

She felt her heart being pulled two ways at once. She felt inclined to have her cake and eat it too, a practice very much frowned on in the Convent of the Bleeding Heart. Angel wondered if there might be a guitarist at the poetry reading. She'd heard sometimes in readings in pubs, guitarists accompanied the poems.

And she would always have Crimea Pass to come back to after Lake Garda. She smiled at the thought of all the high jinks she and Peppy might get up to there, and, of course, all the souls they might save from the fiery furnace in the process.

And usually she enjoyed Mother Agnes's company too. Except that recently, Agnes had seemed so fed up, it was almost as if she had something on her conscience.

It was Agnes who had spoken out against keeping places for vulnerable children in the mansion house convent. Agnes said they wouldn't be able to be open for retreats, since the police vetting rules had become stricter. And the pilgrims did bring in quite a lot more money, to be sure.

But when the last little 'orphan' had been passed on to a foster home, the place had lost a lot of its liveliness. And Agnes had got more and more down in the mouth, in spite of an unexpected coupling of two old rescued donkeys which had yielded a very cute foal, after a few sleepless nights and finally a heroic intervention by Mother Agnes. Angel had got her nose nearly bitten off when she had suggested calling the foal "Harry" because he looked like the royal prince, with long eyelashes and a cheeky expression. Too late, Angel had remembered that Father Harry, Agnes's special friend, had come to a bad end, a really savage end, which they were all trying to forget.

Mother Agnes was even talking about returning to Ireland, where she now knew no-one. Agnes thought she might be happier there. But even Agnes wondered if things would be any better. She had lost the jaunty attitude that had kept her going for so long. She was thinking she might be something of a jinx, because of the tragic events she had been involved in recently. Though nobody blamed her. Nobody at all.

Angel sighed. She didn't know if she was up to Mother Agnes's bad moods. She had enough of her own. But just then, the office door slammed open, and Agnes herself breezed in. She was waving a copy of the Limners and Scriveners' newsletter.

"Look, Angel! There's a poem in this by Frank Childers. That smart detective who sorted things out when Philomena got killed. I hope he's going to Garda! Maybe the trip will be okay! Nine days till we must book up, Angel. We'll just have time to make a *novena* that you and I will have a safe, pleasant, trip! Are you game?"

But Angel was not impressed. She hadn't fancied the looks of Detective Childers. She didn't like detectives much. And Childers, she recalled, from when he'd interviewed Mother Mary Agnes, was sort of slim and greeting-faced, as if he had a pain in his guts. Nosey, too, and always on his high horse! Well, she'd soon sort out Detective Inspector Childers! (She'd heard he'd been promoted because of his investigations into the 'Bleeding Hearts Murder'.) And she would know how to sort him out, if he presumed on their short acquaintance! She'd fix him! And she'd better things to do than make *novenas*. She'd no time for outdated forms anyway! Nine days of set prayers! Let Agnes do that if she liked. Angel had other stuff to do. Cultural stuff! Poetical stuff!

When Mother Agnes had gone, Sister Angel had a little rehearsal of her poems in front of the glass bookcase door, which acted as a mirror if you jammed it ajar.

She found her voice came out in a squeak. That would never do. So she tried projecting the words the way one had to in making the Latin responses of her order's sacred office. There, that was better, although a bit ecclesiastical. It was going to require some work.

She turned her radio on for a little rest, to BBC Radio 4, and was delighted to catch the end of a recital by an old poet. Pascal something. He sounded brilliant, kind of sing song but conversational at the same time. She really adored old poets! She'd been to a reading in the National Library of Poetry in Edinburgh by some brilliant old poets. She might make a poem out of that. Something brief, but musical. Like an extended Haiku. Maybe the other poets would love it, her unwritten poem. Her heart pounded at the thought.

3

Poisonous Poets

Lena Wallace was getting ready to go out, in the en-suite of her bedroom, while the baby was being wheeled round the gardens by Mother Agnes, who had to lean down to reach the handles of the baby buggy. Lena knew that Mother Agnes was secretly trying to teach Joel to say 'Agnes' as his first word. The sounds he made sounded quite like it, she admitted. But was only because he was cutting teeth, she knew.

Lena was finding it a bit difficult to apply her make-up. She had refused all offers of help. But on second thoughts, she should have let Sister Mary of the Angels help, even without Peppy. She didn't seem to be able to get rid of the strange little red veins that had crawled across her cheeks since the birth of Joel. She thought she must have put on too much cover up make-up. Her face was looking ghastly and pale. Perhaps some blush powder would help. She'd heard some on the tip of the nose softened the feature. One thing she was good at, though, was eye make-up. She'd always been good at that, because of her skill in drawing, she thought. So why did her expression seem funny? Sort of surprised, or was it incredulous? Perhaps if she put some self-tanning powder all over it would kind of even everything out, once it started to work.

Lena thought she better give up on the make-up and start to get dressed. She'd wear what she'd worn before to the club. It would still be quite fresh.

But Lena forgot that, in her hurry to be a good mother, she'd rushed to hug Joel when she got home without changing first. She sniffed at her gauzy clothes.

She thought she detected a smell of sickness from them, as well as pee and poo. God, she hoped it was not on her best Indian tunic she was wearing, into the beaded silk. Lena tried dabbing at the embroidered silk with Dettol, then scooshed on "Mania".

She should really have changed, but there wasn't time. This was the big day. The day of her lunch with her new best friend Georgie. She wondered what Georgie did for a living, probably something secretarial. The little black dress she wore was very dull and plain. (Dame Georgie would have been outraged. The dress was her favourite Nicole Farhi.) Lena had heard Georgie's big galoot of a husband mentioning the abattoir where he worked. He had a very posh accent for such an earthy, not to say bloody, occupation. So he was no doubt a manager or supervisor while the other guys blootered the animals. Lena gave a shudder. One of these days she'd go totally vegetarian. Maybe even vegan.

But something nice was niggling at her brain. Something which made the corners of her scarlet lips edge upwards. Apart from the lunch date. Apart from her new membership. Of course, how could she have forgotten? The Sally Gardens, as she had learned to call it, had sold one of her small paintings. If the club had ten shows a year, and she sold as much at each one, her income would increase by thousands of quid. And Sammy had tried to tell her she was not business-like!

Sammy wouldn't be at the Gardens. She hadn't asked him, quite confident about going on her own. Everybody had been so friendly and nice.

32

It had got a little windy, and as she ran down the convent steps to her taxi, the breeze lifted up her gauzy skirt, swirling it around her bottom unflatteringly, she was sure. She hadn't been able to bear the bother of putting on tights. Never mind, an artistic club was sure to be lax about dress standards. In the taxi, her new control garment, her 'magic knickers', started riding up till she felt strangled. Maybe the missing tights would have controlled that. What had she been thinking of, trying them out for the first time on such an important day?

In the entrance vestibule of the Sally Gardens, she managed to get stuck in the swing doors, after a malfunction of her new member's plastic key.

Georgie hadn't arrived yet, she saw. She was early anyway. So she had a little look round the gallery. She was looking for her little 'sold' painting. There would either be a red dot showing its status, or it might have been carried off already. She didn't mind which.

But there the painting was, behind the tea urn, naked of its dot.

"Disappointing, isn't it?" the young housekeeper fiddling with the urn remarked. "I hate it when they bring them back. You were informed?"

"Not as such! But no matter! Tell Georgie I've gone to keep her a place for lunch!"

Lena swaggered into the dining room as though she didn't give a damn. She sat down at a nice table for two at a window, the only one of its kind not occupied.

Time went on, though, and Georgie did not turn up. A tall gentleman she thought she recognised came up and stood imposingly over her table. He had a kind of Punch face, where his nose and his chin did their best to meet in a forced grin. And he had tried to embellish, or disguise, his countenance with a pair of drooping moustaches. The man was tall and so thin that his concave torso could be adduced below his figured silk waistcoat. He grabbed a lady who was passing, and pushed her towards Lena unceremoniously.

"Hi! I'm Guy! Guy Everard! You may have heard of me! And this is my girlfriend Roxanne."

Lena remembered the redheaded plump lady. And he was the club president, come over to her to offer his congratulations. Maybe he and Roxanne would sit down with her. Lena had to admit she found him most unattractive. But after all, a president was a president. And she thought that plump Roxanne looked friendly, maybe even good fun. Lena eagerly scraped her chair back, got hastily to her feet, and was horrified to find she was executing a kind of curtsey to them.

"I'm waiting for Georgie!" she said, "But maybe she's stood me up. Do sit down!"

"Trouble is, Dame Georgie can't make it. And I keep this table for her. So would you mind? Find another table. Look, I'll help you!"

Guy grabbed Lena's awful looking home-made handbag, and her glass of house white. Lena looked round in panic. Conversation died out, and lunchers looked at their plates. "There's my phone!" Guy handed her back her bag and glass and vanished.

Lena caught sight of Dolores sitting, bolt upright, wearing glasses, at a table for four. Roxanne went to plump herself down there. Lena made her way towards it, but as she got there, Dolores dumped her handbag on one free seat, and a large book on the other.

Lena approached a larger group, seated at two tables pushed together. A seat at the middle was vacant, where the legs of both tables made sitting uncomfortable. She had just placed her hand on the carved back of the chair, when a big red bearded guy in the adjoining seat, made a sort of growling noise in his throat. It could have been 'Clear off' he was grunting.

"Oh Binkie! Don't be rude! She'll hear you!" The ladies at the table shrieked with laughter.

The fact was that the members had picked up the truth about Lena. That Dame Georgie had taken her up just because she thought she was a prostitute, to show people how amazingly broadminded she was. And that Dame Georgie was now humiliated to find that although not exactly pure as the un-driven snow, she did not rent out her body by the hour.

The word was that if Dame Georgie had not taken her around as a dear friend, no-one would have voted for her. Her paintings were big and lumpy, and her poems all rhymed.

The fact was that Lena was being given the brush off, socially ostracised by some poets she had thought were terribly sweet, just because she was not a prostitute, as Dame Georgie had erroneously supposed her to be. But how could Lena know that? The poor girl thought it was the baby smell about her, and again sprayed her jacket with "Mania". And who knows, she may have been partly right. At the Gardens there was no worse denigration than to be called 'Mumsy'. And Lena felt her empty stomach begin to rumble shamingly, too.

She climbed onto a high stool at the bar.

"Brandy!" she said to the big bluff barman. "And have one yourself. Any sandwiches?"

"Sorry, no." he answered, "but I have one fish cake left over. We serve them in pairs. It's the odd one out!"

"Just like me!" she said, munching the fishcake in a napkin. (You didn't get cutlery at the bar.) "The odd one out. No, leave the bottle!" she added, cowboy fashion.

The nice young man who had spoken up for her work planked himself down beside her. "Not lunching?" he asked. "Perhaps I'll just have a snack, too."

But a waitress hurried up to him. "Excuse me, Mr. Childers. Ms Kant says she's ordered for you. The last of the shepherd's pie, and if you don't hurry up someone will grab it."

"Drat! I was hoping to do a spot of Pilates in the garden. Still, mustn't be rude."

Lena wrapped herself lovingly around the brandy bottle, pouring out little nips for herself till she was suddenly reminded that alcohol was a powerful diuretic, and dashed for the loos on the ground floor. One was a bathroom with an old bath and washbasin in it as well as a very dodgy looking toilet. The door of this was snibbed, although the light was not on. There were another two battered toilet cubicles alongside the bathroom with its frosted glass panel. But Lena discovered to her horror that neither of them locked. The snibs were all gaping. (Usually the ladies worked in twos, guarding the dodgy doors for each other. It was part of female club bonding.) Oddly genteel little posies of wildflowers balanced on ledges.

Lena tried to stretch out her foot and keep the door closed so she could use the loo, but it was no use. Then she felt sick. Was sick, splashing her elaborately beaded jacket. She felt she was choking, and managed finally to remove the 'magic knickers' that were constricting her flabby after baby tummy. She felt better right away, but clumsily ripped her flimsy skirt getting out of the tight garment. It was a very funny feeling being pant-less. It reminded her of something. Some experience in childhood. Wet pants. Cross mother.

She began to feel cold, her teeth chattered and she sobered up fast. If she wasn't able to handle those poisonous poets before, how would she manage it minus essential underwear? She began to be conscious of a sort of shadow play on the frosted glass of the bathroom, adjacent to which her cubicle was built, sharing the glass panel. Then the sound of slurping bath water, and a series of grunts and sighs as if a couple was fooling around there. She flushed the cistern to cover the sounds and was rewarded by stifled giggles. She still hadn't managed to pee in the unlocked cubicle, which was ridiculous, considering what was going on next door. Neither did she want to collide with the couple should they exit before her.

Finally she pulled herself together and hit on the device of singing to scare intruders off. But before she could launch into song, she heard a sound of zipping and stamping before she heard stiletto heels tripping swiftly to the exit. She heard squeals of laughter from the outer corridor that sounded vaguely familiar. The guy must still be in the bathroom, waiting till the coast was clear. Thank God it wasn't Sammy, anyway. He wasn't like that.

Apart from the accident of fathering her child, it was he who had convinced her she would be able to look after a little child, and bring him or her up properly. Baby Joel was so sweet, and so vulnerable. As she sobered up, Lena began to realise just how childishly she was behaving, and feeling. All she really needed was a pal to hold the door closed! Surely some of her past good acts to the kids she had taught at horrible Saint Jude's had built her up a little credit. A little Karma. She started to sing a watery song loudly. "Moon River" she sang.

Then a thrilling soprano voice joined in "Wherever you're going, I'm going your way..." The sound Diva Georgie made, in the tiled room, reached an amazing full operatic volume. "That you, Lena? Georgie here! These loo doors are the devil. I'll jam it closed for you!"

Dame Georgie had decided to get over her stupid huff, after having crassly mistaken a poet for a prostitute. Her chauffeur had got her to the club in a rush. (And Barry the barman had told him that the big lady had been feeling unwell. Too much brandy, or the fish cake.)

Georgie escorted her to the dining room again. The crowd were just finishing their meal and looked up amazed as Georgie and her still-best-friend came in. Georgie was walking sort of in front of Lena. And Lena was definitely walking kind of funny. Her clothes torn, and her face flushed. The poets began to wonder if perhaps Dame Georgie had been right, and maybe Lena was a kind of a tart, perhaps turning tricks in the club gardens.

Dolores, eavesdropping from the nearest table, was amazed to hear Dame Georgie ask Lena if she would like to join the club trip to Italy later in the year.

Georgie was conscience stricken about ruining what was left of Lena's reputation before she was even through the doors of the club. But she couldn't quite muster the courage to own up. Not just yet.

"Well, what is the Society of Scriveners and Limners coming to," Dolores asked Frank, "if we're forced to make up numbers with a tart like that? I may decide not to go!"

"Well, suit yourself!" said Frank, escaping. "I think I'll sign up. I'll sign the book now!"

Dolores was amazed to hear Dame Georgie outlining the details of a mysterious travel scholarship which was only open to members who were both artists and poets. (Dame Georgie was making up the multiplicity of detail regarding age and qualifications and funding and sponsorships as she went along, all to suit Lena.) When she got to the bit about pocket money, Dolores could stand the rigmarole no longer, and stalked away. If anyone deserved a scholarship, Dolores considered she did. After all she'd done for the club, running raffles and giving brilliant free poetry master classes in the attics. Generally making herself agreeable to plain and boring but powerful men. Never again, she vowed, but then thought better of it, and went slithering over to whisper in Guy Everard's ear a word or two about Lena. She was rolling her eyes, and holding her nose. Well, she was quite right. If Lena hadn't ponged of vomit before, she most certainly did now. But Georgie was lovingly dabbing at the Indian jacket with Chanel No 5. And both ladies were in fits of laughter.

Guy was having second thoughts too. He grabbed a bottle of wine from his elite president's table, and dashed over to Lena and Georgie with it, fixing on his weird grin.

"Was there something special you wanted to say, Guy?" Georgie enquired frostily, "I'm in rather an important discussion with this lady. About the travel scholarships we considered before."

Dolores, behind her pillar, went a whiter shade of her usual pale. So the scholarship was genuine. She wondered if she could manage to daub a few paintings in a hurry.

After lunch (Dame Georgie's special of consommé and grilled sole) the book was brought to Lena, to sign provisionally for the club trip. Lena had had a little white wine and signed anyway, although she was sure it wouldn't work out for her. Things rarely did, for Lena. Georgie showed her protégée the glamorous brochures.

"Lake Garda, dear!" she said. "It's heavenly, isn't it? And you artists and poets so love it!"

One artist, though, would definitely not be going to Garda. Binkie Boyne would be leaving his place to someone else. His huge beard, triumphant winner of the club's annual 'Beardie' competition, would not feature in snapshots from Garda. Because poor Binkie had drowned before he even set out for that treacherous body of water. While the replete lunchers were waving goodbye to each other and jumping into taxis or settling down for snug afternoon naps in the big leather armchairs, Binkie was stretched out naked, turning blue, in the big claw footed bath in the Sally Gardens bathroom, his curling beard fanning out on the surface of the water, tendrils of a foxglove and juniper posy decorating it, as well as his flaccid genitals.

It was Barry the barman who discovered the body as he prepared to lock up. And he had the sense to summon the president Everard, who in turn summoned a club medical man. Who certified death from heart failure. Which was reasonable, although it was not his well-known dodgy heart that had caused the big chap's demise. His end had been more complicated. But had big Binkie not been lured into the sordid room for an assignation, he might have gone on being the life and soul of the Sally Gardens Club for years and years.

The club had got very skilful at covering things up, and Binkie Boyne's gigantic blue body, though fixed in rigor mortis with one arm magisterially extended like a Triton, was wheeled out in a hamper and got into the club minivan by moonlight that midnight.

4

Hell To Pay

Roxanne was the kind of woman who hated to be seen without a man. She would annexe any man, however devotedly mated or devoutly gay, just to take the bare look off her at parties. And guys lost their heads over her regularly. It would have been no use to remind them that they were not in her league, she having been a beauty in her youth, and her later corpulence only having diminished and not destroyed her attractiveness. (Lena had been wrong when she thought Roxanne was friendly, although it was a fact she could sometimes be fun!) Roxanne, well-endowed in the mammary department, got progressively slimmer as she went down. Her hips were narrow, and her ankles tiny, her feet extremely dainty. In fact, just the opposite of Lena Wallace, Lena herself thought, as she glimpsed Roxanne stalking into the gallery. Lena's bosom was maternal rather than voluptuous, her waist thickened, and her hips had always been generous. Somehow, though, on Lena, this distribution of flesh looked okay. Her gently sloping contours were unthreatening, and some guys went for that, her boyfriend, the poet Sammy Plaister being one. He had had a boozy lunch with Lena, and was cuddling her on one of the big couches.

Noticing that, Roxanne Renton decided to have a wee go at him, when the opportunity presented itself. But that evening, Sammy's wife Emilia had decided to turn up too, and she was a harder nut to crack, armoured in her braided tweeds, with her glossy hazel bob.

Roxanne, hardly ever quite sober, and certainly not on that night, prowled the gallery seeking a victim. Her head was leonine, with gilded tresses and sparkling wicked green eyes.

There was a shortage of single guys at the Sally Gardens Club on the evening of the champagne reception for honorary members. So Roxanne went to take up her position between the only two free men in the place, the famous old poet, Pascal Stone, summoned to be honoured, and his life-time companion and former Brother in Arms, Jackie Joad.

Roxanne decided to pick on Pascal Stone to harass, and started to toy with his tarnished waistcoat buttons, while talking dirty in his ear.

"Will I show you over the library?" she was offering. "We have a new collection of antique erotica. I know you're eighty-six, honey, but I can feel that you've still got a wee pulse going, and I think I could give you a good time!"

Fortunately, Pascal had left off his hearing aid (which he thought unsightly), in honour of the event. Otherwise he might have had a heart attack.

"Very nice!" he was replying, "I look forward to that at a later date." The only word he had picked up was 'library'.

When the poets to be honoured had all got themselves on to the platform, they made a pretty picture. There was Pascal and his friend Jackie in identical falling-to-pieces Black Watch evening jackets and black dress trousers. (They had met in an officers' mess.) The elderly lady poet, in a rosy summer frock, had her aged auntie with her, similarly attired. Sister Angel and Mother Agnes rushed in at the last minute. (The convent jeep wouldn't start, and they'd had to get a taxi.) Their white habits completed the dashing picture. And Angel's flushed and rosy face brought gasps of admiration from all and sundry.

Especially from Guy Everard, who tried to triple kiss her. But she deftly turned her head so on each attempt he got a face-full of sharp-edged guimpe and wimple instead of her soft cheek. Amateur photographers clustered round the platform snapping wildly.

The old poets began to feel uneasy, looking round for a means of escape. But one by one, the poets did their bit, although one or two could not have made themselves heard behind the proverbial Glasgow tram ticket. Lena was finally asked to read, and bravely shouted her poem.

She began to be conscious of the fact that she was getting laughs in the right places, and continued with more confidence.

> *"Occasionally sapsy chaps like women*
> *Some big tough lassies only dig guys*
> *It's hard to devise an acid test*
> *Lest you pass by spouse potential*
> *Not every seahorse is bisexual*
> *Nor every damp mollusc hermaphrodite.*
> *Sharp dressers and black and white movie lovers*
> *Are not exclusive to either camp*
> *So to those who are sexually perplexed and shy*
> *Here's your Agony Aunt's reply*
> *Appearances can be deceptive for a start*
> *Try to keep an open mind and heart*
> *But take my advice on love or shove it*
> *Not one of you is above it."*

The sound of laughter and applause reached Samuel Plaister's other, other half, who was propping up the bar in the recess abutting the gallery. Still chic in her Dior style suit.

Emilia Plaister gave a 'horse laugh', looking towards the barman for sympathy.

"How amusing! Don't you think? Christ, I hope Joel doesn't take after her, the half-wit! Did you notice how her verses only half rhyme? And that hair!" She shook out her own sleek bob. "I'll have a double Sambuca, Barry! And would you light it for me, pet? I'm afraid of flames!"

Sister Angel was next at the mike. Her gaze got trapped by Frank on the front row, cradling a violin case. He was programmed to play later. He must be waiting his turn to perform.

"My poem is called 'A Posey of Old Poets'." Angel said, adjusting the mike.

> *"I saw a posy of old poets*
> *Pale complicated and sweet*
> *A Fantin Latour of fine faces*
> *Open and completely*
> *Unworldly other worldly it's true*
> *What they say about poets*
> *Not like me and you."*

She became conscious of Frank's intense gaze, and her eyes became locked again with his, as she began to intone the next verse.

> *"The old poets were dispatched into taxis*
> *In assorted picturesque batches*
> *Left in the library a scent of rose and jasmine*
> *Pressed between leaves of ancient books*
> *Chanel cheroots and Versace*
> *Gauloise and Sobrani cigarettes"*

She paused, and looked out over the audience. Frank, embarrassed, dropped his gaze, too. In fact, he lowered his head, closing his eyes, as the poem ended.

"Like the incense of last kisses
Or the mystics' odour of sanctity."

In the applause that followed, Sister Mary of the Angels was not sure if she should bow. She was saved from this embarrassment as the gong sounded for supper, and the audience at once melted away towards the dining room. The poets were not far behind them. When they had sampled the mock champagne, and discovered that the supper that was being offered was only canapés, the poets, though, quickly decamped. However, Pascal returned, in a tizzy, having mislaid something or other.

Guy Everard pounced on Angel and led her to the library, to show her the erotica, in the hope of turning her on. Guy's special collection was on loan to the club, too, and was stowed away at the top of a spiral staircase, above the main library, in a little alcove.

When Guy saw there was nothing doing, he left her there unceremoniously.

Sister Angel made profuse notes, lost to the world, but after half an hour, she began to be conscious of voices drifting up to her from the Library below. At first the voices were quiet, then they got louder. Angel judged that one person was ascending nearer and nearer her, probably climbing the tall scary library steps. The two people were being forced to speak more loudly to each other, as the distance between them increased.

"I tell you it's here!" a voice growled, it seemed to her, almost in her ear.

"Christ, why didn't they photocopy it?" an amused voice demanded.

"A copy isn't legal!"

"So there's only you and me and him and the three old buffers in it now?"

"And since you two owe me so much cash, old man, only just me and them. Hold the bloody ladder straight!

This is our last chance to find it, before the trip. Wait a minute! I see it! I can reach it if I stretch. Hold the steps steady, can't you, you damn fool!"

There was a grinding noise, then a roar, a crash, and the sound of footsteps. All masked by a loud piano and violin czardas being played in the gallery. And the footsteps were running away, not approaching. Donnie Donald's bulky form was clinging desperately to the unstable ladder, which had become loose at the base and was swinging in wild arcs across the packed shelves of precious books. Angel was petrified, unable to move, and if Mother Agnes had not been coming in to the library to look for her, Donnie Donald would have been catapulted off.

Agnes, however, was able to grasp the ladder and with her considerable muscular power to set it straight. As she did so, though, Donnie lost his grip and started sliding down the ladder, grasping at volumes and tomes and pamphlets in his flight. In a moment of balance he leapt for the ground, falling on top of Agnes, who broke his fall. Agnes got painfully to her feet, but the big man lay still where he lay. Heavy volumes had battered his head.

Donnie came round, though, as Angel appeared, and managed to stagger to his feet. Agnes led him to an armchair, and he looked up at her, not at all gratefully, Agnes thought.

"Look here!" he said, "Don't let on about this! I feel a bit of a fool! I shouldn't have tried to climb up, all by myself, with no-one in the room. No, please don't start to tidy up. Just send the barman in with a double Scotch, I'll be fine. Oh, and thanks! Much obliged to you."

As Sister Angel and Mother Agnes obediently left him he was rubbing a bump on his head, looking more angry than hurt. Angel couldn't wait to tell Agnes about the weird conversation she had overheard. She whispered frantically in Mother Agnes's ear.

In the gallery, Roxanne was being terribly nice to Dame Georgie. She had her eye on Donald and hoped to put Georgie off the scent.

"Excuse me, Roxanne!" said Georgie," I must just collect my friend Lena! We're taking her back to the house to see our collection of Colourists." She meant to separate Lena from Sammy.

Lena Wallace was at that moment flirting with Frank Childers, telling him teacher gags, which he was trying to laugh at, pretending the gags were new to him. He was glad enough when Georgie called her away. He was eager to speak to Angel. And Mother Agnes, who knew the detective well, had been trying to attract his attention. She wanted to talk to him about the accident. Like Cluedo, Professor Donald, in the Library, with eight volumes of Proust, Agnes thought.

There was a bit of a feeding frenzy among the members, when it was discovered that Sister Angel was going on the tour. What a travelling companion! Loads of people who had been swithering about joining the trip, to make the organisers sweat, rushed to join up. Some were disappointed, though, and it was learned that Pascal Stone had signed up for the last two places for himself and Jackie.

"Doesn't let the grass grow under his feet, that old poet!" Roxanne complained, "I wonder if it's legal, him being over eighty, on reduced subscription." Roxanne hadn't managed to elbow aside a skinny lawyer, who was tougher than he looked, to get a place on the trip for herself.

She dashed up to Frank Childers and greeted him, in her own particular way. This meant stretching her body close, the length of his, and kissing him on the lips. She quite liked Frankie Babes, as she called him, and wanted to make sure he was going on the trip.

"Can you get me a place on the plane, Frankie Babes?" she asked him "Next to you?"

Frank was quick witted, though. "I said I'd sit beside Mother Agnes," he said. "She's a friend of mine. But look!" he teased her, "If you'd rather, I don't mind if you sit beside her instead!"

Guy Everard opened a waiting list for those who had left it too late. He loved doing that. Over his dead body would the worst of the switherers be accommodated on 'his' trip.

There was one extra place for Roxanne after all, since Binkie Boyne's name was scored out in black ink on Everard's list. Not that he was admitting to the fact of Binkie's demise. The club was good at turning a blind eye to sudden natural deaths among the membership, many of them being elderly. The bathroom looked the same as usual, unsanitary, and there were vases of old wild flowers still withering tortuously, as usual, on the window ledges.

Roxanne Renton was shocked by the state of the library, though, when she went in to look for Everard there. There would be hell to pay, she told him when she found him mooching around, making heavy weather of sorting it out. It was obvious that some old ledgers had been trashed. When Guy declined to give her a lift home, insisting on staying on to sort out the library, Roxanne had no recourse but to phone up her husband. He turned up eventually, in the huff, a big saturnine salesman who, luckily, hated foreign travel.

While waiting for him, Roxanne amused herself winding Guy up about his bachelor state.

"A man like you should really have a girlfriend. Or even a wife, for convenience, preferably a randy wee wife. Preferably a rich wee wife. Guy Everhard Up, they call you. Did you know that, Honey? What on earth do you do with your income, from your criminal practice?

Or from your criminal practices? Everyone wonders about that."

Guy was getting fed up with her moaning, like a nagging wife, even. He used one sure way he knew of shutting her up. He swung her up in his arms, and, squeezing her ferociously, he bit into her lips with a savage kiss. Then he pinched her plump backside.

Roxanne squealed and jumped backwards, not knowing whether to be pleased or not.

"Sorry," she fumed, reaching up to whisper in his ear, "I'd forgotten you were also known as Wee Willie Everhard! Are you still on the Viagra these days, Honey?"

Frank Childers gave Mother Agnes and Sister Angel a lift home in his black BMW. Agnes sat in the front with him, and Angel, in the back, fell asleep suddenly, like a child. He stole glances at her in his mirror as he talked companionably to Agnes.

She was telling him Angel's tale of the altercation in the Library, and the accident, if accident it was, that followed it. She tried to play down her role in saving Professor Donald from more serious injury. And she clutched her ancient battered briefcase as she whispered.

"So there you go again!" he ribbed her. "Saving life and limb. I wouldn't mind having you out on duty with me. You could be my sidekick."

"But what about that incident at the library, Childers, then? What do you make of it?"

"Sorry, Mother Agnes! My mind was wandering. I was hoping you would tell me!"

His mind had indeed been wandering, and he nearly missed the turning to Mirkhill, which led to the shortcut to the Convent of the Bleeding Heart. He had been watching, mesmerised, as Sister Angel woke up, stretched and yawned, her cheeks rosy with her momentary dreams, and her memories of the applause her poems had received.

He began to wonder, dopily, what it would be like to waken up every morning with that sweet head on the pillow beside you. It shouldn't be legal, he thought, letting one of Christ's dedicatees loose in the world, looking like that, to wreak havoc on the poor unsuspecting heart of a hardworking, newly promoted, Detective Inspector. It was just his bloody luck!

5

Crimea Pass

Crimea Pass was a conserved block of tenement buildings in the heart of the Bridgegate (pronounced Briggait) district, in the heart of Old Glasgow. It was a bridge linking two main streets, supported on cast iron pillars, overhanging another linking road below. The first floor of the tenement, that is, the ground floor of Crimea Pass, accommodated shops. A fruit shop gave a heady musty smell of over-ripe fruit. A dressmaker's and retro wear shop, and below and nearest the Gallowgate, a traditional fish and chip shop were all subsidised as to rates to keep the heart in this conserved heritage site.

Above that were two stories of dwelling houses, single ends, that is, a room and kitchen. Purists might think these would be one room only. But no-one would actually live in one room, and the tenants' association who remodelled the buildings had also slipped in proper bathrooms, too, even in the attic flats. The communal toilets, though, had vanished.

Peppy had been lucky to get a house there, when setting up her outreach convent. A lot of money had been spent in getting the right kind of old-fashioned wall paper, and the correct fitments for the Belfast square cut 'wally' (that is, earthenware) sinks. As to the closes and stairwells, the designers had not been able to resist fitting Art Nouveau shiny embossed tiles there, which the originals would never have risen to.

Sister Peppy was already making friends in the buildings. The old chap next door to her used to knock through the wall companionably to her when she came home in the evening from the drop-in centres, where she tended to the needs of the vulnerable of the district. He was confined to bed at that time, and sent his greetings through his home help, who popped in to give Peppy his history.

In his time he had been quite a dandy, and a man about town. He still had posh visitors. He had been the boyfriend of many young ballet dancers, both girls and boys. The home help said the flat was like an Aladdin's den, though most of the stuff was reproduction. If it hadn't been, the old man would have been a millionaire, she said. As he lay in bed, he was still quite a dandyish figure, with his dress shirt and bow tie and silk dressing gown worn over his pyjama bottoms. The lady said it was a pleasure to look after Mr. Whitbread. Melville Whitbread. Perhaps Peppy had heard the name?

On the floor below, that is, the ground floor of the buildings, lived a few young tarts, but they were good hearted and quite respectable, and never brought clients back to Crimea Pass, making other arrangements with their pimps. And they always took their turn at washing the closes and stairs, and putting whirligigs in white chalk in the correct patterns for the district. Even though they lived under the shadow of the bridge and hardly ever used the stairs themselves.

At the same level there was a garage and workshop which stretched far back to take over part of the back court. The young mechanic there took rather a fancy to Peppy, and promised he would find her a cheap motor,

Melville Whitbread

once her grants were paid. At the very far end of this dark street, there was a jeweller's shop, always brightly lit behind steel mesh, but which hardly ever seemed to be open.

Sister Peppy fitted well into Crimea Pass. Even her nun's habit, brown for ordinary, white for special, didn't amaze the residents too much. 'Black Narcissus' and 'The Song of Bernadette' had been on TV a lot that season. The retro dress shop had tempted many residents to dress up. The clothes were newly cleaned, cheap and chic, and were better stuff than the jumble found in second-hand clothes shops. And Violet, the girl owner, sprayed the shop with her namesake flower perfume, and also had butterscotch and vanilla candles. So the clothes did not have the scent of death that permeated most charity shops.

Benjie, the young guitar player, who, to confuse the Dole, had no surname, had picked up a pale linen Nehru suit for a song. As he strummed his guitar in the close mouth leading to Peppy's flat, he lent the place a touch of class, with his slicked back long hair in a neat pony tail. And he never fell out with the mobsters under whose stern aegis the Pass lay. Some folk claimed they knew for a fact that the Council had dealt directly with the mobsters, so that Crimea Pass could become part of the tourist trail.

At least a couple of the little tarts who lived in the shadowy flats found the skinny silk tea dresses very becoming when going out with their real boyfriends. So some of them thought perhaps Sister Peppy was simply dressing up in her flowing habits. Perhaps that might have been partly true.

Melville Whitbread, the invalid dandy, had no need of the retro boutique. He had chests of expensive male attire of yesteryear, stowed under both his hole-in-the-wall beds. Edna, his head home help and her numerous helpers turned the clothes over regularly, and sprayed them with modern moth repellent which did not smell of moth balls. They also polished his Sheraton furniture and fondly and respectfully burnished his bric-a-brac and gewgaws.

He was very sweet to them all. Each of his lady helps had had a poem dedicated to her, although some had had to be recycled when staff rotas changed. Because the agency had yellow uniforms (sunshine yellow, although much washed they turned into dead daffodil), he was able to use a folksong. He often used Burns, when he ran out.

"A little something for you in our native tongue" he'd say, although he was Cockney born and bred. He thought his Glesca dialect was faultless. "Hae a wee listen...

> *Lassie wi' the yallow coatie*
> *Wilt thou wed a muirland jockey?*
> *Lassie wi' the yallow coatie*
> *Wilt thou bask and gang wi' me?"*

If they were under five foot (which some of them were) he tried 'Bonny Wee Thing'. Though some helpers had heard that at weddings and christenings. One innocent young home help, Polish by nationality, had thought he was proposing, and had burst into tears and phoned in to cancel her next shift, because she really couldn't fancy him, and had a sweetheart in Cracow. Though the gent was so nice. And rich, you could see.

But sometimes, without prior notification, the ladies would find his door latched and their keys would not work. Usually a card would be pinned to the front door saying "Poet at Verse. Do not Disturb! See yiz Chinas!"

His ladies just smiled and went off and had a cup of coffee.

They would have been surprised, though, if they had seen what Melville got up to behind his barred door. Before their wedge-heeled sandals (I don't know why wedges were uniform, perhaps for retro chic) had finished clacking down the stone steps, Melville had sprung out of bed. Dragging out a pair of much damaged squinty wooden stepladders, he had run up them, and was rummaging around in the hatboxes that decorated the tops of his wardrobes. Especially since they had all massaged Melville's white, hairless and stick thin legs with his special Gentleman's Liniment. He making polite appreciative moans, not at all lecherous. Those ladies would have had red faces! They would have been black affronted to discover Melly could scamper about at will.

The jaikies and junkies stretched out immobile below the bridge, and squinting up through the curved wrought iron railings which supported it, were in for a fashion show from the gentry who visited Melville on such days. Gents in city suits and ladies in fake fur coats. One of these ladies on a certain day (as it happens, the day before the Sally Gardens Garda trip) was an absolute knock-out, in her leopard-skin print summer-weight raincoat. The loiterers below, who were in a position to see she was not wearing much beneath the coat (she intended to try on some retro resort wear at Violet's boutique later) gave sharp whistles and low moans as she passed above them. The Crimea Pass homeboys knew Roxanne Renton well, by sight, although nothing would induce Jimmy the mechanic who took charge of her Audi to reveal her identity to them. (Cash occasionally changed hands, but usually Roxanne just threw him a wink and an air kiss as she chucked her car keys to him, to park her car properly inside.) Then she rattled upstairs on her killer heels, and let herself into Melville's flat, now unlatched in expectation of her visit.

That day Roxanne seemed nervous. She really needed cash.

"I know you're eighty, honey, but you've still got a pulse..." she tried her old joke, which did not go down well.

"Enough, madam!" Melville, sitting up in his satin quilted recessed bed in state, spat at her acidly. "My venerable age and the state of my goolies are no business of yours. And would never have been. I had some of the best-toned young bodies in the business in my heyday. I was never a lover of avoirdupois, madam. So you would never have been my *bague*. But looking at you in that unfortunate outfit, bag seems to be the appropriate word. I'd ask you to relieve yourself of the plastic coat, but I shudder to think what might be revealed!"

Throughout his diatribe, Roxanne kept her eyes lowered, not daring to answer back, just waiting for him to finish, like a chastened child, a blank look in her green eyes.

"Well!" Melville roused himself from his dream of times past. "What have you got for me? I take it your visit relates to business, not pleasure!"

"Lovely stuff today, Mr. Whitbread. Some of it you will know. Some may be new to you."

"If it comes from the Sally Gardens, dear, nothing will be new to me. I have everything of any worth listed and filed, in my own way, which you'll never hack into, you silly little tart!"

Roxanne turned out the contents of a large Armani carryall on the counterpane before him.

"Yes, that is rather lovely!" He fingered an upward stretching ivory figurine voluptuously, "but far too well known. Half the dealers have it on their websites wish lists. Do you wish to get me thrown into clink, at my great age, darling? Maybe I'll take the lady anyway, take her and keep her. I have her twin in my corner cabinet."

He reached beneath his pillow for a roll of newish bank notes and peeled some off to toss to Roxanne, who dared to give them a funny look.

"Something wrong, dear? I thought you were off to the Italian Lakes tomorrow. What better place to launder the money? Surely even you will find that not beyond you! Well?"

"Do you mind if I count it?" She fingered the Titian red coils of her hair hesitantly.

"Okay, but what about a nice wee cup of tea first?" In spite of himself, he was falling into the old sweet ways he had for his home helps. Unfortunately, Roxanne was not much of a helping person. She had other talents, she considered, which were lost on a man like him.

"Okay, great!" Roxanne answered absentmindedly.

"I meant perhaps you'd make me one. I've had to send away today's ladies!"

"I'm not so hot on tea." Roxanne admitted. "Too technical! But I can mix you a nice Harvey Wall-banger. A White lady? Or would you prefer a Shirley Temple? I'm never quite sure what your preferences are!" She had got her courage up again since folding the sheaf of notes into her crocodile wallet.

"Well, I would never have preferred you, you slag. My tastes were exquisite. And even if I had been coarse enough to relish fondling pneumatic tits, the knowledge of your foul back-biting spiteful nature would have kept your hulk out of my bed. I'm sure your present crass companions in lust are lucky to wake up with their balls still attached!"

"Well, you will have your wee joke, Honey. I'm sure you don't really mean it! Sure you'd like to have a wee go, wouldn't you, pet? I'm sure you'd find I'd turn you on. Want a wee look? Go on, Melly! You know you do!"

Roxanne, as a Parthian shot before she left, ripped open her raincoat, and flashed him with the full bulk of her chalky white bikini-clad body, layers of curves bouncing up and down, in her mock triumphant gallus dance, as she loomed over him shouting, "I'll get you back, wanker!"

Melville screamed in disgust, pulling the rose silk of his bed spread over his bony head. Roxanne dashed out, slamming the door, laughing vindictively, leaving him sobbing.

It happened that Angel was paying Peppy her farewell visit that day, and Roxanne nearly collided with them on the stair-head. She was hastily zipping up her coat, adjusting her specs.

"Is Mr. Whitbread alright?" Peppy asked. "Was that him screaming?"

"With laughter, dear, with laughter! I feel I have to cheer him up from time to time. Nice old soul that he is, and we're such pals! And I do like tending to his wee needs. I should have been a nurse, like my mammy always said. Well, see ye, girls. As my old granny used to tell me, 'Be good! And if you can't be good be careful!'"

It was not till Roxanne was halfway across Jamaica Bridge on her way home that she remembered where she'd seen the pretty one of the nuns before. The brown habit had fooled her, and she had not recognised Angel at first.

"Jesus! The bloody poet! She can't have recognised me though, with my dark glasses on."

It was not till Angel was driving home past Glasgow Airport that she remembered where she'd seen Mr. Whitbread's visitor before. She was the woman Angel had seen wrestling amorously with Guy Everard in the Sally Gardens Library! The arched eyebrows over her sunglasses had given the game away. As well as the scarlet lips twisted into a mocking smile.

"At least she didn't recognise me," Angel thought. "She would have thought I was spying."

"I wonder if that nun was spying on me?" Roxanne thought. "I wonder who put her up to it! See if it's that Sammy Plaister, I'll kill him. Could be Everard, I suppose, but would he dare?"

At that moment, Sammy Plaister was toiling up the tenement steps at Crimea Pass. He was carrying an extra-large, elephant size, portfolio with the greatest of difficulty, using both hands and also balancing it against his tummy, as he heaved it onto the doormat outside Melville Whitbread's flat. He rang the bell and then waited patiently for some time, the sweat streaming off his face, and dampening his white curls, which stood up round his head like a halo. Eventually, he tried the door, and not finding it open, he produced a massive ring of assorted keys, and quite quickly finding the right ones, got the door to open, and dragged the portfolio inside.

"Hi, there!" shouted Sammy, from the lobby, not liking to advance further uninvited. "Mate! Melly! You there mate? Sammy here! Can I come in?"

Melly emerged from the bathroom where he had been bathing his eyes with witch hazel. When he saw Sammy, he threw himself into the poet's arms, and sobbed some more. He'd always liked Sammy. It was he who had put Sammy up as a member of the Gardens, he remembered. He had been a sophisticated older guy then, and Sammy a young buck.

"Oh Sammy! What a shock I've had! That bitch Roxanne tried to have a go at me!"

"You mean ...?"

"Oh no, not really, but it was still a nasty shock!"

Melville caught sight of the huge portfolio. "Well, that's a big one, ducky! As the actress said to the archbishop. Is it for me? "

"Well maybe, Melly. Maybe you could value it for me."

Melville indicated that Sammy should follow him with a flick of his nail-polished forefinger, and led the way into the kitchen, where an iron kettle was steaming on top of a closed lid on a black-leaded range.

"Put it down there on the bed," he said, swiftly pulling the kettle off the heat. "We'll have a nice cup of tea afterwards."

Sammy dropped the portfolio on top of the bed and the springs of the bed-frame creaked. "Ages since I've heard that sound, Sammy. Creaking bedsprings! Remember Limone?"

"Never forget that summer, mate. How could I? Wrote some of my best work that June. But I'm a married man, you know! Not only that, but I suppose you've heard...?"

"Yes, yes, Sammy. I've heard all about it. Couldn't believe my ears! An infant! And I've heard its mother is an absolute fright! That right, Sammy?"

"No, not at all! Who told you that? She's very nice in her own way. And the baby's lovely! Joel! I let her choose the name, but I like it too. Shall I bring Joel to see you?"

"Shouldn't bother, old man! Thanks all the same." Melville started to untie the tapes of the portfolio, opening the flaps flat. "Before I look," He turned to Sammy. "If you need cash it's not a problem! You don't have to sell your heirlooms, Joel's inheritance!"

"Not exactly his inheritance. I only kind of own them. Go on, take a look!"

Melville turned back the covering sheets of rice paper and gasped at what was revealed below. He had to sit down on the bedside bentwood chair. He looked up at Sammy.

"Are they right?"

"Yes, right as rain! They have the original dust of the Sally Gardens on them. When the place was being done over. I offered to clear the attics, which were full of rubbish. I was young and strong then. They said I could keep anything I wanted, if I took the lot away."

"They didn't mean these though, Sammy, did they? A full set, let me count them, yes, twenty two, twenty three, and the last one, sadly dog-eared, twenty four. First edition art posters! Picturesque Garda! Very fine Stylization! Double Imperial! Did nobody miss them?"

"No-one knew they were there, it seemed. Except Everard. He questioned me about them. I explained I'd always meant to give them back. And then he..."

"Suggested you should sell them for yourself. And for Joel!"

"Melly! How on earth did you know?"

"Have you thought, Sammy, if he's letting you have these, how much is Guy spiriting away for himself, with the same excuses?"

"You see, Melly, I am in a spot of bother over money. This trip to Garda. Lena's going and then Emilia wanted to go too. Pretty expensive."

"If you sell these, you put yourself in Guy's power, and he's a nasty murderous bastard! Do you really want to do that? I'm willing to take the risk over the provenance, but wait a bit. Make up your mind. I'll hold them till I get word from you, and if you say sell, I'll sell!"

Melville shut up the portfolio again, Sammy tacitly giving in by pocketing the cash Melly held out to him. He followed directions in shoving the folio carefully under the bed.

"Just drop me a line, Sammy. Whatever you decide. Send me a postcard from Garda! A picture postcard, preferably from Limone! For old time's sake!"

But Sammy was not so hard-hearted as to leave without brewing Melly his long awaited cup of strong tea. He darted about making it quickly, and yelped comically when he burned the tips of his fingers on the heavy old smoke-blackened kettle on the hob, having ignored the new electric kettle Melly's ladies always used.

"Now where's the condensed milk, mate?" Sam asked. "Tea isn't tea without it."

Melly watched him in a reverie of blissful nostalgia, as Sam speared a slice of bread and held it to the bars of the range. "Do you remember the old studio, Sammy? No mod cons!"

But Sammy hardly lipped his own tea, and was already halfway out the kitchen door.

Impetuously, Sammy Plaister came back and gave his old friend and lover a hug. The sharp light in his piercing brown eyes softened for a moment. He stood there, rather shyly, running his hands through his springing white curls. Then he swooped out of the door, slamming it behind him, and making the stone steps ring from his stout leather brogues.

Melville lay back on his bed, looking perplexed, as he heard Sam's departing yells echoing round the close.

"*Ciao*, Melly! *Arrivederci!*"

"It's almost as if he never expects to see me again." Melville said to himself.

6

High In The Clouds

"Any of you lot feeling just a bit queasy? A little bit under the weather? Nervous? Sweating? Little palpitations? Anyone thinking they might wet themselves with fright when the big bird soars into the wild blue yonder? Come on, little Sister Mary of the Angels! Your wee face looks as white as your habit! Have one of my anti-funk pills. Your travel mates swear by them! I haven't lost a tripper yet, in all my years in charge of foreign trips!"

Guy Everard was strutting up and down the benches packed with his clubmates in the departure lounge of Glasgow Airport, haranguing them. He prided himself on never feeling travel sick, or even anxious. As he approached, most of his companions pasted nonchalant smiles on their faces. Except Sister Angel, who was reciting the rosary to herself, to calm her nerves. She wasn't the world's best traveller, though she would have been roasted on Saint Philomena's gridiron before she would have admitted it to Guy, the big pillock, as she thought of him. She flicked him with a frosty glance as he threw himself down beside her.

Nothing daunted, Guy flung a lanky arm round the nun's shoulder, and pulled her round to face him. He

64

used another approach, more intimate, whispering in her white veiled ear, invisible beneath her wimple, her starched head-dress.

"Seriously, dear!" he murmured, "Better have one of these. You don't want to be sick on the flight. How embarrassing would that be? Here!" He forced a small round pill between her lips and shoved his bottle of water at her, giving it a squeeze so that liquid spurted out, and she was forced to swallow. "Now swallow, there's a good girl!" She did, and, grinning, he produced a red silk handkerchief and dabbed at the front of her guimpe, the stiffened gauze collar of her habit, where a few drops had spilled. "There you go! That wasn't too bad, was it?" he said impudently, getting up suddenly, pretending someone was waving at him. And waving back at the figment, he hurried off, in the direction of the bar.

Really, Angel thought, if he had no respect for her as a poet, as a person, or even as a fellow club member, he might have some respect for her sacred habit, revered near and far, she had found, as a symbol of dedication to holiness! Not that she was very holy, or all that dedicated, she admitted to herself. Now Mother Agnes! She looked at her white-clad saintly companion, whose tall heavy figure loomed at her side. That was another story. Agnes had brought people back from the verge of death. She had helped animals give birth. (She said it wasn't as easy for brute beasts as everybody made out.) She had hand-reared their offspring when animal mothers had succumbed, going without sleep night after night. And of course Mother Agnes had no fear of flying. She had flown all over the world to charity conferences, no bother at all. Except for her legs, and the public speaking. Angel recalled Mother Agnes confiding to her that she was nervous of that. She was sensitive about her Irish brogue, she had said, although everyone thought it was lovely. Patronising, Angel thought, to think one accent more than another was lovely. Guy Everard was always speaking cod Irish (like Father Ted, he thought) to Agnes, to wind her up.

The young cop, Frank Childers, came and stood in front of Sister Angel, as if to protect her from any more attention from Guy Everard. Angel saw his lips move. It was 'Pillock!' he was mouthing, she saw, after Guy's retreating figure. She couldn't help smiling a bit, although she had promised herself to keep her distance from Frank. She gathered he had been able to do Agnes a favour in the past, during the investigation into Sister Philomena's death. Well, he needn't think he could capitalise on it. Guys were always coming on to her. When would they get the message? Not everybody needs to be part of a couple. Some people have their own lives to lead. What did he think she was wearing the great big white frock for? Because she thought she looked good in it? Well, that was true of course, but not her only, or indeed her main, reason. Angel sat up sanctimoniously, with a little prim smile on her face. She noticed Agnes seemed to be giving her a funny look. She was shaking her sleeve to attract her attention.

"I was just saying to Mr. Childers, Angel, would he like to form part of our trinity? We've been told to get into threes for the seating arrangements. That okay, Mr. Childers? We won't embarrass you? And if the plane crashes, sure we'll hear your last confession!"

Just then their flight to Bergamo was called and everyone rushed to form a ragged queue, passengers trying to look as if they were not pushy, while trying to get as near the front as possible (their budget airline not yet having pre-booked numbered seats).

By some chance, the group from the Ancient Society of Scriveners and Limners was called first. Guy tried to take the credit, going up and down the queue winking as he shepherded his party aboard, but it was probably chosen alphabetically. Or perhaps because of the 'Ancient' in the title, the organisers thought all the members were as old as Pascal, who would have qualified for getting in first anyway, and even for a wheelchair, if there had happened to be one around.

With Angel dashing for the window seat, and Agnes preferring to be on the aisle, Frank Childers found himself seated between the nuns. He went goose pimply down the Angel side.

Roxanne was marooned between Jack and Pascal. Lena was stuck in the middle of the august couple, Professor Donald and Lady Georgiana. (Georgie wished Lena would give Sam Plaister the elbow. Of course she had never met baby Joel.) Lena looked in vain for Sammy. He was near the front, with the skinny chap who had taken Emilia's place on the trip. Because Emilia had thrown a tantrum when she learned, not only that Lena was going to Garda, but that she herself would be forced to speak to her, maybe even be polite! And who was to mind Joel, she had screamed. Was he to be put into an orphanage? Should we put the poor little lad in a Home, while all three of his parents were gallivanting round the Italian Lakes? Or maybe, she'd screamed, they should take him with them, where the food wouldn't suit his little tummy, and his little ears would pop on the plane. Emilia had known enough about club trips to time correctly her opting out. In time to get her money back, when someone took up the place. She had actually done it a couple of times before, just to annoy Sammy. Who, to annoy her, pretended hardly to notice her absence. To crown it all, a mother and baby from another party was put on the outside seat next to Sam, the stewardess having thought he had a kind face.

Dolores squirmed in her place between two beautiful Italian students returning from Glasgow University to their home town, Milan. To make matters worse, the two students were very casually dressed. Even for a budget flight, when some members were wearing their static older clothes. Dolores wore a white Armani jacket of a matelot cut, in honour of the lakes, over a black stylish jump suit, which made the other women on the flight cross. No-one without the most subdued and obedient of bladders could have worn that very zippered suit on a long journey. Her make-up was flawless too. She kept her eyes down, peering through her heavy reading glasses at a sheaf of her own poems.

Towards the back there was a rabble of lawyers and advocates, to whom Guy was returning favours. The Gardens Club members worried that he also gave them reduced rates.

Right at the front, to where she and her companions had been ushered, Angel was having a spot of bother, trying to fasten her seat belt over her voluminous habit, although Agnes had no trouble. Angel was feeling a little bit dizzy, and Frank had to twist sideways to assist her, blushing furiously as he did. As the plane started to take off, Angel's mauve eyelids fluttered and her breathing came in gasps. As it at last lurched into the air, Angel gave a long drawn-out scream and grabbed Frank's hand, scratching it, drawing blood with her little pointed pink nails. (Brilliant! he thought shamelessly. Go on, go on, hurt me more!) Then he got a grip of himself, as he caught Guy Everard glancing at him from the opposite aisle, where he was saddled with a couple of large, grey-suited Italian businessmen who had pushed in. Guy was definitely giving him the evil eye.

Almost instantly, though, Angel fell fast asleep, her head nodding on Frank's shoulder. Guy's herbal pill was to blame, actually. His pills were more potent than people realised. And for a joke he'd spiked his water bottle with vodka. Angel wasn't used to alcohol, except

Mother Benigna's Elderflower Wine. And she could even get tipsy on that.

Other members had accepted Guy's herbal pills too, and the atmosphere in the plane as it flew above the patchwork lowland fields became quite dreamy. Friendships were made and quarrels made up. Donnie Donald got so pally with Dame Georgie that Lena was feeling like a gooseberry. When the plane flew among the clouds drifting over the channel an odd euphoria developed, especially among those who had sampled their duty free. Angel, released from her seat belt, collapsed right over Frank's lap, cutting off his circulation. He didn't know whether he was in more pleasure than pain. He was almost relieved when Mother Mary Agnes cried out in agony, having difficulties with her own dodgy circulation. She explained through gritted teeth that her thighs kept going into cramps. It often happened to her, she said. She was sorry to be a bother, but the only way it could be stopped was by massage. Guy quickly scrambled away to find a flight attendant, as Agnes writhed in pain.

Her screams had wakened Angel up, and when she jolted upright, Frank leapt across to crouch at poor Mother Agnes' feet, giving her a very serious massage, with his already tanned strong hands. (Angel couldn't help noticing how nice his hands looked.) Mother Agnes was very grateful, so relieved she was beyond embarrassment, and Frank, too, seemed immune to the catcalls of ridicule and the laughter that was coming from his own travelling companions.

Guy loped back from having a fly fag in the toilet. He'd left it too late to change places with Frank as he'd planned. And Frank was quite the hero of the hour, after all, as he sat coolly discussing Renaissance art with an admiring Sister Angel. In the middle of Masaccio, Sister Angel suddenly fell childishly asleep again, curled trustingly round Frank, holding on to him, and he spent the rest of the flight high as a kite, watching the golden angelic cloud formations form and reform behind her beautiful head. Angel did not awaken till Frank was forced to release himself from her, and balance her upright in her corner, fishing round her to put on her seatbelt for landing.

Lena Wallace was glad she was stuck in the middle seat. She had clocked Sammy craning back towards her from time to time, as he got into contortions trying to avoid the baby. No doubt he thought she would be delighted to change places with him. Well, he had another think coming! But Sammy, fed up with the baby's crying, decided to take matters into his own hands, literally. He scooped the baby up and squashed her against his own padded jacket. The baby burped obligingly and stopped crying, depositing a little regurgitated milk on Sammy's wide cream linen shoulder.

"There you go!" he said to the mother, as he handed the infant back. "You see, you were doing it all wrong! Women made such a fuss over looking after babies!" Sammy sat back complacently, tightening his seat belt, just wondering a bit where the pong of sickness was coming from.

As Frank Childers got Angel's seat belt on, she woke again with a beatific smile.

"Oh, I've been having such lovely dreams!" she exclaimed before she could stop herself. "Is the journey over already?"

Guy Everard stood up illegally early to be sure to be first out when the doors opened, and nodded grimly at his creased and sleepy group to follow suit.

Being first out did make disembarking and Customs easier, though Everard made rather a meal of counting his group when aboard their bus, racing across the motorway to their hotel.

"I'd just hate to lose any one of you!" he explained, with his jackal-like leer.

Frank had sat beside Angel on the bus, and did not come down from his high till he was showered and lounging on his hotel bed in his grey silk pyjamas. He didn't feel like dressing for dinner yet. Next door to him he could hear the chant of ritual prayers. Mother Agnes and Sister Angel had been given the room next to his. (Halleluiah! he joined in fervently.)

He had earlier refused an invitation from the gang of lawyers to go out 'on the town' with them. Rudely, their avowed aim had been to pick up pretty girls, and they had, to a man, swaggered off, leaving the single women in the party stranded. Frank didn't think the lawyers would have much luck, in the picturesque castled town of Malcesine. There weren't all that many low tourist dives there, of the kind they were looking for. Anyway, Frank considered lawyers to be his natural enemies. Very wrong of him, but there it was. So he stayed put where he was. He himself was ungallantly anxious to avoid Dolores, whom he rightly guessed would be hanging around the bar downstairs, hoping he would turn up.

Dolores and Roxanne sat at the bar sipping champagne cocktails. In the mirror behind the bar they could track the progress of the only handsome Italians in the place. Both tall, with blonde hair and red moustaches. The taller of the two was explaining something to his companion, under his breath. Then they both burst out laughing.

The other man was searching for the right word. He was miming a curvaceous outline which Roxanne took to be hers, and turned round to glance at him provocatively.

Roxanne leant over to whisper in Dolores's ear. "I think the big one fancies me!"

"Don't bank on it," Dolores advised, "The pair of them look like a couple to me!"

They both laughed loudly and rudely, hoping to grab the men's attention. At which they were unsuccessful. Dolores leaned over to Roxanne.

"Or gigolos?" she suggested, swivelling on her stool to stare at them. "Do you think they're a pair of gigolos? Looking for business? Could we afford them, do you think?"

"Oh, I do hope so, darling. Rough trade is always so interesting!"

In response to this, the two men at the other table simply slid from their seats in one movement, and walked languidly out the glass front doors. Roxanne turned her attention to Pascal and Jackie, who had come down, all spruced up, for a nightcap.

She bounced down off her stool to not quite kiss each of them elaborately.

"I heard they've put the two of you in bunk beds, in the attics. What a sin!"

"We don't mind!" said Jackie gamely, "and it's only till tomorrow. Then we'll get a room with a view!" He looked fondly at pale frail Pascal.

"A room with a view! You're lucky!" Roxanne was jealous. "We've got three double beds and views of a friggin' wardrobe! But tell me, which of you is going to get on top tonight?"

"Look here, why don't you gentlemen come into our beds?" Dolores broke in poisonously. "We have two spare, or you could double up in one! Do you like doubling up?"

"Well, there's a first time for everything!" Roxanne muttered. "Seriously, chaps. You two ever tried women? It's better late than never. We women have our points, you know!"

The two refined gentlemen fled from the bar, which of course had been the whole idea.

"I wonder if that bastard Frank Childers intends to come down tonight?" mused Dolores, "I'm a sucker for young fit men like him, and I thought he was sweet and really liked me. But he was just like all the other genteel guys who shag you a couple of times and then dump you. And you thought you were doing them a great big favour!"

"And as for that big pillock Guy. Guy Everard! Everhard!? He wishes!" Roxanne seethed.

They both sighed. They both knew all about Guy Everard. And for a while there was silence between the two ladies, as they both considered the problem of how and when they would manage to get their revenge on big shot Mr. President, Guy frigging Everard!

Upstairs, on the first floor, with a view (a view at present dusky and blue and broken by the fairy tale turrets of the castle, with inky blue lake waters lapping its ramparts), Detective Childers had been awakened by the raucous laughter from the bar. He was padding up and down on his balcony, his interconnecting balcony with the holy Sisters next door. He could hear their murmured prayers starting again. He even recognised some of it. The Litany of the Virgin, they were reciting. He was on cloud nine. He was in paradise! If there was one part of the old rituals he loved it was the litanies, and especially he loved the Litany of the Virgin!

The two female voices chimed. One treble and bright. One alto and husky and weary, like two instruments, maybe a violin and a cello. He deciphered a few phrases floating past.

"Mother most pure," the words were all coming back to him now in a rush,

"Mother most chaste," that his wee mammy had taught him sitting on her knee.

"Mother most amiable." Sounds like Agnes, good Mother Agnes of the Holy Child.

"Mother most admirable." Yes, that too, but she'd hate him, if she knew his secret.

"Virgin most venerable." Not Angel, no!

"Virgin most merciful." Nor merciful either! Christ no!

"Mystical Rose." Yes little rosebud, pearly rosebud!

"Tower of David." Now you're talking!

"Tower of Ivory." At last a couple of phallic symbols!

"Ark of the Covenant." Whatever that means but okay, whatever you say I'll covenant!

"Gate of heaven." Your gate my heaven!

"Morning Star." So stay then till dawn! Why rush away?

"Health of the sick." The lovesick need not health,

"Refuge of sinners." but a refuge for their sick sins.

"Mirror of justice." shining like a fair cop, in an unjust world,

"Seat of wisdom." I'll teach your soul my wisdom.

"Cause of our joy." My joy! Your joy! Oh boy!

"Singular vessel of devotion." I'll pour my grace into your vessel.

"Queen of Angels." My Angel! My Queen!

"Queen of peace." No Peace without you my Queen! To misquote a lovesick poet laureate.

The voices died to a murmur and, fevered, ashamed, he lost track of the rest of the verses.

"Pray for us! Amen!" The voices ceased.

Frank modestly shut his balcony doors and went back to lie on his bed. He had a problem. He was falling for a nun! And acting like a stalker! And worse, he suspected he was falling for her because she was a nun! The purer she was the more he liked it. It looked as if his problem might have no solution.

He heard a rustling at his door. A scrap of paper was pushed under it.

He picked it up and took it to his bedside lamp to read it.

"Dear Mr. Childers," he read. "I have a problem, a serious one. I would like your help."

Frank got to the door and threw it open. A figure in a brown habit was just turning away. A large figure. Frank Childers had never quite lost the good manners his mammy had insisted on.

"Please come in, Mother Agnes!" he called. "I'll be very pleased to do anything I can to help you. With your problem, whatever it is. No, of course it's not too late. I haven't even said my bed-time prayers yet!"

Mother Agnes did not laugh at his little joke. She looked worried. She sat down on Frank's bed without asking permission, and from the voluminous brown sleeve of her habit, she fished out a narrow scroll of vellum. She grabbed various of his toiletries from his dressing table and used them to batten down the unrolled parchment, on top of his silk bedspread.

"Can you make head or tail of that, could you tell me?" she asked Frank, her southern Irish accent more pronounced, he noticed. "I fear it may be a matter of life and death! But it looks as if it was written in Elvish! Sure I thought to myself you'd be the very wee man to translate it for me, so I did! Would you just cast your eye over it?"

Frank came down to earth with a bump as he studied the stained and tattered document. He could read the scrawling ink blotted vellum page right away, even without holding it up to the mirror, which he now did, so Agnes could read it properly too.

She gasped. "Just what I thought!" she said. "A Tontine! The survivor gets all."

"It would make sense of the 'accident' in the library. And I've heard there has been another 'accident', this time fatal, that they've kept well hushed up. I hope we're not due any more!"

"Can we meet tomorrow to discuss this?" Frank asked. "There may be no time to lose. We'll have to miss the boat trip to Isola Del Garda. Angel will have to go by herself!"

It was almost a relief to Frank to rule out his crazy romance, even just for a day.

"Oh, Angel will be disappointed!" Mother Agnes said kindly, giving him what he saw, as his olive cheeks burned, was an unmistakably compassionate look. "Sure, what will she do without us, me her Mother in Christ, and you her dear kind friend? She'll be all at sea!"

"Christ, so she knows all about it!" Frank moaned as Agnes left, closing the door gently.

It opened again immediately. Mother Agnes was smiling sweetly.

"By the way, I suspect I heard you make some antiphonic responses to the litany of the Virgin. How unusual that you were acquainted with such abstruse verses. Unless, of course, Frank, you were making up your own, impromptu. How clever!"

Frank sat back on his bed, blushing, his head in his hands, coming down from his dreams with a crash.

7

In Convent Gardens

On the private launch crossing the narrow channel between Gardone and Isola del Garda, Angel held forth to her fellow club members. She didn't have much time, therefore, and made her remarks as short and pithy as she could. She was stung by the very late arrival of Roxanne at Gardone, and the way no-one had objected (probably because she had been made up to the nines, in their hotel's spa). Angel's face on the other hand was innocent of make-up, and she was the one girl in a hundred, she couldn't help acknowledging, who could get away with that.

"Signora Gardone is a sophisticate," she told them, in the narrow cabin of the launch. "We wonder how she was funded, but the money has lasted long enough to keep the lady looking fine, to date! She's a heartbreaker, just past her prime!" Her eyes flickered over Roxanne, who took the glance as an envious compliment. "Her casinos have vistas of mirrors, like *Last Year in Marienbad*, that magic film, directed, as you know, by Alain Resnais."

There was a murmur of appreciation from her eager audience of artists and poets. They nodded at each other in satisfaction. Their glances seemed to say that they had done well to pay for Angel's services. No common guide could have strung such evocative phrases together, flattering her listeners with a knowledge of Nouvelle Vague cinema too.

Sister Mary of the Angels blushed prettily at the encouraging comments, and went on.

"We are now approaching Gardone's sweet little sister, whom she snootily ignores. Floating, as you can see, like a mirage just above the waves, partly man made, and I think you'll agree, ravishingly fake. Like a modest lady who has had to use every cosmetic device at her disposal to increase her attractions! And is still, perhaps, lonely, and waiting to be kissed!" Her eyes skimmed Lena, with her wildly ringletted hairstyle. "Some writers have reported that the islet was even more lovely in the past, when the monastic and conventual rule of Saint Francis was still thriving. When the landscape, untended, was more simple and graceful, a refuge for fishermen and lake birds, during stormy weather."

Angel was absolutely furious with Frank Childers for not being there to listen to her carefully-chosen phrases. She had been shocked to find both he and Mother Mary Agnes had left before breakfast, to go to the convent at Toscolano Mademo, where Agnes intended to stay. They might have told her, although she admitted it was nice of Frank to accompany Agnes and help her with her luggage. Although Agnes didn't usually need help like that.

Sister Angel had even got a few gags ready, comparing Frank with Saint Francis, his namesake. It was hardly worth trotting them out now, she thought, and was relieved when the little boat bumped up against the small wooden dock head. Guy Everard helped her off with a mocking bow, as if her habit must be impeding her.

As Angel spoke a few more words on the terrace balcony of the formal gardens below the Venetian style villa, Guy kept his eye relentlessly on her, standing in the first row of the circles round her, in spite of his height. He was trying to put her off, she knew, as she outlined the complex history of the residence, from monastery to palace to villa.

But Guy managed to trap her against a marble balustrade, under the excuse of his precious video, making her point that way and this, turning her face to the light with his long fingers, openly sighing in admiration.

"Now that will make a lovely shot!" he kept saying. "Looks ravishing, as you said. And the view's charming too!"

Angel began to feel really edgy, and a bit resentful both of Frank and Mother Agnes.

Guy shoved his Punchinello face ever nearer her, and she could feel his drooping moustaches brushing her cheek. But a ship's horn sounded just then, through the violet mist that was beginning to descend, and both turned their heads towards it. Somehow, Angel got the feeling that the sailors just visible lining up on board could actually see them. Perhaps they could, through field glasses. They gave Angel the impression of being watched, and it looked as if Guy felt that too. Anyway, he turned away from her to capture the image of the Junk, with square cut sails set, as it skimmed across the ruffled surface of the lake, from behind a screen of spruce. All nature seemed still, the sun hanging high in the sky, hot enough to melt the wings of any Icarus. Everyone stood frozen, watching the silver dream ship in silence, till it disappeared at last behind the farthest groves of trees. As if departing from Cythera.

Later, the birds in the sanctuary below flocked round Angel uncannily as she spoke, waving her arms to point out the varieties of trees. Maybe it was their feeding time then, but they made brilliant pictures for the video cameras, as they fluttered round her equally light figure, against the dark trunks of the swamp trees reflected in random pools.

Guy Everard came rushing down, but missed the best shots. And Guy wasn't the only one to have a go at the newly-vulnerable Sister Mary of the Angels. Professor Donald patted her paternally, and got her to pose beside him for snapshots, towering over her, his huge arm slung round her shoulder.

Really, Sammy Plaister was the only chap who was nice to her, talking about poetry to her and reading out some of his own. And Lena Wallace was the only lady who did not mind her partner talking to her. She went around making lightning sketches of beauty spots. They looked incomprehensible, Angel thought, but no doubt meant something to her.

Dame Georgie was the only one who thought of buying Angel a cup of tea in the little shabby tearoom. Sister Mary of the Angels had forgotten to bring any money with her. Usually, she didn't need any. She felt her face crumple a little bit when her millionairess friend generously bought some pastries for Angel to choose from.

"Never mind, dear!" Dame Georgie said briskly. "You've done well! Your talks went well! I'm so glad we asked you to come with us!"

"I'm used to Mother Agnes being with me." Angel admitted. "Nuns are not usually let out on their own."

"No wonder, dear!" said Georgie, "if they're as pretty as you! Was that the boat's hooter I heard? We'd better get back to it, before the mist gets any worse! So where's Donald?"

The mist that the guide books said often 'bathed the island with mystery' was enveloping the little artificial promontories and curling round the ramparts and turrets of the villa. Only the tops of the enormous cypress trees that guarded the driveways showed as silhouettes on the terraces above.

It occurred to Angel that Georgie was keeping a stiff upper lip herself, about something. Angel glimpsed Dolores framed suddenly in a misty archway as she and Georgie passed. Dolores turned to jeer at someone walking behind her. The person came into view, through the arch, in his turn. The shambling figure of bulky Professor Donald appeared, remonstrating, it seemed, pathetically, and not in his usual comical mode.

When they got back to the landing stage, Guy Everard was running up and down the line of his travel mates, shouting at them and counting them. The trouble was, two were missing. Then Sammy Plaister appeared with Lena Wallace, who'd stupidly got herself trapped in a toilet cabin. He'd had to wrench the door open to get her out. Dolores was already aboard, and was standing behind the skipper as he sat at his controls, leaning on him, and tipping his cap over his eyes playfully.

"Hurry up, you landlubbers!" yelled Guy, taking over the function of a Captain, as he hurried his crew of poets aboard. "Step lively now! Unless you want to be marooned!"

He was using his semi-official status to slip his hands round all the ladies' waists as he helped them aboard, over the small ramp that acted as a gangway.

Suddenly there was a surge in the choppy water, and the line tied fast to the stanchion vibrated. At the same time, for some unknown reason, there was a surge in the heaving crowd trying to board. How it happened no-one knew, but first Donnie Donald did a sort of crazy cake walk on the ramp, stumbling and nearly slipping off the edge, on his quite surprisingly small and dainty sandaled feet. Then his much smaller wife managed, with a superhuman heave, to send him skittering over the threshold and into the boat.

But she herself, with a kind of bark, took a nose-dive into the steep space between boat and the dock, and, submerging in the deep-cut channel, did not reappear at once.

Everyone stood petrified, then Roxanne began to scream, and Guy Everard started shouting for a lifebelt. They all watched as the skipper wrestled the shabby circlet off its rusted clamps.

Until Angel hit the water, no-one had even noticed she had torn off her outer vestments and dived from the pier. She went down into the water just as Georgie bobbed to the surface, having freed herself from weed. Then Angel, in her turn, bobbed up, looking weird in her close-fitting white cap, without her wimple, like a toy seagull, as she rolled against the waves. Then Guy threw off his blazer and flannels and lowered himself carefully into the water. He floated effortlessly. Bizarrely, as Lady Georgie did not seem to require help, all three swimmers made their way, energetically, at once to the slimy steps that led out of the basin. Sammy was halfway down, clinging to iron rings set in the stone, ready to help them out. The rest of the group crowded round, congratulating and commiserating. Except Donnie. Seated in the cabin, almost fainting with fear and shock, he covered his face with his hands.

"That could have been me!" he kept repeating. "And I can't swim!"

Then, "It's not my fault!" he moaned. "I tripped over something. I've got strange eyesight. Natural monocularism. I can't judge distances. I'm rotten with steps and ramps. I often trip up going down steps! Georgie was hurrying me!" Then he started again, complaining, looking round for sympathy. Dolores must have made up her quarrel with him, because she came over and patted his large pallid hand with her tanned, be-ringed claw.

He began to recover. "What was the hurry, anyway? There's the mist lifting. We won't even be late for dinner now." He got up suddenly, as the rest of the group came aboard. "So where's that naughty little wife of mine? What a good job you're as strong as a channel swimmer, love!"

An irrational thought came into Angel's head, as she shivered under the greasy blanket the Skipper had shoved around her, and they were powering back to Gardone.

"It's all Frank Childers' fault!" she said to herself. "He should have been here to look out for me! I hope he's sorry now!"

The next thought that came into her head was, "I wonder who shoved Professor Donnie?"

She got Sammy to find the number of the convent in Toscolano and phone Mother Agnes.

In the garden of the Convent of the Star of the Sea, Frank received the scary news from Mother Agnes, and jumped up, upsetting the papers that he and Agnes had spread out on the folding table between them.

The first irrational thought to enter his head was, "I should have been there to look after Angel. It's all my fault!"

But Agnes forestalled him.

"But what good would you do, rushing back? Worse things happen at sea. Pick up those papers now, that's a good chap, and let's go over our deliberations again, and see if we can't come up with a solution at last. Sure you wouldn't want Angel to think we were treating her like a ninny!"

Frank still stood there irresolute, still eager to return to Malcesine and Angel.

"And to be honest with you, young man!" Mother Agnes stared into his eyes strictly, "It's not exactly your place! Is it now?"

But Frank's mind was in a whirl since he'd got news of the accident. Even before that, if he was honest. He looked round the peaceful garden, with its pergolas overhung with rose and jasmine, clematis twining its way up the chestnut trees, with the little grove of olive trees that climbed the hill behind. He had just kept wishing Angel was there with him. He now saw how foolish he looked, and pulled himself together. He scrabbled the papers they had been examining off the grass, and anchored them with pebbles.

"Let's start again!" he cried, getting out his good pen to make notes. "Back to this document. By the way, how did you find this, Mother Agnes? It's called a Tontine, a kind of Group Life Assurance policy. The survivor inherits all the combined investment."

"Find it, nothing! Sure I stole it from the club library. Donnie Donald had it in his hand when he fell on me. I was due that at least for the bumps and bruises I got from the learned fellow. It's a wonder I survived. And then I tidied up a few more documents that were lying doing nothing!"

"Look, Mother Agnes, it's no good! My brain won't work till I get things sorted out with Angel. Tell me, can nuns revoke their vows? Or are their contracts binding for life?"

"It's supposed to be, that if you knew what you were vowing when you made the vows, that yes, they're binding. But if you held back something and didn't really mean it, not so much! I don't totally 'get' that myself. As you know, Mr. Childers, I have had my own problems in the past. Love doesn't just strike beautiful people like you and Angel. It strikes old codgers as well. And this mess we've landed in here on our lovely Italian holiday. Is it all about love, Mr. Childers, or is it all about money? This Tontine, as you say it is, is it binding for life? The survivor inherits all? Now what all is that?"

"Both, I should think, Mother Agnes, maybe about the money you need to buy love! It seems someone doesn't love our Donald. One accident could have been carelessness. Two look like malice aforethought! But a Tontine is not necessarily for life. There is a date. A Tontine date, when it finishes. And this states," Frank took up another folded paper, "that date is exactly a week tomorrow! And the Tontine's Investment was the clubhouse of the Ancient Society of Scriveners and Limners! Bought when it was at rock bottom. This, folded up inside, is an extract from the Register of Sassines, an obsolete body which still retains the force of law. Whoever wins the Tontine, wins the Sally Gardens."

"And the investors? I can't make those names out even with my glasses."

"The first is clear enough. The accident-prone Professor Donald Donald. This loopy one, I see, is Guy Byron Everard. And this tiny spidery one I recognise without reading it. It is the well-known signature of the poet Pascal Stone. This one, looking a bit nibbled by mice, I don't recognise. It looks like Stanislaus Pasternak. Unknown to me. There are also several chaps who, if they are not already dead, are due the Queen's telegram, judging by their dates of birth. And Bryn K Boyne, Binkie Boyne, is accidentally deceased, I heard at the club."

"The last is Melville J P Whitbread! I think that's the famous critic, Melly Whitbread!"

"I'd say he and all the survivors are in danger. All except the accident maker. He's determined. Soon he'll pull one off, and we'll have a murderer on our hands!" Frank concluded grimly.

"To add to our personal problems, Frank!" said Mother Agnes. "Will we go for a walk in the garden, and you can tell me all about your affairs of the heart. Maybe I can help!"

As they strolled among the silver grey groves of gnarled olive trees, Frank boyishly ran ahead, jumping up now and then to swing from the branches, and dislodge a hail of green unripe olives, which he picked up to chew, then spat out.

"Come here a wee minute, Frank!" Mother Agnes called to him, smiling at his antics in spite of the load of worries and regret crowding her mind. "Do you see this garden?"

Frank returned to stand obediently by her side like a good puppy or a nice small boy.

"This garden here, Frankie, could be likened to the conventual life. The life that Angel, for the time being at least, may not want to leave. In many ways this garden would seem to have everything. Hundreds of types of perfumed plants. Angel could rhyme them all off to you, smart wee girl that she is. There is shade from the sun, and open spaces when it's the sun you want about you. It has little creatures in it that you may cherish, but only if you choose to. You can bring books here to read, or you can sing or make music here. But here you don't break hearts if you decide to leave, and go to a colder or a warmer place."

"Can you see the attraction a place like this would have for a young girl? A clever girl who wants to make her mark in the world. Without a husband to catch her and pull her back. And especially, without children, screaming and yelling blue murder. I don't think Angel has ever wanted children. Of her own."

"Oh Christ, Mother Agnes, are you sure? She seems to me like a girl that would like kids!"

"Of course I'm not sure, Frank! And young women do change their minds. But she's been a Sister for five years now. Five years is a long time. I think you might know in five years!"

"You'd think so!" agreed Frank, sharply striding away up the garden path to the convent building, and then turning and striding all the way back.

"Mother Mary Agnes! Are you saying I should give up all hope?"

"Not at all, my boy. Quite the reverse, but you should cultivate only reasonable hope!"

"As you did yourself, Mother Agnes? Which perhaps led you in such terrible pathways after all? You told me about them! As I see it, you should have hoped more!"

"You may be right, Detective Inspector Childers!" Agnes flinched as she looked at him.

Frank stood his ground. Glad to have hurt her. She was great at handing out plenty of home truths, right enough. But she wasn't so good at taking them! Just like a nun!

Agnes turned to go. "In my case, I'm sure you are right! But don't forget, all the same, I was always a plain big girl. And Sister Mary of the Angels is much cleverer than me, too. She has far more options! And by the way, I thought the things I told you in the past were in the strictest confidence, as though in the confessional! Was I mistaken?" Mother Mary Agnes turned her back on him, and stalked off.

But she too, turned back. "Listen, Frank! Where there's life, there's hope! The greatest sin of all is despair! So they say!"

Frank went and sat down on the wooden bench in the rose garden. Not English style roses, cut and clipped, but spilling mounds of climbers and ramblers. They reminded him of Angel. Snatching his mobile out of his pocket, he rang a number. He got straight through to Angel.

"You okay?" He asked casually, but unknowingly like a schoolboy. "Listen, are you still going on the trip to

Limone tomorrow? You up to it? Good! Well, Mother Agnes asked me to invite you to lunch here first," he lied. "It's really lovely here. The gardens are beautiful. You should see them! And the Sisters make the most delicious food, and amazing home-made wines. But watch out for them, they're lethal. Especially the elderflower. I'd stick to the cordials if I were you! I'll meet the ferry at eleven. Okay?" He rang off before she could reply, never once having mentioned the accident and her bravery. He couldn't believe he'd done that.

Lunch in a garden sounded lovely, Angel thought. But what on earth could she wear? Sodden parts of her white habit were still floating round the landing place at the Island. Her brown habit was far too warm. She wouldn't wear it as a penance the way Agnes wore hers! She'd see if Dolores could lend her something. They were about the same size.

8

Al Fresco

Frank Childers was disappointed that when he went to meet Sister Mary of the Angels at the quay at Toscolano, Mother Agnes was already there, looking out for the ferry from Malcesine. He had wanted to have Angel all to himself on the way to the convent for lunch.

Mother Agnes would turn out to be the least of his troubles. Because when the ferry had docked, amid all the bustle and excitement (as if it were the last boat that would ever make its way to the little pier), down the ramp came not just Angel (strangely dressed in a tiny, revealing, strawberry pink sun dress lent by Dolores) but most of the Sally Gardens trippers, too.

First off was Dame Georgie with Donald by the hand. Then Dolores, closely followed by Everard, Roxanne having been pushed to the back. Then Lena Wallace managed to jump off, hot and sulky, in an impossibly heavy paint covered artist's smock, and painfully tight jeans. Her face was bright red, not from sunburn (she avoided every ray she could) but from heat, which it was impossible to avoid. Sammy Plaister wrestled Lena's easel and painting gear down the ramp with comic difficulty. A few poets scurried quietly ashore, as if anxious not to be left behind. Roxanne Renton nearly was, and had to leap from the ramp to the bleached planks of the pier, to hilarious laughter from the party.

Only the solicitors and advocates were not present. They had not fancied lunch at a convent, thank you very much, on their precious trip away from their wives. They had nonetheless been nettled when it became clear that Mother Agnes had not invited them. The lunch was Agnes's treat, to repay hospitality she had received from the Scriveners and Limners when she accompanied Angel to the Sally Gardens.

It turned out that the lawyers did not know what they were missing. If they had, they would have curried favour with Agnes, to gain an invitation, instead of going into all kinds of huffs. Several Sisters of the Convent of the Star of the Sea, or Stella del Mare, lined the driveway, white aprons over their brown work habits, to welcome the guests, out of respect for Agnes. They led the guests up to the long table, set under the shade of a large chestnut tree, on the main terrace at the back of the convent, and waited for everyone to take their places.

The nuns watching tittered when all the guests hesitated as to where to sit down. You would have thought there was a bomb hidden under some seat or other. The guests tripped along, or slouched, and at one point, some even ran, to secure the seats they wanted. That is, the seats beside the best people, according to their taste.

Angel had casually sat down near the end of the table. And Guy and Donnie Donald hastened to sit on either side of her. Frank glared down the dazzlingly white-clad length of the table reproachfully in her direction. He was sitting at the top, next to Mother Agnes. He was always next to Mother Agnes, it seemed. But Agnes deserted him, too. He felt a real idiot in solitary splendour at the top of the table. Agnes stood calling for Angel to come and help her with something. It was the napkins, Frank saw, the white damask napkins. Angel, in a pretty flurry, gave out the last of the napkins, and was two short. She hesitated, then disappeared through the back door to the kitchens and came back with a paper roll of kitchen towel. She tore off two long sections, and, coming up behind Frank, tucked one in the neck of his silk shirt, like a bib. The other she put on herself, and casually dropped into the seat Mother Agnes had vacated. Frank's eyes dimmed with delight. When Agnes came back to chat for a moment, he made to rise and offer her his seat, but she shoved him down again unceremoniously, without interrupting her flow of chatter.

Just then the nuns dashed out with trays of antipasto. And at the same time, Pascal and Jackie turned up off the later ferry, having had a nostalgic breakfast alone on their balcony, staring out over the lake, and remembering holidays past on Garda, when they were two fit young guys, and everyone had been mad for them. At a loss as to what ferry to get, they had gone the long way across the lake.

Roxanne had grabbed the seat between Donnie Donald and Guy Everard. Dolores was sitting on Sammy's knee, and Lena and Dame Georgie were discussing the difficulties of sketching in the open air. Two young Italian postulants, allowed the festive lunch as a special treat, faced Jackie and Pascal across the flower decked table.

After the antipasto of *frutti di mare*, the courses that followed were equally delicious. For *primo piatto*, there was a choice, *spaghetti con vongole* or *minestrone con pesto*. For *il secondo* there was *pesce di lago*, simply crisped and seared with olive oil. And there were platters of exotic salad stuffs grown in the convent kitchen gardens.

And all the while, Asti was passed up and down the tables, as well as the home made peach wines and cordials for which the convent was famous, made by secret processes from the Convent's own peach orchard. There was soda water too, for anyone bold enough to commit the sacrilege of diluting the wines and cordials, which, with seeming innocuousness, slipped over the throat like the lemonade of childhood. The *gelati* went well with them.

Mother Agnes took her place for a time, as hostess, at the very head of the table, looking down genially at the high jinks, occasionally throwing Frank an ironic look.

The mood of the party grew hilarious, with guests changing seats, and eating from each other's dishes. From hilarious they moved to tender. Friendly kisses were given and received quite above board. Below board, games of footsie were being played.

Guy Everard, landing up with Dolores on one side and Roxanne on the other, played with Dolores's fingers, while Roxanne rubbed her plump bare foot over Guy's sandaled toes.

Guy gave Roxanne an annoyed look.

"To quote a joke of Proust's!" he brayed in a voice meant to carry the length of the table, "Tell me straight away you love me, Madam! But do not tread on my feet like this!"

Roxanne punched Guy playfully in his skinny belly, but she blushed scarlet.

Sammy came up and pulled Dolores to her feet, putting his arm round her waist, and whispering in her ear. Donnie Donald so far forgot himself as to plant a passing kiss on his own wife's sweet little nose. Pascal was reciting Dante to the two pretty postulants.

The Sisters brought their precious hand-cranked record player onto the paved terrace just in front of the house. And Mother Annunziata, who had brought it into the convent as part of her dowry, played her prized records of Neapolitan songs, and waltzes and tangos, on it.

Jackie bowed to Lena and got her up for a dance, while Pascal jotted down a few lines of verse in honour of the occasion. And Roxanne stooped over tiny Mother Annunziata, leading her round in a decorous slow tango. "I've always loved nuns!" she confided to the tiny Sister. "I wanted at one point to be a nun myself, but my then boyfriend wouldn't let me." She guided Annunziata back to the walnut record cabinet. "I wish now I hadn't listened to him, considering he hopped on a plane to Buenos Aires shortly after!"

The Sisters had arranged a specially early lunch, so that their guests could catch the ferry for Limone. The sun was really high overhead, and the large tree was not casting so much shadow. So the party took their tiny cups of espresso or tiny glasses of limoncello up to the orchards and olive groves spreading uphill at the back. Angel was dashing about, helping the nuns to clear the tables, her white skin revealed by the flimsy pink sun dress.

Agnes sat down beside Frank, who had been devouring Angel with his eyes.

"It's a funny thing!" she said without preamble, "Sometimes when things are really nice, I get to wondering if they are suddenly about to go really wrong. It's a terrible habit of mine. But look what happened when we let Angel out of our sight! She could have been drowned! And how would I have explained that to Mother Benigna?"

"You'd have been defrocked, or dehabited, I suppose."

"And I suddenly remember sad things in the midst of happy times. And I sometimes worry, when I'm feeling at my holiest, that I've never in my life made a really true confession. Have I actually confessed my sins, not things that counted as sins?"

"I used to make up my sins, Mother Agnes, when I was a wee boy. I never had any sins, you see, being horribly good. And I had to make some up. So I lied about my sins.

"Or another thing I did, Mother Agnes, I used to say things like, 'I quarrelled with my school friend after he punched my nose' and 'I wasn't kind enough to my mother when she shouted at me when she was tired and crabby' to let the priest know what a saint I was. I have no proper sins even now, but you can tell to look at me, can't you?"

Mother Agnes did not bother to acknowledge Frank's remarks. She went on with her own stream of thought.

"I thought what I might do was go and make my confession to an Italian priest, preferably one who doesn't speak English. I could get everything off my chest and still get absolution. What do you think, Frank?"

"I think you don't need absolution, Mother Agnes, from anyone but yourself!"

Leaving Mother Agnes to her thoughts, Frank climbed up to the furthest terrace, where an iron swing was set into concrete amid gravel paths. He had an itching desire for exercise. He hoisted himself up to the top bar, and began to do chin ups.

Dolores Kant materialised from the grassy slopes above. She reached up lithely, to swing too. Her hair, coming out of its chignon, flew in a scented curtain across his face.

"Do you still like that?" she asked, placing a hand delicately on his sweat dampened shirt, just over his heart. "I though perhaps your heart had grown cold!"

She flipped his shirt out of his shorts and laughed as he dropped down in panic, his breathing fast from irritation, and whatever else.

"Let's go and cool down, or whatever," Dolores whispered coyly, "up there. There's a sweet little arbour behind the trees. How about it? You liked it before *al fresco*! No-one would see us, but if the poor nuns did have spy glasses they would be grateful for the education. What do you say, Frankie? Just a quick one? Short time, Mister?" She laughed appealingly.

"Dolores! The last thing on earth I want from you is a short time, or a long one. I used to like you, and I was sorry for you. I thought you were sad and you were up for it. It would have been rude not to! You are also as lovely as a film star. One of the wonders of the poetic world. But I don't care any more about that! And what about all your other admirers?"

"I prefer you, Frankie. You know I do!"

"You only prefer me because you can't have me!"

"No, you're wrong! I would prefer you, if I had you every day. I must hold that thought!"

Even in such a humiliating encounter, Dolores was calm. Not cool, but perversely calm. And her chiselled face was not even flushed. He felt furious, and determined to put her off.

"And there's so many years between us!" he spat out.

"So you prefer to cradle snatch young Sister Mary of the Angels!"

"As a matter of fact, Angel is only months younger than me, and it's none of your business."

Frank went striding off up the hill. Dolores went striding after him. He turned on her then, warding her off with angry gestures.

"And I swear to God, Dolores, if you spoil this for me, if I lose this chance of happiness through your meddling, I swear to God, I will kill you!"

"Frankie, really!" Dolores turned her beautiful face away from him, as he held her at arm's length. "Let's not drag God into this!" She leaned out to pass her hands over his body.

If she thought she would engender sensual longing in him, she was wrong. He felt himself shrivel, and he waited there, shuddering, till he was quite sure she had disappeared downhill.

When Frank re-joined the others, lying about on the lawn, he discovered that Dolores had gone to catch an earlier ferry. It seemed she had an appointment at Limone.

The group had rather lost track of time. Everyone had to run, finally, to get the planned ferry to Limone. The vessel was crowded. He wasn't even sure if Angel had made it aboard.

At every stop he kept a weather eye out for her, crowding to the rail in case she decided to disembark at one of the other beautiful ports.

Pascal Stone came and stood beside him. Frank got the feeling he was reading his mind, and indeed it looked as if he was. He patted Frank encouragingly on the shoulder.

"Why don't you jump off here, my boy?" Pascal suggested. "Who knows what might be waiting here? What new adventures? Myself, I always jumped, in my glorious distant youth!"

Frank came across Dame Georgie downing a stiff gin and tonic at the tiny bar.

"Now, Frank, you won't let a lady drink alone", she said, diving into her handbag for cash. "Is gin okay? Or would you prefer brandy?"

"Where's Professor Donald?" he asked as he sipped his Fine.

"Ask somebody who gives a damn!" Lady Georgie muttered hoarsely.

Frank put an arm round her to cheer her up. She really was such a nice little lady, he thought, cheering up a bit himself. He liked the old-fashioned perfume she was wearing.

And then to reward him, as they came into sight of Limone's ultramarine ridges, he caught sight of the back of Angel's head, her spiky hair mussed in the offshore wind and spray. She seemed to be attempting to do watercolour sketches of the approaching landfall, amid all the upheaval of jostling tourists around her. Then she was waving her pale slender arms in excitement, pointing out the beauties of the scene to Mother Agnes, showing her the separate sheets of paintings. Suddenly the playful breeze whipped up, and the paintings went flying around, eagerly retrieved by the passengers dying to scrape acquaintance with her. Angel was laughing, and thanking them all politely. On top of the flimsy pink dress, Frank saw she was wearing a huge white cable knit cardigan which Frank recognized as belonging to Mother Agnes. Whether from modesty or exposure to the chilly breeze, Frank couldn't figure out.

What a pathetic little clown she looked, Frank thought, the breeze making his eyes water.

9

Shy Sly Limone

After the deceptively intoxicating lunch, Frank Childers' head was swimming as the ferry disgorged the afternoon passengers at tourist-bait Limone. He had read in his guide book that 'Shy sly Limone stretched out suggestively over the azure inlet.' The phrase summoned lascivious images to his overheated brain and overactive libido as he hurried over the steep gangplank, anxious to keep Angel in sight, but not to appear to be doing so.

As he was swept off the ferry, Frank had had just a glimpse close up of the flower decked balconies, awnings fluttering like sails, and the ancient narrow stone houses that backed the lake side arcades and bridged promenades. It was dazzlingly beautiful and overpoweringly pretty. Just like the newly revealed Angel.

But in a moment his whole attention was taken up by the necessity of not losing sight of her in the crowd. Sometimes he would glimpse her turning round, her head in profile. Might be checking if he was still in pursuit, he wondered. And then she'd be gone as he shyly loitered further behind. A whole ferry load of French tourists at one time intervened, cut out in front of him, while the advance guard of his own party leapt nimbly ahead.

He pushed frantically forward, and saw her for a second, just within friendly calling out distance, and then she disappeared into a warren of electrically lit boutiques under the darkest part of the tunnelled arcades. He sauntered up and down, peering into souvenir shops and boutiques. Sometimes he dashed in, did a sweep round, and not finding Angel there, decamped without courtesy, just muttering the odd '*Scusi!*' and '*Prego!*' Frank's mother, who had brought him up to have the most exquisite manners (like his charming Irish father, God rest his soul), would have disowned him.

When he discovered he was going into the same shop several times, and thereby meeting several times other unwanted members of his group, he gave up. He returned to the main open promenade, with the heart-breaking views of the distant stern indigo mountain ridges. Their majesty reprimanded his recent frenetic, morally suspect, activity in pursuing the poor girl, who had happened to take his fancy, through no fault, certainly through no collusion, of her own.

Other beautiful young women passed him as he sat on a low wall. Some in ridiculously short shorts and skimpy tops. Loads of them beauties. He might have fallen for any number of them. He often fell violently for some attractive young woman, but never quite managed to follow through. He got a few glances from the half-naked beauties too. For Frank had his manly attractions. His trim muscular body and a reflective expression made women want to trust him. (Though it often turned out they were mistaken in assuming his faithfulness and his docility. Sometimes Frank's mammy had had to apologise to some nice girl's mammy when thing didn't turn out right.) Apart from these often misleading signs of niceness, Frank took a deep tan quite easily, and didn't go bright red with blotches like some of the tourists, broiling like lobsters, painfully, in the sun. And the beard he was growing suited him, too.

Frank rose and stretched, running his hand over his abdomen to reassure himself that his six pack had not melted away under the indolent Italian sun. He longed for exercise. He'd heard there was a path up the mountainside, to the lemon groves. He stared upwards, over the head of a dark beauty in a bikini and sarong, who had brushed against him.

But Frank's eyes were searching for a figure in more modest attire. And suddenly there she was, on her own, waving and smiling cheerfully at him. She'd obviously been shopping in the boutiques, and was wearing new baggy elasticated lemon shorts, surely designed for large children, Frank thought, with a long sleeved blue and white striped sailor jersey, far too large for her. The jersey had a kind of masculine cut to it, but not in a good way. What funny taste she had, he thought, nearly weeping with joy at the strange sight of her as he whipped on his sunglasses to disguise his delight. He had to sit down on his wall again.

She came and sat beside him.

"Nice clobber, lady!" he complimented her. "Are you here for a fashion shoot?"

She slapped him nicely. "Mother Mary Agnes insisted on buying this stuff for me. I didn't like to hurt her feelings and not wear it, since she'd spent so much of her pocket money on it. I was perfectly happy with my borrowed finery. It was kind of Dolores to lend it."

Yeah, right, he thought. Dolores must have expected the sun dress to be ludicrously revealing.

Angel was searching in her rucksack. She had some eatables and drinkables squashed in there. She had two wine bottles of pink liquid too. The nuns' peach cordial again!

Angel raised her slim arms to ruffle her spiky urchin cut hair. Real urchin cut, by herself with nail scissors. It had worked okay. A flying bug had landed in it. He delicately plucked it off, noticing the darker ash blonde at the roots, where the sun hadn't struck. Darkened with sweat too. His forefinger probing tenderly at her hairline, where her hair stuck up on end, was moist as he flicked the insect away. It flew off. That was a good sign, he crazily thought. She had noticed the tiny bug's escape too. She flashed him a shy smile.

"It's supposed to be cooler up there, at the lemon groves. I was thinking of ..."

She hesitated. He had stopped breathing. She was about to suggest a picnic.

"Yeah! I was thinking!" Frank was trying to play it cool. "It might be worth ... "

But Angel was not listening any more. He followed her gaze to the far promenade, where Dame Georgie and Donnie Donald were walking along, pointing to the beauties of the view. In their wake trailed Lena Wallace, kitted out in new dark gauzy clothes, bought by Dame Georgie. Swathes of designer veils like Death in Venice. She had a large black straw hat on to keep the sun off her oddly pale face, smeared in thick lotion. Frank remembered seeing the outfit in the window of the only upmarket boutique in the tunnelled arcade.

Dame Georgie uttered glad cries and trotted towards them, still chic in the heat, in sleeveless black linen and fashionable sandals, holding a Japanese parasol over her head.

"Thank goodness we've found you in time, Sister Angel!" she chirped. "Now do come along. I've booked a posh tea at that bistro you said you liked the look of. The one with the red sails."

"Oh, but you mustn't, really. I didn't mean I wanted to eat there. I just thought Lena might make a nice sketch from the balcony."

Georgie threw an arm impulsively round Angel's shoulder. "It's the very least we can do, after your saving my life yesterday. We were both very lucky not to have been swept under the barge, with those currents. I've taken the liberty of ordering their best champagne. You'd be allowed a little champers my dear, wouldn't you? Not against your vows?"

That was all Frank needed, Georgie reminding Angel of her vows.

"We've left Lena's painting gear there. Sammy is minding it. I wish I could invite you too, Mr. Childers, but I'm afraid Lena's easel takes up most of the booth!"

"S'awright!" Frank's voice caught in his throat, as he waved them off. Donnie Donald was shouting jocular insults at his wife, pointing at his watch and shaking his fist.

After saying they were in such a hurry, the group dawdled back along the promenade, Jovial Donald in his holiday golfing gear of huge Bermuda shorts, checked shirt and white baseball cap, trying out his Italian on passers-by, being a really good sport. Frank Childers wondered why he didn't take to the man.

Frank watched the oddly assorted group till they merged with the crowd at the ferry station. Angel from time to time seemed to look backwards over her shoulder, but maybe he was kidding himself. He went into a large touristy cafe and ordered a beer, which he downed while his heart slowed. As he sat scowling at his guidebook unseeingly, he heard laughter from a nearby table of young Italians. Were they laughing at him? Taking one last look at the brilliant panorama of scintillating lakeside views, he sighed and made for the cobbled path up the steep hillside.

"Too beautiful for me, anyway," he thought aloud, "much too beautiful."

In the lower reaches of the mountain pathway, streams of tourists zigzagged from side to side, and Frank was prevented from striding out as he would have liked. At one point he made out Dolores's sleek dark head, above the crowd. She was clinging to some wolfish Italian. She turned her delicate profile, and her hair, swinging out, touched her smiling mouth.

The crowd thinned as the walk became steeper. The high narrow buildings with their balconies seemed to meet overhead in the heat, and tourists dropped off into the little cafes that were set back in gardens off the road. Frank trudged on, in a lather. As he toiled upwards, his thighs started to cramp, and he had to walk backwards to ease them, realising how unfit he was becoming since he hadn't had a chance to do his usual amount of training.

Quite suddenly he was in an open space. A round *piazetta* in front of a tiny chapel canted against the rocky hillside. The rough little church of San Rocco sprang out before him like a stage set flown into place between acts.

On the steps leading up to the chapel Angel was sitting, sketching the view below. A noisy crowd of tourists had gathered round as she worked, in pastel. Of course, she was also an artist! He should have remembered she was multi-talented. She was also sipping from a bottle of peach cordial. She had a blue pastel smudge across her nose.

"What took you so long?" Angel asked, holding the bottle out to him, smiling mischievously sideways from her almond eyes, a bit like Audrey Hepburn in Roman Holiday, Frank thought, although her regular features were different, and prettier. And of course she was flaxen blonde. 'La Fille aux Cheveux de Lin', he thought.

"I came to look for Mother Agnes." Angel explained, and Frank's face fell. "I thought she had mentioned coming here, but she's nowhere to be seen. Do you want to share my picnic? I couldn't face a big tea, after all."

But Frank had gone a bit huffy, in spite of himself. A minute before they had met, the merest glimpse of her was all he'd hoped for. Maybe a few friendly words. Why he had refused the bottle she'd been drinking from, that her sweet curved lips had curled round, he'd never work out.

"I'll just go in and see the famous murals they speak about. And the Reredos."

It was fairly safe to assume there would be murals. He couldn't remember what a Reredos was. But he didn't want to admit he'd only come hoping to meet her.

"I'd like to see the interior since I've come so far. Maybe I'll get an Indulgence!"

There he went again, insulting her religion. His religion in a kind of a way, because he'd been baptized in Saint Jude's church, and there was no way he knew you could get yourself un-baptised.

As he strode off into the dusky entrance, a marvellous aroma met his nostrils. Incense of course. And a smell of the theatre. Perhaps they'd been touching up the murals. Because there were murals, all united by a haunting dusky blue and an earthy brown colour. Saint Roch, on the altar piece, was leaning on his pilgrim staff. The saint of hopeful travel, with his pilgrim's tricorne hat and his conch shell, and his faithful dog smiling up at him.

Something else, too. Before the altar, branches of trees bearing leaf and small immature lemons decorated the podium. The perfume was enchanting, resinous and tangy.

Angel appeared beside him, in the half light. She had followed him in, wondering if she had offended him in some way.

"Look!" she whispered. "The altarpiece you wanted to see. San Rocco looks just like you. Your mammy should have called you Rocco!"

The altarpiece was only a few metres away from the entrance, so small was the church.

He turned to look at her in the comforting half-light, where his grey eyes could open wide, and his soul could reach out to her, staring into her slanting smiling blue eyes.

"My mammy wanted to call me Ambrose, actually. And you look like Botticelli's Venus, the one in the nude on the shell. Except for the hair, the shell, and of course the nude." He put his hand up to touch her spiky hair, and she didn't move away.

In that heartbeat of time, a door hidden by the choir screen opened and a figure emerged. A figure in a brown cloak. A bulky figure. Mother Agnes hurried out with her hands half over her eyes, tears running down from between her fingers. She was making little moaning noises, and repeating something. "Mea culpa! Mea culpa! Mea maxima culpa!" she chanted under her breath, as she fled from the confessional, not seeing the couple behind the screen.

Mother Mary Agnes had disappeared from view when Frank led Angel outside. The place was deserted. And as they sat down on the church steps they knew why. The ferry's whistle sounded way below at the landing site.

"Mother Agnes must have caught the ferry. I don't think we'll make it." Frank said slyly.

They hiked up the track that led beyond San Rocco's, where the lemon groves sprawled above the winding pathways, among the long grass. Angel staggered a bit and clutched Frank's arm. He steadied her and they looked down at the landing place, where, with a last shriek, their ferry was scooting off through the lake water, now silvery green in the fading light. They felt cool as they sat down under the trees, the lovely aroma wafting over them.

Frank refused the sticky peach cordial, but Angel had a can of coke in her bag. Opening the can, he took a slurp. The fizzy liquid exploded as he did so, warm and gassy from its time in the heat. Frank gagged, and choked. He was unable to get his breath back, and the coke erupted from his throat, out his nose as well as his mouth, and sprayed all over his clothes.

Angel slapped him smartly between his shoulders and, emitting the last of the gassy coke in an embarrassing spray, he managed to grab a gasp of air. As he came to his senses, Frank saw that Angel was laughing helplessly.

"What are you like?" she inquired, slapping his back again. "Can't take you anywhere!"

The slaps on his back became more like pats, and she wiped his face and beard, a bit roughly and then playfully, then began to caress him sweetly instead.

"There, there!" she said. "All better now?"

Then, holding his face between her hands she pressed her lips to his. Bizarrely, Frank struggled to break free. They rolled over and over in the long grass like two kids, as he protested, and tried to shake her off.

At last he gave in and gave her, as it were, the upper hand. She kissed him again, tenderly, and seraphically. As he returned her kiss, she smelled of peaches. Of very strong peach wine.

Lying back among the unknown purple flowers growing around them in the meadow, he opened his mouth to sigh, and Angel slipped her tongue between his lips like the sacrament.

Frank pulled out of the long kiss at last, and turned her within his embrace so that they both could admire Limone's huge moon rising behind the mountains. They remained languid for a time, uttering little random words and phrases. Then Angel turned to confront him. She began to place little kisses all over his glowing face. Then at a point just under his ear, where the muscle swelled. Then down to a hollow just under the collar bone. She began to pull off his coke saturated shirt. And then nuzzled his pecs, then his six pack. When she started to loosen his ruined linen trousers, he cried out more in pain than pleasure, and more in exasperation than lust.

"What the hell do you think you're doing, you stupid woman? Did they not teach you anything about sex at your convent school?" And he pushed her roughly away.

"No, I don't suppose they did." She spoke huskily through swollen lips, her eyes dazed.

Frank jumped up, with a curse of protest, and turning away from her, strode to the edge of the hillside, getting himself somehow back into his stained clothes, in a rage.

Shocked, Angel came to stand penitently beside him, and he passed his arm round her waist, forgivingly. He kissed the top of her head as she laid it on his shoulder.

"Never mind! Never mind, Angel," he crooned, "It will be alright! We'll work something out! Would it help if I became a priest? Then I could give you absolution! Give us both absolution?"

They looked over the edge towards the pathways below. At some distance away, harshly revealed in the moonlight, a couple were spread out in the throes of a wild encounter. The girl, pale and glimmering, lay athwart the man, whose copper skin glowed from beneath her. As their cries of passion rose towards him, Frank recognised not only the voice of Dolores Kant, but her elegant shape, and her long hair now in disarray. Only too well known to him.

He turned quickly away. He dragged Angel down the slope fiercely, and, in the espadrilles they both wore, dangerously, and did not stop till they reached the boutiques, opening again below. He pushed her inside the posh one, and insisted on buying the fluted white dress in the window. It was the shop he had been into several times on his own, looking for her. She looked divine in it. Literally, he thought, like a Greek Goddess. She chose a pair of flat golden strappy sandals, too. He was relieved she didn't go for high heels which would have made her taller than himself. Frank quickly acquired new white trousers to replace the coke soaked ones, and dithered over a Mickey Mouse Tee shirt which he quite fancied, but wondered if it was too dear and too silly.

Angel insisted on having her shorts and jersey packaged in a posh boutique carrier bag. And, not to be outdone in generosity, she spent the last of her pocket money that Mother Benigna had given her from the Convent of the Bleeding heart, to buy Frank the Mickey Mouse Tee shirt.

By the lake, all was bleached white or smoky grey, Angel's face as delicate and luminescent in the flooding moonlight as alabaster held up against the light. Angel started to run along the small crescent of shingle that the wicked high tide was rapidly covering. Like an Atalanta against the agate frieze of the waves. She had decided not to risk any more kisses. He had to sprint to reach her.

Frank put out a hand to stop her mid stride, and told her that he loved her.

10

O Sirmione!

Lena Wallace had planned her campaign already, as the boat party from the Sally Gardens alighted at Sirmione, near the crenelated castle of Cangrande della Scala. She was, in her own way, just as ready to do battle as the Lombards and Guelphs who had skirmished there. She wasn't quite sure who had crossed swords with whom. She hoped she had attended to enough of Sister Angel's little lecture on the boat to impress the horrid Guy Everard, who, she had noticed, had been listening eagerly, and taking notes.

Lena hastened after Guy, who had marched ahead of the main party. They were squabbling over the choice of cafe for pre-archaeological stroll drinks, before tackling the long roadway that led to the Roman ruins of the Grottos of Catullus. She had looked it up on the map, and she reckoned that it was much longer in reality than it seemed. She had devised a plan to isolate Guy from his pals, and then give him a piece of her mind. And she had arranged with a rickshaw rider to pick her up at a certain point, just before the arcade, and rescue her from the tedious walk. With her gear packed neatly in her back pack, and stout walking shoes, she looked energetic, if not trim.

Lena had devised a way of getting her revenge on Guy Everard, for his original insult to her at her first club luncheon, and his continuing scornful treatment of her, despite Dame Georgie's intercession. Since he had discovered that Dolores held Lena in contempt for her rhyming poetry, and Roxanne despised her lack of glamour, Everard had got courage enough to show his dislike for her, by making rude faces to the others. And even letting his squint eyes glaze, to her face, when she was telling one of her funny school stories. He hadn't been able to keep his face straight when he saw Lena in her walking gear, her orange-peel thighs emerging from her short shorts.

Guy, on the other hand, had aimed at a more relaxed, resort-style costume. He had on his usual navy-blue blazer and his white flannels, and crisp white shirt, with his panama hat. For a slim, fit, man like himself, the roadway, with its panoramic views, looked inviting. The glistening lakeside path would be ideal for a relaxed stroll.

His brow furrowed with annoyance beneath his panama's shading brim, as Lena, springing out at him, plucked at his sleeve, ready to impress him. Like Sirmione, she also had a sensual and romantic side. And she had learned a few lines of Catullus to prove it, in translation of course.

"O Sirmione, flower of all the peninsulas and all the islands that double dealing Neptune rules over," she quoted to him in ringing tones.

Everard wondered if she referred to his numerous affairs with Sally Gardens ladies when she referred to 'double dealing.' He wished she wouldn't shout so much. Some of the other tourists, thronging the pathway, were beginning to stare. And why in the name of all the sea gods, had she decided to have her hair curled like that? Sweat made it writhe as if it were made of sea snakes, slithering Medusa-like over her poppy pink face and shoulders.

She was acting differently, too. Guy had thought his unremitting rudeness had beaten her into submission. Now he had a feeling she was about to revolt, and he didn't think he'd like it.

Guy was right! Lena was planning a showdown. She was fed up swallowing insults. She was keeping another poem of Catullus (something about a lady lying in the lake waves with her lover, being kissed) for later, when she met Sammy at the Lido below the grottos. She had put her Tee shirt and shorts over her bikini. She aimed to surprise Sammy there. He had often boasted what a wonderful swimmer he was, and she had at last learned to swim, at classes at the Western Baths, which had cost an arm and a leg.

And as Lena marched along smartly beside Guy, she imagined a languorous swim later. Guy was feeling dizzy, under the broiling sun. There was hardly any shade. He had to take off his panama to mop his brow, and then the sweat ran into his eyes and stung them. He tugged at Lena's arm to get her to slow down, but she only smiled oddly, patted his hand, and went on, buoyed up by malice, and her desire for revenge.

The reason for her smile was that she had played a trick on Guy. She had put some drops of her own sleeping draught in his fruit smoothie that morning, and was waiting for the results.

Guy suddenly staggered to the side of the road and sat down. Lena could see that his face had gone a funny mottled red.

"What on earth's the matter?" she asked sweetly. "I thought you liked exercise."

She sat down beside him. It really was broiling hot, and her heavy shoes were making her feet swell up. She noticed, with alarm, that other people were sitting down too. Young healthy looking people, quite hiking-looking types were gasping for air, and lobster red.

The pedestrians still streaming past jumped to one side as a little motorised buggy came tootling round the corner. There was screaming and yelling and laughing coming from it.

Most of the screaming was coming from Roxanne, who was shouting at the driver to stop.

"There's room for one more!" she said, waving to Lena and Guy. "Which feels worst?"

Before the words were out of her mouth, Guy had recovered miraculously, enough to leap into the buggy, which zoomed off, to cheers for him and jeers for Lena.

It took a minute for Lena to get herself to her feet, and join in the archaeological stroll again.

As usual, none of her plans for sticking up for herself had worked out.

The wonderful views out over the lake ceased to exist for Lena as she limped on, her eyes on the stony pathway ahead of her. Around her, people were helping each other, younger helping older, fitter helping weaker. There was a babble of different languages, as fair skinned races deplored the sizzling heat they had travelled so many miles to access. As she reached the meeting point she'd arranged with the young rickshaw man, she realised he wouldn't be waiting around for her, with so many potential, exhausted, clients on hand.

Her footsteps started to drag. More and more people overtook her. Finally Frank Childers, who had stopped at the cafe for a cool drink, overtook her too. Frank looked stunned, but it was not with the heat. He had been shocked all morning, since he had first seen Sister Angel, back in a (borrowed) white habit, lecturing coolly on the love poems of Catullus. She had given him a vague smile and her eyes had flicked away from him. He had thought perhaps it was the presence of Mother Agnes close beside her. No doubt she was embarrassed to recall the romantic evening she had shared with him in Limone. Why was she not wearing her funny yellow shorts and striped top? He was wearing the Mickey Mouse Tee shirt she had bought him. Now he felt a perfect fool.

In a way it was a comfort to see poor Lena in such a state. Luckily he had three bottles of water in his knapsack. The first he gave her to drink. The second he poured over her head. And with the third he bathed her feet, like a male Mary Magdalene, after removing her socks and shoes. He had a spare pair of espadrilles too. Lena had thought he was a cool young man. Now she thought he was a kind of saint, as he ruffled her wet curly hair kindly. He was suddenly overcome by an excess of pity for the poor distressed woman, and taking her by the hand, led her to the partial shade of a tree on the extreme right of the road way, where, reaching across, he kissed her tenderly. Lena nearly passed out with delight, and reciprocated with several hot passionate kisses, not realizing she and Frank were in the way of another motorized buggy, carrying lucky tourists downhill to the groves of Catullus. Which looked as it were bound to run them over, as the packed occupants screamed a warning.

Unfortunately for Frank, Sister Angel and Mother Agnes were two of the lucky tourists. As Frank leapt for safety, shoving Lena aside, his horrified gaze met that of Sister Angel for a nanosecond before he ran after the buggy, and nearly killed himself trying to catch it up.

Lena abandoned the marked road way and walked randomly around the historical sites following areas of shade. The crumbling remains of the huge villa looked sinister, and the sudden dazzling glimpses of the lake beneath gave her vertigo. She didn't like to ask for directions from other tourists, as she couldn't speak French or German, and they all looked rather foreign. And her Italian was minimal, too. She took out her camera to snap some views, so she wouldn't look lost.

She began to feel like crying. But as she was painfully sneaking along the shadow side of a huge noble double arcade, she saw a familiar couple approaching. Donnie Donald and Dame Georgie were strolling in the opposite direction. But they looked as if they'd had a quarrel, and weren't talking.

Then Lena heard Dame Georgie shout over her shoulder at her husband.

"Well, have it your own way, as usual! But I tell you, you'll live to regret it!"

"Yes, Dear! Yes, Dear! Yes, Dear!" Donald grunted sardonically from behind her.

Embarrassed to recognise Lena, they simply slowed down as they passed her.

"Don't miss the grottos!" Donald advised her. "They're crumbly and horrid! But you'll love them! Live dangerously! One false step and you're in the lake."

"Oh do shut up, you silly old fool!" Georgie cried, dashing ahead in tears.

Professor Donald doubled back though, to have a few words.

"We're actually out scouting for young Pascal! He flounced off in the huff, in his swimmers. Roxanne upset him with something she said. I would have gone after him, but bossy Guy Everard stopped me. He said we should wait, the path was a dead end. He'd have to come back sometime, with a red face. Serve him right, he said. Georgie's mad at me. When she and Jackie came back from their swim they dashed up the path. What do you think? Not a sign of him! He'd vanished off the face of the earth! Georgie's sure he's wandering somewhere boiling hot, among spiky cacti, lost and miserable! So keep an eye out for him. It's easy for old people to get lost!"

And for youngish people too, Lena thought, stifling cries of panic as she let the couple go, too embarrassed to ask for help. Lena started to walk very quickly downhill.

Downhill must at least lead to the lake. She might find Pascal, miserable, hot and scared, and rescue him.

But Pascal was not, at that moment, any of those things, though he had been all three. Especially boiling hot! With rage welling up from inside, as well as the fierce Sirmione sun aiming directly at his poor scrambled brains, through his eggshell thin skull and its wisps of white hair. As he'd toiled upwards, he'd come across clumps of cactus, and nearly turned back then. But he couldn't bear to do so, to be humiliated in front of Jackie. And by Sam, who he'd done so much for! Tears and sweat had poured down his face and down the knotted and scrawny muscles of his torso.

"How sharper than a serpent's tooth to have a thankless friend!" he'd cried in rage, and mustered the courage to negotiate his way round the huge jagged plants. But only to emerge onto a long dusty bleached pathway. He might as well try to fly to the moon!

But along the path, like Friendly Visions from his youth, had come a gang of boys, on scooters, single file, with a few girls clinging to pillions. All the skinny youngsters looked nude, though they wore some scraps of clothing. The lead rider had stopped short, with arms out flung in dismay, as he'd seen the state of the old man stranded there.

They'd given him water, and a girl pulled off her flower-decked straw hat, and set it on his head. They'd helped him onto the pillion of the leader, a big boy they called Dirk. A Dutch boy, then. Pascal had known a big Dutch boy. Had he been called Dirk? Or was it Jan?

So Pascal was carried off in triumph, and when Jackie returned forlornly uphill later, to check the surrounding rocky slopes, he was nowhere to be seen, and the path was empty.

The youngsters were headed for a smaller beach they knew. They set up Pascal there, against a rock and in its shade, the hat tilted over his face.

"We take you home later, Papa!" Dirk crouched beside him. "Have snooze! Okay?"

Pascal pretended to snooze, but through half closed eyes, and through the fringed straw of his borrowed hat, he could see the amorous dalliances of the youngsters, embracing in the pale aquamarine shallows.

The words of Catullus came into his mind. "*Vivamus Lesbia mea atque amemus!*"

He himself had translated it as, "Let us make love! While we're young who can blame us?"

There might be a better way of putting it, Pascal thought, his poetic muse taking over, as he watched the lithe golden bodies of his rescuers, like Angels, or Gods. And his dreams eased him into eternity, as a little breeze from the lake sprang up.

The same breeze cooled poor Lena as she stood irresolute, watching the retreating figures of Donnie and Georgie become tiny in the vast perspective of the colonnade.

So Lena hadn't got up her courage to ask Donnie and Georgie the way. Nor how Guy had made it to the lido. So there was nothing for it but to keep going till she reached it, or fell off the end. No-one would miss her. They wouldn't even notice she was gone.

Why on earth was she so determined to get her own back on Guy Everard? Even though he was a selfish boor and a callous brute? The reason, she acknowledged to herself, was childish spite. She should have known better.

Lena turned away from the hot roofless colonnade, and took a little pathway into deep undergrowth, where bougainvilleas and oleanders contrasted with the cypresses. It was cool there, and on an irrational impulse, Lena slipped off her Tee shirt and shorts to get even cooler, and rolled in the damp grasses in her bikini. She reached up into the scented brightness of the overhead garlands. She did a few dance aerobic leaps.

"Lovely!" she called out in delight! "Magic!"

Then, for the first time, she noticed, through a gap in the flowery bushes, a sinister grey bearded man, gaunt though handsome, was snap-snap-snapping his camera off at her.

He approached quite openly, and in dumb show asked her to stay where she was and pose for him again. In the dense green shade she did look wild and dramatically picturesque.

"No!" Lena cried. "Non! Nein! Niet! Pas possible!"

"Sorry!" said the man. "Not a problem!" detecting her specific accent, then "You Scottish? You maybe from Glasgow? Glesca, ha ha?"

Lena nodded dumbly, shielding herself with her arms.

"I know Glasgow. West End. Queensborrow Gardeens! You from there? I recognise nice lady voice. Like my old geerlfren!"

"Queensborough Gardens! Nowhere near where I live!" she laughed, ironically. "I'm from way round the corner in Partickhill Road!"

"Parteeckheel Road! Loveliest road in all Glasgow! So many many 'appy memory! Look!"

He produced some snapshots from his wallet which he took from a pocket in his Baggies.

"Look! Me! Geerlfren! Nice big lady. In Parteeckheel rose gardeen! Ex geerlfren. I get dump."

Lena could understand why.

"I'm headed for the lido!" she explained. "That's why I'm in bathing togs, as you see!"

"Yes, I see, madam! Most lovely! Bellissima!" He kissed his fingers to her.

"No, I'm not! I'm not at all! And my hair was a mistake!"

"Hair very nice! Very artistic, no? Bottom like Rubens lady, too! One last shot?"

In spite of herself, Lena obliged. Then she remembered Sammy.

"I'm supposed to meet my boyfriend, I mean my fiancé, at the lido. I must rush!"

Lena started to rush, then slipped on the pine needles and skidded for several feet.

The stranger helped her up carefully. When she tried to start off again he held her back, quite firmly. He was fumbling in another pocket in his wide jeans. She saw it was only a battered tube of Ambre Solaire he was getting out.

"You pale like Madonna." he said. "You boil. You fry. Allow me, madam."

Lena had to stand while he slathered the cream all over her arms and chest, tears of embarrassment coming into her eyes as she stood still like a small child.

"Now I really must be on my way! Arrivederci!" she cried brightly.

"*Permette? Versi. Mi chiamo Enzio!*"

"*Io sono Lena!*"

"Catch you later, Lena! Lenabella!"

Lena made off along the first pathway she saw.

"Lena! *Signora! Madame!*"

And she had thought she'd got away. She looked back unwillingly.

"Wronk way! You goink wronk way! I showink you!"

Enzio led her towards the outer edge of the precipitous slope. Lena went, meek as a lost lamb, she felt. He stopped suddenly at a gap in the gnarled formation of an ancient chestnut tree, and pulled the clematis back from it. "There! Look!"

A panorama of the azure waters glittering under the sun, swirling round a beach of white sand, among giant rocks, appeared, with terraces of olive groves reaching down.

He rummaged in his backpack and brought out a pair of field glasses, which he handed to her. He leaned over her to help her adjust the focus. Into view came several groups of figures. Her eye was instantly drawn to a couple reclining in the shallows. The man was splashing water over the woman, who retaliated. Lena adjusted the focus again for greater clarity. Guy and Roxanne came into view, cavorting around a lilo. Roxanne in a very skimpy bikini. Guy in very baggy shorts. Sam Plaister and Dolores came to paddle, and the other couple moved into deeper water. Their mock fighting became more serious. Guy pushed the woman's head roughly under the waves. She came up gasping, and kicked him. Then their activities became really sexual. And although the waves screened them from other swimmers, from above, the azure waters became transparent as Lena scanned downwards. She could not believe her eyes.

"You bastard!" she cried, as she saw Sammy and Dolores locked in a watery embrace, too.

"You bastard! How could you?" she cried as she dashed and slithered down the slope.

From above, the beach had looked like a stone's throw away, but it took Lena ages to reach it. When she did the sun was setting, a fiery ball just above the horizon, and the shadows of the huge columns and arches spread over the small beach. The place was empty. There was not a soul in sight. An abandoned yellow Lilo bobbed about.

Then she noticed some clothing on the sand. A jacket and a panama hat. Lena slowly waded into the shallows, and then further out, looking for swimmers. She caught sight of clothing being swept against the half submerged rocks. She recognised Guy's good blazer, the white shirt. The tide must have swept them out. He'd be furious to lose them. Guy would probably find some way to blame someone else, as he usually did when things went wrong.

But the party would be spared an outburst of Guy's temper this time.

Because it was not just Guy's clothing snagged against a rock, and being slapped at by the incoming tide. It was Guy himself, shockingly half-naked, and floating, his long face downward, in the limpid water.

Lena waded out as far as she dared, and just managed to get a grip of the inert form. But she found she could not budge the water-soaked body one inch from the rocks it was entangled with. She'd seen plenty of action films where rescuers did just that. But she could not, try as she would, get Everard back to the shore. He was a dead weight. The tide grew stronger, flooding the inlet. It floated her right on top of Guy's body, and as she struggled ferociously to free him, she had a horrible memory of the recent nasty trick she had played. Then an energetic wave toppled her off the body, and threw her several feet up the sliding sandy shingle. The wave without difficulty dislodged the partly-clothed body and set it spinning further out into the lake.

Self-preservation took over, and she found she had scrabbled up to the scrubland, pulling herself out of the dragging waves.

When she looked back, the body had been tossed further in, and was floating on its back, the blazer half off, the shirt billowing out behind it.

Lena turned wearily, to climb back up the hill in the half light.

Halfway up she met Enzio, crouching in the shadows, waiting for her. He jumped out suddenly, to intercept her.

"Enzio not bastard! You notta nice girl to say so. Why you say bastard, Signora?"

"Not bastard, I know, Enzio. I meant someone else. You're a nice guy! Have you a phone? Listen, you've got to help me!"

Lena and Enzio stood looking down at the bay. And all at once the rain which the humid weather had foretold came slashing down, then lightning, and then a growl of thunder. As if old Benaco, fathoms down in his lake, had risen up to complain about the pollution of his pristine divine waters with human passions and human trash.

Waiting with Enzio by the lake for the Polizia to turn up (which they seemed in no hurry to do) Lena decided not to go back to the hotel at Malcesine, to report the accident. For which she might even have been to blame, after spiking his smoothie with a barbiturate.

"Come home with me!" Enzio pleaded. "My wife very nice lady! Very hospitable!"

So Lena agreed, and when Enzio took her in his arms she let him kiss her, too. And as they subsided onto the still warm soft sand, she suddenly remembered the lovely lines of the poet Catullus that Angel had quoted to them on the motor launch to Sirmione. The returning tide curled round both their recumbent bodies as, swooning, she recalled them word perfect.

The lines had described Sirmione as
A beautiful woman lying on her side
Being whipped and then caressed
By the divine impudent tide.
Lashed by the rain and the waves, Lena thought she knew exactly what the poet meant. In her snatched moments with Sammy Plaister, she had never felt anything like this.

Pascal Stone, still propped against his rock just round the inlet, was already stiffening in death, his usual gentle smile hardened into a rigor, when Dirk bent over him to waken him.

Not looking for trouble, the shocked kids jumped on their illegally-ridden scooters and zoomed off. Just delaying long enough to cover Pascal's body with a bright beach towel. A towel delightfully impregnated with the scent of young love and sun oil.

Perhaps Pascal's soul, not quite received into eternity, delighted in clinging on, for a few extra seconds, to its fragrant earthly refuge.

11

Thunder and Lightning

The summer storm that had targeted Sirmione rolled the length of Lake Garda and spent its last spiteful powers bombarding Malcesine, and especially the fortress there, which had turrets and towers and flagpoles that pricked the lightning's pride and made the thunder roar with disdain at human fortifications. The hotel where the Sally Gardens Club members were staying was built into the coastal embankment just under the castle. So its terraces were lashed with rain, and the little boats at anchor in the marina bobbed up and down piteously, being dragged back by their chains.

In the large dining room looking out over the water, the assembled club members had headaches and dined together in silence. Professor Donald presided over the table, in the absence of Guy Everard, whom the members suspected of going off with Sam's girlfriend Lena to another resort, leaving them in the lurch. None of them then knew about his unfortunate fate. They had in fact been apprised of the death of Pascal Stone, and were trying to suppress their feelings of guilt because they didn't feel exactly grief-stricken about the event. The general consensus was that the old poet had had quite a good run for his money. And Roxanne put into words what many of them were feeling, when she murmured to Professor Donald as she stopped by his chair on her way out.

"Anyway, the old queen died the way he always liked to live, surrounded by cute skinny young men!"

Pascal's new and last friend Dirk and a few of his mates had dropped in at the hotel to return Pascal's diary, which he had dropped on the beach where he died. Jackie had gone off, livid with anguish, to identify the body, all by himself.

But once the club members had separated and gone off to their sleeping quarters, the tensions that had been building up during the day began to erupt, and the stabs of rage and invective rivalled the forked lightning outside. And the hoarse roaring of anger and contempt could hardly be covered by the thunder still growling overhead.

Even Frank Childers got snappy. He grabbed the diary of the dead poet (for further investigation, he said, as though he were in charge of a murder enquiry), and would not yield it to Donnie Donald, who wished to take charge of it. Frank was not in the best of moods. Mother Agnes, who Angel had brought back with her from Sirmione, couldn't return to the convent as the ferries there were no longer running because of the storm.

Dame Georgie, of all people, had the most spectacular row of all. At one point she opened her balcony door, risking being struck by lightning, in order to scream to the Club members and hotel residents at large that she was married to a Big Fat Skinflint.

"But you don't need the money!" she screamed, as raucously as the seagulls which were screeching over the town, trying to find a refuge from the raging storm. "What the hell do you need the bloody money for? You are supposed to be wealthy!"

There were *basso profundo* rumblings which Roxanne, in the room next door, could hardly make out. She caught the words. 'Matters of Principle', and 'in my judgement'.

"Your judgement, don't make me bloody laugh! What judgement have you ever shown? You got lucky, that was all, and maybe your luck's about to change!"

Then Roxanne, her ear pressed to the partition wall heard a roar of rage and "Are you threatening me, you bitch?" and then Dame Georgie's voice got kind of muffled, almost as if she were being strangled.

Roxanne was about to go and hammer on the furious couple's door, but suddenly she heard Georgie's voice again, shriller and louder than before, as the door was flung open.

"And another thing!" Georgie screamed at her spouse, "Have you no respect for beautiful objects? Would you raze Art Nouveau architecture? Just for cash?"

But Sir Donnie wasn't taking this lying down. "I would remind you how you got your Honours! Cash, darling, cash! My cash! Did you think it was your wee chooky birdie voice? As to beauty, you never had the kind of figure I like, even when we were young. The only reason I married you was because I thought you were pregnant!"

"You brute! How can you say that? After all I've been through trying to get pregnant! Some hope! And now we're on the subject, the only reason I married you was that I thought you were rich! And now after a wasted youth, it seems I was wrong!"

Then the door and the widows were slammed shut simultaneously and silence reigned.

But the quarrelling contagion seemed to have spread through the ceiling to the room above, where Dolores was getting herself into a rage, waiting for Sammy Plaister to come back to his room from the cocktail bar downstairs. When he did, she first went into the huff, and when Sammy didn't notice, sniffed loudly and contemptuously.

"Something wrong, Dolores?" Sammy got the message, under Dolores's furious gaze.

"No, not a thing! Except how much of your dirty business am I supposed to do? And how much are my services worth? One way and another? And poor bloody Pascal? He was supposed to be a great friend? And a wonderful poet, you said!"

Sammy sought to turn the argument into a literary discussion.

"In his early days, yes. But his work has fallen off sadly of late. I don't believe we would have got much of poetic value from Mr. Stone in the future. Had he had one!"

" 'Had he had one!' What a horrible way to speak! I think your veneer of niceness is cracking! Soon everyone will see the rotten stuff beneath. And Pascal liked my work!"

"Did he? Are you sure? Look, Dolores you better make yourself scarce. Lena might turn up tonight, that's if I haven't done her in, as you probably imagine!"

But Dolores returned to the attack again. "And what about the carry-on in the sand?"

"What sand? What carry-on? A term I hate! You're picking up Parliamo Glesca, I hear! When we were digging each other in, covering each other up to the neck? I thought that was fun! I quite enjoyed it! I don't suppose you enjoyed my later efforts, either?"

"Quite!" Dolores replied tersely. "Neither of your lakeside efforts was fun for me. But if I had not been dug in, I would have run after poor Pascal, and brought him back, and given him iced Martini out of my coolbag! And maybe Pascal wouldn't be dead!"

"Iced Martini! No-one drinks iced Martini! For a sophisticated young woman, you have vulgar habits. Quite frankly, Dolores, you're getting to be more trouble than you're worth!"

Here the disembodied screeching started, and objects were flung round the room. Sammy decamped again for the bar. His bow tie was squint, and a bruise was coming up over one eye.

But in the bar another quarrel was going on. People had been getting at Roxanne, for being rude to Pascal, and making him stomp off. She stood it for a while, then she turned on her accusers. Her mane fiery, she was one rosy glow of pink, from guilt, rage and sunburn.

"I was always nice to him. I was always trying to cheer him up. Maybe I was a bit cheeky but that's just my way. I was only doing it for a laugh. And I introduced him to some nice young guys at the bar the other day. I understood him, the wee soul! Are you trying to make out I don't like Gays? I love them. My best friend is one."

"I hope you don't mean me!" Dolores came in. "No-one has ever said that about me!"

"No, darling!" her friend countered, "But they've said plenty of other things!"

"Well, if you're going to be like that I'll bugger off. I was only staying because of you. To make sure you didn't pick up a couple of truckers and get yourself gang-banged, but maybe that was what you were hoping for."

Roxanne, after a pause of incoherent rage, got her voice back.

"Bitch!" she shrieked "You were the one out looking for Gigolos!"

"Cow! How dare you? I never paid for it in my life." Dolores quaked with rage.

Roxanne sidled up to her insultingly closely and whispered vehemently in her ear, words which the eager audience of drunken lawyers and poets could hardly make out, "services rendered", "nothing you wouldn't stoop to", "God help the poor bugger!"

With a face so white it was greenish, and tears beginning to slide down its porcelain planes, Dolores stamped out of the bar, slamming the Tiffany-style glass panelled door behind her, so hard it nearly shattered. Her spike-heeled shoes nearly got caught on the carpeted stairs as, not waiting for the lift, she scrambled upstairs, to her room, to pack.

The odd thing was, as Dolores reached her room, the tears rolled backwards into her gleaming dark eyes, and a slight smirk compressed her scarlet lips. And when she looked about, the smile became complacent. She had hardly any packing left to do. Her cases were already packed and stashed in wardrobes. She only had her Paloma Picasso toiletries to stash.

The only one who did not quarrel with anyone was Jackie, who had to pack up his best friend's things. He found an old tatty booklet of poems Pascal had written about Lake Garda. It had been dedicated to Samuel Plaister. Jackie slipped this into his inside breast pocket.

And things went from bad to worse between Frank and Angel. Frank forgot himself enough to accuse Angel of shamelessly leading him on, which he knew in his heart of hearts to be not exactly true. And Angel tearfully denied it, although she knew in heart of hearts she had been the one who had tried to seduce Frank, in spite of himself.

Then Angel exploded and asked Frank why, after hanging around her so long, he had decided to dump her when she had that difficult tour of Isola del Garda to do. And look how that had ended! She might have been drowned and he hadn't even come back to see how she was that night.

Then Mother Agnes got involved and owned up to persuading Frank to stay on at the Convent. She said they'd had important matters to discuss.

"Important matters, Mother Agnes! And what could those matters be? Too important to tell me? I, who chose you as my holiday companion!" fumed Angel.

"I, who agreed to mind you and keep you from doing anything silly! Not that I've had a great deal of success in that regard!"

"And what have you to say for yourself, Mr. Childers? Perhaps we should hear your opinions round about now!" Agnes went on, but Frank merely tossed his handsome head.

Relenting, Agnes suggested that Angel and Frank should make time to have an honest talk with each other and thrash things out. You couldn't just bury problems. It was no use hiding their heads in the sand. They should avoid digging up the past.

Angel thought Mother Agnes's metaphors were a bit funereal, but anyway she agreed.

Then Frank had a brilliant idea. He could get two tickets for the Arena di Verona, for the next day. Would Angel like to go with him, and they could discuss their differences there?

It started at nine. The motor launch would pick them up at the harbour at seven. There was a nice bistro he knew round the corner from the Arena, where they could have a quick bite to eat first.

Angel said very seriously that that seemed to be a good idea. Unless of course Mother Agnes would like to go in her place. She believed it was 'Norma' that was on.

Mother Agnes threw her hands up in the air. Young people! Could you ever get an honest answer out of any of them? With a tender but rueful smile playing about her wide lips, Agnes took herself off to say her office on her own. As a matter of fact, and not that Angel or Frank would give a damn, Norma was her very favourite opera. One in which she thought the plot was rather relevant to her own life, in a way. She sighed as she got out her prayer book and rosary. Perhaps Angel would find it enlightening. It might bring her some insights into her own nature.

Angel came into the room later, smiling and humming. When she saw Mother Agnes still at her prayers, solemn and quiet, seated in the corner, Angel stopped humming 'Casta Diva', and assumed a little sanctimonious, pious frown, as she got out her own mother-of-pearl prayer book.

Mother Agnes put away her prayer book, and took out the notebook in which she was noting events related to the mysterious document she had found, the Tontine. From the list she had noted down, she scored out one name. The name of the member who had been first to succumb, as she had feared, Pascal Stone. But of course in this calculation she was wrong. Guy Everard had succumbed just half an hour before him.

Everything seemed to settle down throughout the hotel, as the storm blew itself out over the marina at last. But towards dawn the quarrel between Dame Georgie and Donald Donald sprang up again. Roxanne heard Georgie's voice again, high and staccato.

"You don't mean to tell me you fancy that tart? That big stookie?"

And Donnie's voice, low and hollow, like in the sound track of the Exorcist.

"And what do you care, anyway, since you've only ever fancied your tiny self?" he boomed, as the sound of wardrobe doors being slammed made Roxanne quake.

"Anyway, I'm leaving here at first light. I can't bear to face the others after this. I'm getting out of here!" squeaked Dame Georgie.

"And so bloody well am I!" rasped Donnie, "You can forget bloody Norma!"

Next morning Mother Agnes met Frank as they were walking about on the terrace waiting for breakfast. The rain had washed the summer dust from the surroundings, and the lake spread out before them, limpid and blue, the sky above pearly, almost colourless. For someone with the weight of the world on his shoulders, as he had appeared the night before, Frank was doing rather a lot of abstracted smiling. As they stood there chatting they were treated to the spectacle of Dame Georgie D'Amato-Donald and Professor Sir Donald McDonald Donald of that Ilk getting into a tatty hired car.

"The airport. Bergamo Airport." they heard Donnie growl.

Neither the Professor nor the Dame acknowledged them, and neither waved back at the pair on the terrace as they sped off.

"Well, that makes two we don't have to worry about!" Frank noted cheerfully.

But Mother Agnes was still in her sombre mood. "I wouldn't be too sure of that!" she said darkly.

"Could I have a wee look at Mr. Pascal Stone's diary?" she asked as they sat down at one of the small tables. "I could have a squint at it while you and Angel are away. There's a problem I'm itching to solve. Perhaps Pascal will lend his aid, posthumously."

Mother Agnes switched on her most charming smile as Angel descended some steps to the terrace. "And here's the bold girl herself! And all smiles! So the quarrel is made up!" Agnes said, turning away to whisper to Frank complicitly.

Angel was wearing the baggy yellow shorts and the striped Tee shirt Mother Agnes had bought her, both as an olive branch to her, and to Frank.

They had both risen to greet Angel, in honour of their triune reconciliation, and of Angel's dazzlingly pretty, though absurd, appearance in the cheap resort clothes. All three stood as the morning sun pierced the plants above them with light, making them luminous and transparent, as it tried to round the terrace and dazzle them. All three stood smiling. The young man and young woman beaming, while Mother Agnes looked from one to the other, smiling wistfully and uncertainly.

Then Sister Mary of the Angels remembered she had another bone to pick with Childers.

"And Lena? Big Lena Wallace?" she whispered "Why were you snogging, well, kissing, her?"

Frank, turning away, annoyed, rasped over his shoulder, "So you're jealous of poor Lena?"

Frank turned back, and glimpsing their reflections in the glass doors leading to the terrace, spun Angel round so his dark visage appeared in the glass behind her glowing features.

"Do you think I could ever prefer anyone to you? I mean, be reasonable!" he groaned.

And Angel turned to kiss the tender lips under his fragrantly after-shaved moustache, just as the shadow of Mother Agnes whisked out of sight.

12

Moon Over Verona

Angel was looking like a million dollars, Frank thought, as they sat on the broad stone steps of the Arena di Verona, overlooking the seething masses of opera-going tourists. She looked better than all of them, than any of them, in her chic white dress, the one he had bought for her in the boutique in Limone. Most of the tourists wore baggy shorts and jumpers to keep off the chill night air they expected. What were they afraid of? That someone would actually think they liked opera and were dressing up for it? And as for night chills, the air was as mellow as the inside of a water melon from a street stall.

Frank hoped it was a good sign that Angel had opted for the dress, rather than the borrowed white habit she'd taken to wearing again. But you never knew with Angel, and her first remark did little to dispel his fears.

"This might turn out to be our last night together!"

Frank did some speedy thinking. He'd avoid the tragic role if he could.

"If it is our last night, can we pretend? Pretend this is our first night?"

"How do you mean?" Angel was wary.

"Pretend I bought you your pretty dress! Pretend you love it!"

"Pretend I bought you the iconic Tee shirt. Pretend you will never wear anything else to go to the opera, right!"

"And to football matches, of course!" He pointed out the green striped shirt his Topolino (the Italian version of Mickey Mouse) wore with his gondola costume, emblazoned on the front of the Tee shirt. "Old Firm matches, Celtic versus Rangers. Do you dare me?"

"I'd stick to the Celtic stands if I were you!"

Frank thought he looked rather good in the Mickey Mouse Tee shirt, anyway, under his white evening suit. He had got some admiring glances from the fashionable ladies who had passed them on their way to the cushioned armchairs laid out for them on the floor of the Arena. He hoped Angel had caught that. He had got his dark curls spiked and gelled at the barbershop in the hotel, and his beard trimmed Italian style. Though maybe the ladies had been amused to see the elegant couple roughing it in the heaving throng of tourists waiting for entrance number four to open, the one for the cheapest seats, way high up. They were all Frank could get at short notice, when he traded in his solitary expensive ticket for both seats. Angel had gone silent. He started the game again.

"Pretend we've known each other since primary school. You were the big snidey girl in the desk in front of me. I put your pigtails in the inkwells."

"There were no inkwells. Is this *Back to the Future*? We used horrible biros."

"I see, you didn't have calligraphy lessons in your school, then! But the pigtails?"

"Certainly not! I had a baby perm. Since then I've had a perm every year. That is why I only have two inches of hair left now!"

Angel broke off to stop a vendor passing and grab two cans of beer from his tray. She had, as usual, forgotten about the money part of the transaction. Frankie rushed to get the right money out. Vendors were not keen on giving change.

"Grazie, signor!" said the vendor, as Frank pressed too many coins into his hand, for luck.

"Prego!" answered Angel, taking the credit.

"You're not very good at sums!" she remarked to Frank.

"I am so good at sums!"

"I am double good at big hard sums, teacher says."

"You are not. You're just teacher's pet. She lets you off with wrong answers."

"I'm going to tell teacher on you. She'll give you the belt! Pretend I'm the teacher, I'll give you the belt! I have one from the Museum of Childhood in my handbag."

"Okay then, but later." Frank began to think the tourists were giving him funny looks. He wondered how many of them spoke English, or the Glasgow version he and Angel were using. He started on another tack.

"Did you have a boyfriend? When you were sixteen, did you?"

"No."

"Really?"

"No, I had a man-friend. I went out with my music teacher's boyfriend. He didn't know he was her boyfriend, though. I told her how he was doing. I said he was asking after her. I made it sound as if he was a bit in love with her. Which he was."

"How old was he, this man-friend?"

"Twenty-six."

"The music teacher?"

"Thirty-six."

"Nice and neat. I swear you're making this up!"

"I swear to God I'm not!"

"Let's not swear to God, okay!" The atmosphere in the Arena had suddenly got tense and quiet, as officials came out to place the music sheets on the orchestra's music stands, set out right across the front of the auditorium. Frank's voice sounded oddly snappy and loud. But he couldn't seem to stop himself going on. "Let's not swear to God. You've done enough swearing to God for one life time!" By this time the orchestra members had settled, and the conductor entered to applause. As the applause was dying away, Frank was still hissing in Angel's ear. "You should have waited for me, before you decided to swear your life away!"

"Shush!" said Angel, and the audience lit up the candles they'd bought, as the blue dusk deepened, and the overture began. Around them, though, people were still chewing their *bruschetta*, and downing the last of their wine. The stage lighting intensified, and the chorus was revealed. "The pretend curtain is going up!" Angel gasped as the candle flames went out all at once, and the spotlights picked out the sacred groves, looking a bit like Limone.

He could have wept for relief, as she, delighted by the spectacle of the mass of tiny flames put out in one puff, squeezed his hand in forgiveness for his stupid earlier outburst. And Frank Childers, who had read the score, and usually had a sharp ear for any mistake in pitch or tempi, sat unheedingly, wrapped in the harmonies undifferentiated by him, except as a swelling mass of emotion. He sat rapt in the sound, and in the heady musky perfume Angel was wearing, while the drama of Rome and Gaul played out before his unseeing eyes.

He came to his senses again as the moon rose behind the massive circular arena, floating out on cue behind the truncated arched wall and the tower in the distance. At the moment when Norma started her famous aria, 'Casta Diva', as if guided by the conductor's baton. Angel was pale as a ghost, investing all her emotions and sympathy with the heroine, Norma, the druid priestess. She turned to Frank, as if for explanation. Not of the plot, but for the surge of emotion she was feeling. Like at Limone, but without the peach cordial.

For Frank's part, he felt he had the pure chaste Goddess beside him in human form, as her delicate profile was touched by silver points of moonlight, the spiky tips of her hair glittering.

"Casta Diva che inargenti
queste sacre antichi piante
a noi volgi il bel sembiante
senza nube e senza vel."

The aria ended to tumultuous applause, which rocked the looser parts of masonry in the ancient stadium. Frank glanced at his programme for the English translation.

"Chaste Goddess, who doth bathe in silver
these ancient hallowed trees
turn thy fair face upon us
unveiled and unclouded."

Angel turned the page with her small forefinger, and kept the finger there under his as the music resumed. He felt first his finger, then his hand, then his whole arm begin to shake. He was almost glad when the first act came to an end, and the audience lit their candles again.

The *gelati* vendors swung into action. Angel was the first in the row to grab two cornettos.

"Now where were we?" she asked, as she finished hers, and licked her fingers.

"We were pretending. Pretending it was our first night."

"First night at the opera?"

"First night of our" he lowered his voice dramatically, huskily, in her ear "honeymoon!"

"So can we?" Frank broke a little silence.

"I'll see!"

"No you won't! You're just saying that! You've no intention! None at all! I can't bear it!"

"Frank!"

"Yes dear?" Frank looked up, mock cheerfully.

"We're just pretending! You can't be pretend upset! You can only be pretend nice. That is, really nice but pretend!"

"Okay! I see! Look, the pretend curtain is going up again."

As the opera unfolded, the irony was not lost on Angel that Norma was torn between carnal love, and her vows. She suspected Frank had chosen the opera on purpose, which, if he had chosen to demean himself, he could have proved was not true. He had booked in advance. There were some uncanny similarities, he admitted, as when the young priestess Adalgisa is urged by Norma to give up her sacred life for human love. Angel was sure, that if she had asked Mother Agnes's advice, it might be similar. Not that she ever would. She had, in fact, made up her mind to turn Frank down. So she became annoyed with him when he was charming, and relaxed when he turned grumpy. Not that he had asked her. She had managed to put him off. But in the interval before the last act, he sneakily did.

"If you weren't a nun, would you marry me? Or would you just go out and get the very handsomest and richest man you could find, and try him out?"

"Is that a proposal?"

"It's a pretending one!"

"Well, then pretending yes!"

"Only pretending yes?"

"For a real answer you have to start again at the beginning. There's the pretend curtain about to go up on the real stage. But where's the real moon?"

The moon had hidden herself behind a cloud and the arena was in shadow. Only a few beams filtered through, alighting on random spots in the open air arena.

Towards the end, when Norma was about to sacrifice herself, ascending into the flames, Angel's eyes happened to light on a profile in the crowd several rows ahead, and an aisle to the side. The profile momentarily outlined by moonlight was familiar to her. She thought she recognised the jowly face, and as she peered forward, she saw the white waistcoat-clad abdomen bulging out over the tartan trews. And she recognised the slim elegant figure with him. Dolores Kant was leaning against Professor Donald, languishingly, lovingly. They were both laughing at the melodramatic ending. Maybe that was what had made Angel notice them. Their burbling laughter was growing quite loud.

She turned to alert Frank, but he had already followed her gaze, and was staring in the same direction. She judged, from the furious expression on his face, that he had recognised the couple too.

"Sneaks!" he whispered, as the applause started. "Sneaking back here when they were supposed to have gone home. And Mother Agnes was actually worried about both of them, him especially."

"I wonder where poor Dame Georgie is. Does she know, do you think?"

But the snooty couple were causing a bit of commotion in their row. In breach of audience protocol, they had risen from their seats, and were pushing past the rest of their row to get to the exit. People had to draw their legs right up on the seats to let them pass by. Hissing and expletives went unnoticed by the couple who were lost in conversation. The audience turned back to its cheering and stamping and screaming applause, but Angel and Frank followed them with their eyes as the illicit couple started down the chipped, brutally steep, stone steps leading to the exit. So they witnessed what happened next. Donald seemed to be holding back, looking for handrails, of which there were none. Angel expected

Dolores to stretch out her hand and help him down. But Dolores seemed to turn to him sharply, making annoyed gestures to him, pointing at her watch. Donald seemed to be frozen, petrified, as if suffering from vertigo. Dolores did stretch out her hand. Donald gave a sharp yell, and waving his arms like sails of windmills, seemed to be trying to recover his balance. Frank stood up, ready to go to his aid, and was in time to see a red high-heeled shoe fly off Dolores's foot colliding with Donnie's sandaled foot. The large man went sailing out over the stairway, and in falling turned a somersault, finally being reunited with the staircase, to bang his head repeatedly on the high marble treads. His heavy body juddered downwards, to the very bottom.

If the incident had taken place a few moments later, it would have been much worse. Not worse for Donnie. It couldn't have been any worse for him. The attendants who leapt out to pick up the body saw that. His skull was smashed in many and various ways, each precluding life. And he had already no vital signs when the medic on duty checked, before enlisting his whole crew to manhandle the body away out of the entrance and into the ambulance that waited there. (A little lady on sticks who was always allowed to escape early from her ground floor seat screamed as she saw the huge prostrate form on the stretcher six men struggled to carry. The poor man with the twisted neck and staring open eyes.) The ambulance was usually used for opera buffs who had had heart attacks with delight, or for ladies going into labour. But there might have ensued a crowd disaster, with a number of deaths not witnessed since Christians were thrown to the lions in Roman times. The arena marble, sometimes seeming thirsty for the blood it had been slaked with, was denied a libation on this occasion. And if Donnie's huge body had fallen among lighter mortals he might have carried many off with him to the Elysian Fields. Or across the River Styx, who knows which. Panics are easily started. And for that reason, the attendants hastened to mop up Donald Donald's blood before the houselights came up to advise the audience to stop clapping and get home to their beds, it being nearly midnight.

Frank and Angel had slipped out as fast as they could, among the mercifully small group who had witnessed the accident and had gone to crowd round. Still, before Frank had managed to contact the *Polizia* on duty, Donnie had been trundled away, and the lovely Dolores was nowhere to be seen.

"Listen, Angel!" Frank shouted, as he ran her out of the exit to the dying applause from the auditorium, ahead of the rush that was moments away. "Don't for God's sake argue with me, but come round this side street. Let's run! I'll have to get hold of the police again."

The desk clerk at the Arena Hotel, tiny premises across from the Arena, had a superior smile on his face when Frank dashed to the desk, panting, to book in. He had seen eager young men before, but this was ridiculous!

When they got to the tiny room on the fourth floor, Frank sat down on the bed instantly, ripping off his jacket, and kicking off his shoes, leaving Angel to her own devices.

"*Pronto! Polizia! Sonno Detective Inspector Childers, Escozia!*" he barked into his mobile.

Angel eased off her shoes and lay down beside him. The conversation looked as if it would take a long time. She fell asleep and when she woke her posh white dress lay folded carefully on the chair beside her. She remembered it had been too hot for underwear. All she was wearing was a little thin gold chain Frank had bought her for the occasion. A white coverlet was spread over her, right up to her chin. She felt like Snow White.

There was a note on the pillow. And an opened bottle of champagne in a bucket.

"Dear Angel," the note said, "I felt it my bounden duty to go and help the local cops. I know more than they do. I'm sorry I had to dash away. And this was supposed to be our first or our last night together, our pretend honeymoon. Sorry for the pretend disappointment. I'll be back soon, I hope. Have a nice nap. Ring room service if you get hungry.

Your loving pretend husband, Frank."

When Frank got back he didn't want to talk about Donnie. Or Dolores. He said he was dog-tired and he would explain later. He swigged half the champagne from the bottle. Then he lay down on the cover and fell asleep fully dressed.

When he woke up his clothes were stacked neatly beside the bed, all his clothes, including his silk socks and his designer boxers.

And the bottle of champagne was empty.

"Does this mean ... ?" he whispered

"Well, I dunno!" She jettisoned the hotel dressing gown from her pale gold shoulders and lay down close beside him. Embracing him, she murmured in his ear. "Just a few questions first. Have you ever had a girlfriend?"

"Heavens no!"

"Not even a music teacher?" She ran her hands through the damp curls of his hair.

"Certainly not in the carnal sense! I'm pure as the driven snow. I'm not even sure how it works! I could try to get sex therapy, but it would cost you. Perhaps we should go for trial and error. Maybe you could just start easy with me, and we'll see how we get on?"

He rolled on top of her and tried to stop her talking with his kisses.

"One more question. Who would you choose, me or Adalgesa? If I was Norma?"

"You! In whatever guise! Even in a white habit! Of course I'd prefer you as Minnie Mouse."

When she woke up next morning, Angel opened the curtains to a lovely view of the battlements of the Arena. She sent a message to the convent to say she was staying in Malcesine. Then she phoned Malcesine to say Frank was staying at the convent.

The deferred sexual encounter had gone very well, considering Angel's lack of experience.

Her reading of historic erotic literature had certainly given her some bright ideas, new even to Frank. Finally he had rebelled.

"Angel!" he had complained, "Take it easy, darling! I'm supposed to be in charge!"

As the sun peeped into the attic, Angel, after a struggle, got the tricky coffee percolator to work. She carried a cup carefully over to the bedside table. In the narrow bed, Frank was stirring, golden and bearded like a Sea God, thrashing out as he wakened, stirring the sheets like a sea storm, in triumph. One muscular tanned leg was exposed. And round his slender ankle gleamed Angel's thin gold chain, which she had wound round and round, as a token of his slavery to herself. She traced the line of his instep with her finger tip, and he jumped, nearly upsetting the coffee.

"Do you take milk or sugar," Angel asked, "Mister ... I didn't quite catch your name?"

Frank insisted on switching both their phones off, so neither Dame Georgie, nor the Polizia could get through to them. Angel thought of phoning Mother Agnes, but finally decided against it. Instead she went back to the narrow little bed.

13

Cards On The Table

Detective Inspector Frank Childers faced Mother Mary Agnes across the polished rosewood table of the reception room in the Convent of Stella del Mare in Toscolano Maderno.

To Frank, the aromas in the room were overpowering. He felt he was drowning in them. Lavender wax from the parquet floors. Scent from the waxy lilies in the flower arrangements that Mother Annunziata spent so much of her time refurbishing, so that foetid water was never among the disturbing smells. Then the smell of the convent's famous peach cordial, made by an elaborate secret process from the harvest of the convent's own peach orchards. And then the delicious whiff of lunch simmering in the basement kitchens.

It seemed a long time till lunch. Frank's stomach growled. And he had a lot to get through before that. If, that is, he was invited to partake of that almost sacerdotal meal which the Sisters and their visitors enjoyed in the early afternoon, usually around two o'clock.

Mother Agnes sat with her back to the light, which was floridly diffused through the clematis that wreathed the French windows. He couldn't tell what Agnes was thinking. He felt a sudden impulse to take her hand. He could have learned a lot from her hand. His Mammy had taught him to read palms, a traditionally female skill, as she had no daughter to whom to pass the psychic information.

As if reading his mind, Agnes withdrew her hands from before her on the table, and slid each in the opposite sleeve of her habit. She even blushed. Frank had a sudden image of her, first as the nicest big girl in her class, then as a funny young nun. Mother Agnes seemed to snap her face shut on him.

"Well, Frank, lay your cards on the table! Have you anything to confess?"

Frank remained silent, still staring at her, as if to fathom her innermost thoughts.

"Put it this way," Agnes went on more brusquely, "Are your intentions towards our little Sister Mary of the Angels strictly honourable?"

"Of course, honourable!" Frank cut in before the words were out of her mouth. "Why do you think I'd be sitting here waiting for a shiricking from you, if my intentions were not? Honourable and even matrimonial!"

"So did anything happen between you and Sister Angel, at Verona? Anything sexual?"

"I don't kiss and tell, Mother Agnes. You'd have to ask Angel. But anything else, I'll tell you. I'm not a wealthy man, but I have my police salary, and no debts. I don't gamble or smoke or drink, except parsnip and elderflower wine, and peach cordial. My only excess is exercise, and I'm trying to cut back on that."

"I have no appendix, but all my other parts are intact. I have a mortgage on a flat in the Merchant City. But it gets a bit rowdy there at night, after the bistros and concert halls empty. So I wouldn't mind moving to the suburbs, or even to the country, if we have kids. We might get a nice farmhouse, or...."

"Steady there, young man! Hold your horses! This is the million dollar question. Is it at all likely you will? Have a child? Possible? Probable?"

To her distress Frank coloured up. He couldn't get a word out. He seemed to be choking. His breath came out in little rasping gasps. He fumbled in the inner pocket of his beige linen suit, and produced a Ventolin inhaler.

"Excuse me!" he wheezed, and went over to the windows to use it. Agnes sat waiting in patience while he did.

As his breathing returned to normal, he resumed his place opposite her.

"A child?" Agnes reiterated. "A possibility?"

"Certainly not! Maybe! I don't know!"

"Did you take precautions?"

"That's a very old-fashioned phrase!"

"Did you use contraception, then? A condom?"

"No, not exactly. It all came up so suddenly! And I was afraid I'd put her off. But I swear I tried to sort of ..."

"Saints above! You're not talking about Coitus Interruptus? In this day and age?"

"I suppose I am!"

"So Angel could be pregnant?"

"I suppose she could!"

"Well, Frank! That's the whole point! That's what I'm coming to! I think in that case, the authorities will be in rather a hurry to release her from her vows. A speedy wedding might be in order. You might swing it if the two of you went to Rome, to hurry things up."

"As to that, you'd have to ask Angel. I mean, I'd have to ask her. Look, Mother Agnes, have you any idea what she'd say?"

"I think the idea may have occurred to her. I eavesdropped on her phoning Sister Mary of Perpetual Succour. She was asking Peppy to be her bridesmaid."

"But what about you, Mother Agnes of the Holy Child?"

"Me? Why naturally I was a bit upset, not to be asked. I had my bridesmaid outfit all planned, but there you are, Frankie! Some you win and some you lose!"

"No, I meant, if Angel and I go off to Rome, who looks after you, Childie?" he used the nickname he had for her, "There is a murderer on the loose, don't forget."

"There are probably several murderers on the loose in Rome, too. Don't you worry your pretty little head over me, Childers, my boy!" She reciprocated, using his matching pet name.

When Frank didn't respond to her jest Mother Agnes went on more seriously. "You see, I'm not afraid of anything, any more. I used to be afraid of my own shadow. But now I snap my fingers at fate. Let the evildoers be afraid of me, I say!"

"And who do you think they are, these evildoers? While Angel and I were off gallivanting, did you come to any conclusions?"

Agnes sorted out the papers on the table in front of her.

"I would have bet my best Wellington boots on Donnie Donald! Poor big Donnie! I was so wrong!" Mother Agnes scrabbled among her notes, and sternly scratched a name out. "From what you've told me, Dolores seems a likely suspect, but she was not near Donald in the crush to board the launch. But she was at the Lido when Pascal was bullied. As to Pascal's death, morally Roxanne is to blame, bullying him and taunting him till he dashed off into the sun and got sunstroke. Guy was equally to blame, I think, in not going after him. What is Guy up to? Has he gone off with Lena Wallace? I hope she's alright. Yes, I think I suspect Guy Everard! But then again, Roxanne Renton has been acting very strangely. I came across her kicking Everard's shins at the convent luncheon party. Then there's the mystery of the big bearded fellow from the club, Binkie Boyne. Did he drown? Barry the barman told me he was a very odd colour. Bright blue. Cyanosed? Poisoning? Digitalis?"

"And the sweet little bouquet of foxgloves and bryony? Dolores arranged them."

"Why did I not think of that, Frank? But anyone could have administered poison seeds. As to Sam Plaister, he was at all the accident hotspots, and Lena was usually with him. So they are both suspects, and not to be instantly ruled out. They were both at the landing site in the throng trying to board. But only he was on the Lido when poor old Pascal Stone ran off, I've been told." She looked up enquiringly, and when Frank nodded, she went on.

"The few old-fashioned rhymesters, and sad out of date artists who make up our group seem to me to be too demented to promulgate any plan of action, criminal or otherwise. You'll agree we have to rule out our own good selves, you, me and our Angel, practically and theoretically. Right, Detective Inspector?" Agnes asked, smiling disarmingly.

"Now that leaves the solicitors and the advocates, Friends of the Glasgow School of Art, who care nothing about the Sally Gardens. Not members. Then there is sad little Jackie!"

"Jackie? Don't be ridiculous. Jackie is crushed by Pascal's death. It looks as if it may kill him! And you've forgotten Dame Georgie!"

"Why, yes, I have! You're up to speed today, Frank. I suppose we shouldn't rule her out! I've glanced through Pascal's diary. He seems to have had a great big thing for the unknown signatory to the Tontine, Stanislaus Pasternak."

"Pasternak! Pasternak, Mother Agnes, sounds like wishful thinking! A *nom de plume*?"

Agnes smiled. The brain storming was working. She felt an arc of energy was leaping from Frank's tanned smooth forehead, to her own wimple-encased furrowed brow.

She took Frank's long fingered hand between her broad paws.

"Atta boy, Frankie!" she said. "Well done, Childers! I'll work on that, while you're away. Angel has made the travel arrangements for Rome. Did I not mention that? You are to meet her at Bergamo airport at noon. You'd better get your skates on!"

After lunch, and quite a long nap on top of her bed in her luxuriously simple cell on the top floor, Mother Agnes returned to the reception room, and spread out her notebooks and index cards over the table again. She had enjoyed a stunningly deep sleep, and had to force herself to continue her work. The dusk was dropping behind the plant-screened French windows. She procrastinated by not switching on the lamps, but staring out at the larches and bougainvillea that decorated the steep driveway of the front garden. She suddenly became conscious of a form moving in the garden, close behind the windows. She was embarrassed to see that someone was staring in, pulling the clematis aside to do so. She realised that the would-be observer did not realise anyone was in the room. Agnes shrank back towards the interior doorway, and at the same time, the French windows swung open silently. The figure, a loping ungainly man, shuffled to the table and started squinting at the documents laid out there.

Mother Agnes reached out to turn on the overhead light switch.

Sammy Plaister stood there, his hand stretched out, poised to grab something from the pile of papers on the central table.

"Mother Mary Agnes!" From a mischievously eager expression, Sammy's face adopted a hangdog aspect. "I wonder if you can help me!" He stood away from the table, while Mother Agnes sat down.

"Well, I'll try my best, Mr. Plaister. How can I help you?" she asked formally.

Sammy sprawled onto a chair on the same side of the table as Mother Agnes, and put his head in his hands, his white hair haloed in the evening light.

Mother Agnes stared at him steadfastly. She had the impression that she was being observed through the man's obscuring fingers. "Is something on the table of interest to you?" she asked directly.

"Yes, indeed Mother Agnes!" Sammy made a play of wiping his eyes and nose with a large white cotton hanky. "That diary there. That one of Pascal Stone's. That is of interest to me. You see ..." he turned away from her and spoke to the small Aubusson rug at his feet. "I fear it may contain some references to me. References that might upset both my wife and my girlfriend, and who knows, my little son, in years to come. Pascal is not known for his discretion. Several years ago, Mother Agnes, I had an affair with Pascal Stone. It didn't last long, but when I tried to break it off, Pascal threatened to 'out' me to my friends and family. So I went back to him from time to time, to keep him sweet. And I fear he may have chronicled these meetings. May I ask you, Mother Agnes, to tell me, has he done so? To be honest, I'd rather wade out into the lake, if he has. I've thought of drugging myself and lying down on a Lil-lo, to let the tide sweep me away."

"I'm happy to put your mind at ease, Mr. Plaister. I suppose I shouldn't really tell you, since it's confidential information. But it surely can't do any harm to reassure you. Pascal Stone never once mentions you in his diary."

"God bless you, Mother, for that! I can't tell you how badly I feel about Pascal. The spat he had with Roxanne went right over my head. I was playing a silly game with one of the ladies. Dolores, I think. We were burying each other in sand making sand statues. By the time we had extricated ourselves, Pascal had decamped."

Sam stared into Mother Agnes's dark eyes. He stretched out his hand to shake hers.

"I'll take my leave now. Mother Agnes! I'm so sorry to have interrupted you."

Plaister hesitated for a moment, not knowing whether or not to push his luck. Finally he decided to take the chance.

Looking longingly at Pascal Stone's diary in Mother Agnes's hand, he broke out with, "I suppose you couldn't possibly ... let me see that for a moment?"

"No, I'm sorry, Sam, I couldn't do that. Do you want to say anything else to me?"

"No! Wait a minute, yes!" Sammy sounded peeved. "I'm worried about Roxanne. She seems to be losing the plot. Have you seen the amount of watches she's buying? Money laundering, obviously. She seems to be quarrelling with everybody! First she was forever coming on to Guy Everard, then she quarrelled with him, at the Lido, shouting and screaming, vile things. I won't sully your ears. Could you have a few words with her, Mother Agnes? Maybe give her a few words of spiritual advice?"

"That would not be up to me, Mr. Plaister, but I'll remember her in my prayers, as I will you and all our companions."

Without another word, Sammy Plaister bowed himself out by the French windows.

Mother Agnes sighed as she made a few notes. It saddened her that death and illness and accidents always seemed to bring out the worst in people, not the best. She had Pascal Stone's diary in her hand again when Mother Annunziata bobbed in to the room, closely followed by Roxanne Renton.

"Scusi Mother Agnes!" was all the nun got out before Roxanne threw herself down in front of Mother Agnes, with cries of despair. Annunziata flounced out in high dudgeon.

"Oh, Mother Agnes!" sobbed Roxanne, laying her head on Mother Agnes's knees. "I want you to hear my confession. Can you do that?"

"Come now, Roxanne!" Agnes raised her up, quite sharply. "I'll discuss anything that's troubling you, of course. But I can't hear confessions. What's the matter?"

Roxanne leaned over the table and grabbed Agnes's hands. "They're all out to get me! But you'll give me a fair hearing, won't you? I hate them all! First that Everard comes on to me, on the lido, the dirty bastard. Nearly drowned me. Then Sammy Plaister took his part and told me to shut up about it. He wouldn't listen to me. And when Dame Georgie told Everard off, Lord Donnie told her to mind her own business, that they'd other more important stuff to worry about. He didn't want to get on the wrong side of Everard. It's my belief they were patching up some kind of dubious business deal between them. And it's something to do with the Sally Gardens, I know. Something about building works. I reckon they've decided to take backhanders over the firms contracted to repair the mouldy place. And now everybody's blaming me for old Pascal snuffing it. As if it were my fault. And only the other day, I heard Sammy shouting at him. Threatening him about something. And I was always nice to the old man, in my own way, offering to cheer him up, if you know what I mean. No, I suppose you don't! And I thought I could rely on my pal, Dolores. (Kant, she still calls herself, although Jonnie Kant was two husbands ago). I even lent her the money to get one of her daft wee books of poetry published. She was always asking Donnie Donald for a grant to help her. The stupid big fool thought she fancied him, and the poetry was just an excuse for her to get together with him. She followed him and Georgie to the airport, when they left the hotel, to have a last go at him. I think she fancied herself as his next wee wifie. Or his widow!"

"But listen, Mother Agnes, apart from that, she's still a pal. And I'm getting worried about her. She hasn't turned up again. And she hasn't got the cash to get herself back to Glasgow on her own. Should I go to the Polizia? Sammy says no. What do you think?"

"Well, my dear, I think you'll find the police are already looking for her, but I suppose you could tell them what you know. Would you like a wee cup of tea, Roxanne?"

"No thanks, Mother Agnes. I've got a friend of Dolores's waiting outside. Aldo was very fond of her, although they only met last week. He's promised to help me find her. We're going to check on the lakeside bars for a start. Thanks, Mother Agnes. You've been very good to me. I've always loved nuns. I don't suppose you'd ever think, though, that I used to be in the Children of Mary?

"One thing is on my conscience, Mother Agnes. I played a joke on Guy Everard, and I think that's why he went AWOL. I stole his trousers and pants, to embarrass him, while he was stretched out on his Li-lo, blind drunk, snoring, fully dressed, in the sunshine. Guy must have had a job buying more at that time of night. I wish now I hadn't done that."

"Roxanne," Agnes called her back as she headed for the door. "I wouldn't buy any more watches, dear, and then return them, they'll say it's money laundering."

"Right enough, Mother Agnes. I never thought of that!" Roxanne clapped her hand over her luscious mouth in self-deprecation. "How stupid can I get?" she said, dashing out.

Agnes heard a few chirpy words from Roxanne Renton outside.

"*Pronto*, Aldo!" she heard, "*Pronto!*"

And she heard the screech of a sports car burning rubber on the paved driveway. Mother Agnes gathered up her documents and went wearily back to her room, and locked her door.

So Jackie Joad was too late when he called at the Convent, asking to see Mother Agnes. He had something important to tell her, he tried to explain in his halting Italian.

"*Cosa importanta!*" he cried.

When he couldn't get in, Jackie slid a tatty leaflet under Mother Agnes's bedroom door.

And Sammy, too, was sent away with a flea in his ear, by a convent gardener, when he turned up again. He found himself shoved outside the wrought iron gates which were closed at nightfall. And were only opened electronically thereafter to sophisticated voiceprints.

In her room, Mother Agnes sat reciting her daily prayers. Thoughts kept intruding on her devotions. Patterns of names swirled before her eyes. Vague suspicions took shape, only to be superseded by others. At the moment nothing fitted. Perhaps everything would be made clear tomorrow. She picked up the leaflet, a volume of poems like the one she had.

Agnes put away her prayer book, and took up Pascal Stone's diary again. She felt sure the solution lay somewhere in the closely written daily entries, full of dates and quotations and scraps of his own poetry. She started to read it methodically at the first of January. After one o'clock, the diary fell from her hand, and she'd only reached May.

14

Roman Holiday

Rome was sultry. Rome was dusty. Rome was stifling. No wonder the citizens of Rome had constructed so many fountains. Frank Childers had forgotten his sunglasses, and the flight from Bergamo, though short and sweet, with his arm round Angel, had nevertheless still made his ears pop and his head ache. And what the hell was he doing in Rome, anyway? He had sworn no fealty to Rome, although baptised in the Catholic Church. And although he had long ago shuffled off the coils of his strict Catholic education, people still treated him as if he was a daily communicant. And in a way, he acted as though he were, constantly questioning any impulsive action, for a secret malice towards others. Some people liked that trait, and some did not. His fellow police officers, on the whole, did not. Some went so far as to call him a big Jessie, because of his excess of scruples.

Frank and Angel, in the crowd round the Trevi fountain, were pushed and buffeted right up to the edge. Tourists were literally screaming in excitement at the vision of the baroque monument full of sea creatures, presided over by the sea God. But it left Frank cold, or rather hot. Why on earth had he worn a jacket?

(Actually, it was to keep his stuff in the pockets. He had never taken to men's handbags, and to stuff wallets and cards in trouser pockets spoiled the perfect line of his new designer slacks.)

Angel, too, hemmed in behind Frank, did not look her usually cool self. What had Mother Agnes been thinking of, to buy such a frightful dress for her *protégée* Angel? Frank thought it really odd, and not in a fashionable way. It was brown with a white collar, and draped from under the bust, which made Angel look, what was the word? Yes, pregnant! So that had been Agnes's idea!

Frank leant over to trail a finger in the famously cold water in the shallow stone basin. He might have been swimming in Lake Garda, the fins of lake fishes brushing his heels. The glamorous fountain meant no more to him than a paddling pool set up in his back garden, as a little boy, when he had longed for the seaside, in a summer heatwave. The sun struck off the white horses rearing up from the stone froth, and the waters gushing over the Nereids reaching up to him dazzled his aching eyes. He felt as much a fish out of water, as the fat dolphins leaping from the spray. The Triton, poised majestically nude, made him feel stupidly overdressed in his linen jacket. The imposing white palace behind seemed to trap the heat and noise. The sun rays fragmented the light into spectrums which made the crowd gasp, but which gave Frank no joy. He felt a zigzag of neon energy sear across his right eye. He reeled. He wasn't sure if he could still see from the left one.

All he wanted to do was to go and lie down in a darkened room. He didn't even want any lunch, he thought childishly. He hoped Angel would enquire, so he could refuse.

"You won't want any lunch, will you, darling?" she said, instead, "I'll have to dash off in five minutes. I have an appointment with the Grand Inquisitor! You don't mind, do you?"

"I thought I was supposed to attend the '*Auto da Fe*' with you. I could probably combust spontaneously, in this hateful heat! Otherwise, why would I be here? I might be swimming!"

"Just to prove you exist that's all. That I'm not claiming a virgin birth. That I'm not making you up to get out of the Convent of the Bleeding Heart! As if I'd want to!"

"To make me up?"

"No, to leave the convent. The convent is lovely!"

"And I'm not?"

Angel was feeling sweltered and weird too.

"Do you want to go back to Malcesine and leave me here?"

"No."

"Do you want us both to go back?"

"Not since we've come so far."

"Do you think I'm pregnant?"

"Haven't given it a thought!"

"Have you ever got any one into trouble?"

"No trouble, at all. They just have abortions. No trouble to me! Only joking, no."

"Then why did you chance it with me?"

"Ask Mother Agnes! I told her! I'm beginning to think it might be easier to marry Agnes!"

Frank sat down on the edge of the basin.

"I really am feeling awful, sick and dizzy!"

"They'll think you are the one who is pregnant!" Angel remarked unsympathetically.

"And listen, Angel, I think I may be going blind! You'll have to lead me about."

"Very funny!"

"No, I mean really, would you? Could you get me to an hotel, before I'm sick?"

"It's probably just a migraine. I have pills for them in my bag. I have them all the time. So you'll have to get used to leading me about! Don't be a big baby, Frank!"

That was the beginning of their unplanned Roman holiday. Angel pushed and shoved till she got Frank out of the circle of tourists round the fountain, and led him down the stylish Via Condotti. How she would have liked to stay there, and penetrate the mysteries of one of the chic boutiques, dusky behind smoked glass, and cool, probably, with air conditioning. Frank had decided to forge ahead grimly, sweeping strollers out of his way. Angel stumbled behind him, her eyes either lowered or giving mute apologies to the people Frank barged into.

Chic Roman ladies murmured "*Mama Mia*" as he ricocheted off them. Aussie back packers wanted to know if he was looking for a fight. Italian teenagers talking into their *telefoninos* screeched to their friends in amusement, thinking he was drunk.

"Now, here we are!" said Angel, when they emerged into a small beautiful piazza, where a fountain played and flower sellers had their carts placed picturesquely. "We're at the Spanish Steps. The convent where I'll be staying is right at the top!"

"The convent, where you'll be staying." Frank repeated loutishly. "Does that mean I have to stay in a monastery?"

"No of course not. Don't act obtuse! You don't count!"

"I gathered that."

Frank sat down on the lip of the fountain, where a galleon, as if sinking, spouted water from gashes in its side. This was more to Frank's taste that afternoon. He felt like a sinking galleon himself. The image sent him spinning off into a sensation of *déjà vu*. Where had he seen the galleon before? And the steps, they appeared to him to start to move. And the flower sellers. He began to sneeze too. Some old film, no doubt. He'd give up watching black and white films, he vowed. He had the repeated feeling he should be somewhere else.

Something was happening somewhere else that he should know about. He supposed that detectives often felt that. Good detectives, that is.

"Frank, listen, there are sweet little hotels just round the corner from the convent. You can rest there, and take some pills. I won't be long. I'm simply going to tell them my plans. I'm not going to grovel, or anything. I've never grovelled in my life. I won't start now!"

"So you're really worried about it, Angel?" Frank asked. "You're worried they'll make you change your mind. That's why you're acting so funny!"

Angel made no reply, and Frank started up the fantastic stone staircase, sweeping down towards him in subtle splaying lines, as light and airy as silken fans held by dancers.

"Bloody Spanish Steps," he grunted to himself. Looking upwards to the church towering above, he could not resist the impulse to put his hand up to shield his eyes. He steered his erratic course through the enraptured pairs of lovers taking their ease there, as they took in the view, pointing features out to each other.

Most of the ladies were carrying little posies of flowers. (Some flower sellers had their baskets balanced in corners between the marble balustrades. But Frank blundered rudely past them.) Angel squeezed up her features, to get rid of a tear balanced on her pink cheek.

Angel had looked up a little hotel in the next street to the Franciscan Convent she had been told to report to. She had booked a double room at the hotel, The Hotel 'Chummy'. She thought they were after the English trade, and Frank might find it funny. (They promised high tea with muffins.) Frank, however, did not seem disposed to find anything funny.

So Angel, not being used to putting up with anyone else's bad moods, dumped Frank in the lobby there, among the potted palms, not even seeing him up to his room.

The minute she had left Frank, Angel began to feel better. She gave in to her grumpiness. She was the one who was supposed to be pregnant, and he was the one who was feeling sick and dizzy! She'd heard of that before, sympathetic pregnancy. Although Frank didn't seem very sympathetic. Not that she was pregnant. She'd know if she was. They said that the girl knew right away. No, that was merely a ruse thought up by Mother Agnes, who had confided to her that she didn't think she, Angel, was suited to the conventual life. She wondered why Agnes was saying that. She'd always been beautifully suited. She'd been a great nun, doing loads of good deeds, and at the same time making everyone laugh. She'd nothing to accuse herself of on that score!

She made her way disconsolately along to the convent, which looked lovely from the outside, very restful and peaceful, its stone frontage painted a pale apricot. A tiny but elaborate front garden, enclosed by wrought iron gates, led to a square recessed entrance. Angel thought she saw the outline through the glazed inner doorway of a Sister waiting to welcome her.

Frank, when Angel had departed, felt better instantly. He got himself up in the rackety lift, and even managed to turn the air conditioning on, without summoning help. He swallowed a couple of the tablets Angel had given him, and twisting himself out of the jacket, collapsed on the bed in a heap and zonked out.

In the second floor parlour of the convent, Angel asked the nun who had admitted her for a cup of tea. Apparently, though, the Sister did not speak English, because she returned silently with a small bottle of fizzy cream soda, very sweet. After that, Angel was left on her own for quite a while. The parlour was immaculate but scantily furnished. The furniture was old without being antique, and the walls were decorated with lithographs of the Pontiffs. It was, however, cool, with only a few rush mats over the tiled floors. And a window was open to let in the evening air. Angel was shocked by the view suddenly presented to her. The whole panorama of the most sacred part of the Holy City was spread before her eyes.

The prospect was divided into two, the azure of the sky with the pastel colours of roofs and walls of interconnected buildings that were struck and bleached by the last force of the declining sun. And a deep rose shadow encompassed those parts of the architecture which were flung into obscurity. A flock of birds flew up as Angel threw up the window wider. The sun made points of brilliant light over the ancient buildings. Church bells began to toll together, at various pitches as she watched, perhaps from Saint Peter's itself and neighbouring churches, whose domes stood out against the skyline.

On cue a dark soutaned figure entered the parlour and came up behind Angel, placing an arm carefully over her shoulder. Angel looked up, shocked, her eyes still full of wonder at the view.

"It's a marvellous place, this Holy City of ours! This Catholic City! And wonderful to have a place within this amazing body we call the Catholic Church! Don't you agree, Sister?"

The priest took hold of both her hands and led her away from the window, returning to slam it shut. "And so sad to be shut out of it!"

"Cardinal McCreish!" The cleric announced himself. He was in a cyclamen-edged and buttoned black soutane, with a Cardinal's ceremonial Biretta on his head. He placed Angel on a couch into which she sank. He himself perched on the arm of an armchair.

"Why should I be shut out?"

"You yourself have requested it, Sister. Little Sister Mary of the Angels. What a lovely name you chose when you made your vows! Come now, Angel, as your many friends in religion sometimes call you, you yourself have asked to be released from your vows. The vows you took so eagerly not so long ago. Of Poverty, Chastity and Prayer."

But Angel was not the girl to be bullied so easily.

"I'm sorry about the Chastity, but I can't help that! That just sort of happened without my meaning to. And being a girl, that might have repercussions that the Church might not be happy with. But as for the Charity and the Prayer, I don't see why I should give those up. I certainly don't intend to."

"Oh, a temper, I see! Your Mother Superior warned me about that! But what on earth have you been up to, Sister Mary of the Angels? What are you like, girl? One swallow, as they say, does not make a summer!"

He suddenly sat down beside her, and threw a burly arm round her slender shoulders.

"Anyway, girlie, you don't know everything. It's more than likely, if it was the first time, and you were maybe all nervous and wanting it over with and jumping up in hysterics, I've no doubt, to run and tell your Father Confessor all about it..." He paused for a moment, and wiped his streaming brow with a white handkerchief, "As I say, you're more than likely not pregnant at all, perhaps even still *virgo intacta.*"

Cardinal McCreish got up and paced the room, in some agitation.

"We could arrange to have you examined, by a catholic doctor, in the presence of clergy, to find out if that is the case. If it is, your troubles are over. Now!" He sat down on the sofa beside Angel again, "I think we're due a nice cup of tea."

He rang a tasselled bell, and when the silent nun answered it he ordered, without looking at her. "Earl Grey, in the pot. Your china cups and muffins."

"Yes, Cardinal McCreish," the nun replied meekly, understanding English perfectly now. "Lemon? Butter on the muffins?"

The Cardinal nodded curtly.

Angel couldn't help smiling. That was the second time that day she'd been promised muffins.

The Cardinal acted Mother and poured the tea. He drank and scoffed in silence. But when McCreish had finished he pushed the tea trolley away, and took the cup that Angel was raising again to her lips, and put it down. He put his arm around her again, and whispered in her ear.

"Is your problem that you liked it? The sex act? Did you enjoy it?"

"It was okay. My boyfriend says you get better with practice."

The aroma of the Cardinal's gorgeous aftershave hit Angel. A delightful mixture of melon and musk. Unfortunately it was also Frank's favourite aftershave, which he had on at Norma.

She began to long for Frank, and sat up, hoping for a quick getaway.

"But let's get down to brass tacks." The cleric sensed her mood. "Either you're pregnant, and the Church will manage to do without you, or you're not, then you'll have to pay back any student loans that Mother Benigna took over for you. Two degrees, you took at the convent's expense. There's your living expenses for the past five years. That adds up to a pretty penny. You brought no dowry, I believe, Sister Mary of the Angels." he chuckled teasingly.

"Now do you still want to renounce your vows?" he was suddenly grim faced.

"I don't know. I'll have to wait to see if I'm pregnant."

"I wondered when we'd come to that. As you must know, there's no need to wait. And I, too, would like to know."

He rang the bell again, two pulls this time, and the same Sister entered, this time with a tray covered with a white cloth, over what looked like a kidney dish and a measuring cup. She also had a pink cardboard packaged unit, unopened, on the top. A pregnancy testing kit, Angel saw. She blushed with embarrassment and anger. The nun shot her a piercing look.

The Cardinal went to stand looking out of the window, as the nun led Angel off.

"Even if you've never used one of these before," she said snidely, in a neutral accent, "You can follow the pictorial instructions. Just shout if you need any help. I'll be right outside."

Frank was in the shower at the hotel when the phone rang. A lovely cool shower. And he had found, when he wakened up, that he could see again, from both eyes. So it must just have been sunstroke and not a brain haemorrhage, after all. He dashed out, dripping, and got to the hotel phone just before Angel was going to give up and ring off.

"Do you want the good news first, or the bad news?"

"Good, then bad."

"The good news is that I'm pregnant. The bad news is that I'm pregnant!"

Frank had got over the shock, and stopped sneezing, when he got up from his banquette at the Cafe Greco in the Via Condotti. His eyes swam when he saw Angel. His heart pounded. She was wearing a skimpy pink silk dress. (She had bought it at the boutique right next door, with money the Cardinal had pressed into her hand, for the baby's layette, he had said.) Angel considered that Frank had better pay for his own baby's layette.

Angel could see right away that Frank had got over his brain tumour, or whatever it was he'd imagined he was suffering from. And he seemed to have managed to get his clothes laundered too. Trust Frank. He was never happy unless he looked as if he was just out of the proverbial bandbox.

They had a lovely light meal, although afterwards neither of them remembered what it was. Frank had managed to get hold of a tiny ring to take the bare look off her finger. He slid his hand under the table and traced a line along her bare thigh under the little silk dress.

15

Postcards From Garda

The most popular postcard on sale at Garda resorts that year was one of Limone. It had been made from an antique photograph, hand coloured. That, or a modern photograph had been digitally tweaked to give that impression. Either way, the end result was charming. The peaks rose, outlined in indigo, behind the village, clouds swirling madly overhead. Red roofs jostled below, and in the foreground lemon trees offered clusters of surreal lemons.

Sister Mary of the Angels, when she still felt justified in using the title, had promised Sister Peppy that she would send loads of postcards. As she was then a nun of her word, she sent lots of antique looking cards to the convent at Crimea Pass. There was a scheme in place at that time among the more enterprising shopkeepers of the resorts, to sell ready stamped postcards which could be filled in and posted on the spot, and which were collected and sent by private light aircraft across the channel to the Royal Mail in London. After that the cards took their chances with the erratic postal services, but it was still better than the three weeks cards would normally take. Sister Angel spent lots of her pocket money on this expensive service. But she reckoned it was worth it to keep her best friend up to date with her exciting holiday, while both were temporarily denied use of the Internet.

The service was called OK Speedico and the only drawback was that the sender was only allowed five words, apart from the name and address of the recipient. Sister Peppy preferred to be addressed as 'The occupant' of flat 2B, 3 Crimea Pass so as not to give away her solitary feminine status. Anyway the five words could be intriguing! And apart from the five words allowed, the cards were printed with loads of email and telephone numbers, all useful, and sometimes even poems which could only be read by the aid of a magnifying glass.

The good natured Postie for Crimea Pass used to ring the doorbell for Sister Mary of Perpetual Succour (as the handwritten label pinned to Peppy's Convent door named her), to let her know her daily postcard had arrived. One day he delivered three cards. One was of Juliet's balcony in Verona and one of the Grottos of Catullus at Sirmione. And one was a coloured in Victorian lithograph of Isola del Garda, giant waves dashing against the shore.

Sister Peppy was in for a shock when she read the Verona one.

"Engaged. Renouncing Vows. Explanation Follows." it was signed SMA (the traditional Convent abbreviation of Sister Mary of the Angel.) The Post Mark was August 27th.

The postcard from Sirmione was more puzzling.

"Poor Guy Dead." it announced tersely, and not in Angel's hand. "Sell Posters."

This card was signed SAM. The postmark was August 25th.

The third card looked smudged and wet. It alarmed Peppy, too.

"Jumped in Lake." it said. "New Habit?" The Post Mark was August 23rd.

She decided to phone Angel, but Angel had her phone turned off. Mother Agnes didn't believe in mobiles, but Peppy got through to her quickly at the Stella del Mare Convent.

Mother Agnes explained how Angel had courageously jumped in the lake to save Dame Georgie. She said she was all for the convent ordering Angel a new habit. But when Peppy read out the card about renouncing vows, it went quiet at the other end.

"I wonder if Angel really means it." was all Agnes said. "You can never tell with her."

"And there's another card here. It says some poor guy's dead. And something about selling posters. What would that be about?" Peppy asked.

"I reckon that would be about Pascal Stone, the poet. He died of sun stroke, poor guy."

"It might be for old Melly, next door." Peppy had noticed that the card was addressed to Flat 2A, not 2B. "I'll just pop it through his letter box," and she hung up.

Agnes kept trying to get through to Angel or to Frank's phone, both of which were charging. She had lists and notebooks and diaries spread out on the polished desk in the convent dining room. She scrabbled feverishly writing lists of names, then scored one out. Pascal Stone, the first signatory of the Tontine to die, she thought.

This first error in her calculations always put her off.

Agnes opened Pascal's diary again. It was not an up to date journal. It was decades out of date, stained and creased, dog eared, with the ink fading. Pascal Stone must have carried it around for sentimental reasons. As she pored over it again, Mother Agnes felt guilty at intruding on such a personal account of Pascal Stone's life. It told the details of his love affairs, especially one that had been played out at Limone. That must have been why Pascal carried it about with him, to relive the

Sister Mary of the Angels

heady days of his youth while revisiting romantic places from his past.

The name of his lover was Stanislaus Pasternak. The unknown name on the Tontine.

Agnes flicked open at another page, and one entry sprang into focus before her eyes.

"Today I dedicated my Limone poems to 'Stanislaus Pasternak'." it read. "S does not care to have his real name to be on the flyleaf! Not very flattering for me. Why do I go on?"

And there was an entry about Stan being grateful at being given a share in the Tontine.

Sam Plaister's name crept into the diary from time to time. And the name of Sam's wife, Emilia. It was obvious Pascal hated Sam's wife, and also that he was terrified of her. Agnes would have to read right through the diary.

But the main questions in Agnes's mind were, where was Everard and where was Lena?

Both of Agnes's questions were answered right away. Mother Annunziata, the little bowed, creamy-skinned old nun, her hostess at Stella del Mare Convent, ducked into the study, with a postcard in her hand. It had been posted in the main door by a motorcycle courier.

"Guy Everard drowned. Sorry! I just found him, although I really hated him. Love Lena."

A cutting from the Corriere della Sierra was clipped on, about an unidentified male body having been picked up by lake fishermen. It said the corpse's bloated face was decorated by a large moustache. Tiny hand printed script impinged on the swirling clouds on the Limone card.

"Lena did not do this thing. I, her loving friend, Enzio, am witness. Amore to Escocia!"

Back in Escocia, to which all the other cards were directed, Mother Benigna had received a postcard from Garda too. A Limone one, also, from Angel.

"Burned Boats!" it said, "Can Never Return!"

So when Peppy phoned her with the added news of the engagement, Mother Benigna wasn't exactly surprised. In fact, as she put the phone down, Benigna was taken with such a fit of the giggles that she had to rest her head in her hands. What was Sister Angel like?

Sister Evangeline came in at that moment, and thought Mother Benigna was overcome with grief, or that her tremors had become worse.

"Sorry to intrude, Mother Benigna," she whispered, "but there's a young gentleman, that I know you're very fond of, come to see you again, with his auntie, I think!"

And Emilia Plaister stumbled in, carrying baby Joel, who had got so big and obstreperous that she could hardly manage him.

Emilia too had received a postcard.

"Please Phone. Necessary Discuss Divorce." which was signed tersely "Sam"

No wonder the poor lady was upset! No, she would not discuss divorce! But she did have a long grim phone call. The shock had made her feel ill. On top of looking after Joel, all by herself. He was getting to be such a big boy, and she herself seemed to be shrinking. And getting dizzy and confused. She blamed it on the menopause! She staggered and lurched as she carried big little Joel into Mother Benigna's office. Joel immediately reached forward for a gypsy cream from Benigna's saucer, to gnaw with his emerging front tooth.

Mother Benigna could see her visitor was disturbed. Her hair had large areas of grey roots impinging on the nut brown. And her tweed suit looked as if she had slept in it, alongside a fretful baby. There were splodges of smelly stuff on it, whose odours mingled with the scent of lavender water. Her ringed eyes showed she hadn't slept for a long while.

And she seemed to have come out in her carpet slippers, which were large soft bootees, beribboned like the baby's footwear. Sister Evangeline swooped upon Joel.

"Oh my wee darling! Would you look how long his curls have got! He'll be a heart breaker one of these days! Could I take him, Mother Benigna, and play with him for a bit?"

Sister Evangeline's words provoked the reaction of Emilia relaxing, and leaning her head against the high backed chair she was supported by, letting the tears slide out from under her drooping eyelids, down her gaunt cheeks. Then she smiled slowly, revealing uneven teeth.

"I think that's a 'yes', Sister Evangeline!" said Mother Benigna, "Could you get someone to bring some fresh tea for me and my visitor?"

Evangeline carried Joel off in triumph. She had disposable nappies in the kitchen dresser, as well as talcum and nappy-rash cream, none of which Emilia Plaister believed in, and of which Joel was sorely in need. She dropped the greying cloth nappies stashed in the baby's hold-all into the huge kitchen bin, with the used one, ready for the furnace.

Joel stretched out to try to grab her glasses off her snub nose, and kicked his fat legs.

She and Sister Ursula started a game with him. A walking game. One holding out her arms, and one setting him on his feet, and urging him forward.

The chunky baby boy made a dash for it, like a rugby player trying to score a try, and Ursula caught him. Evangeline felt they should own up, and carried Joel back into Mother Benigna's office.

"I'm afraid we've taught the baby to walk!" she said to Emilia. "I hope you don't mind!"

Emilia was explaining that she was a friend of Lena and Sister Mary of the Angels. They had met at the Scriveners and Limners Society. She herself was a Scrivener. So was her husband, Samuel Plaister. He was away abroad at the moment. And she'd begun to find it almost impossible to look after Joel, now that he was cutting teeth, and getting into all kinds of things. It had been easier when he was a babe in arms. It had been easy. A half spoonful of Calpol, and he had been down for the night! She herself should take pills, but they made her sleepy. And then this morning she'd got an upsetting postcard from her hubby Sammy. And when she'd phoned him she'd realised that the problem was a business matter that Sam was involved in, and that she could sort out if she had a little time to herself. And she'd then remembered Angel telling her that the Sisters used to look after Joel for Lena when she got upset. Could she possibly ask them to look after little Joel, just till she got things sorted?

Benigna felt herself justified in taking the baby. The woman looked distraught, she thought, as she limped out to see Emilia off in the battered shooting brake. She hoped she was fit to drive.

Sister Evangeline made Joel wave his little fist in goodbye.

"Now!" she coaxed him, "Wave bye-bye to Auntie. See you soon!"

Emilia hoped it wouldn't be all that soon. She wasn't even Joel's real auntie. And it didn't seem to matter to Sammy if she looked after the baby or not. She was beginning to wonder if she was cut out to be a baby-minder, any more than big sloppy Lena. It would have been different if Joel had been her own child, she mused, getting onto the motorway quite efficiently. The car seemed to be driving itself. If she sorted out this little problem for Sammy, he would definitely have to come back to her. She swallowed an anti-depressant. Then she drove home to her country cottage, fell into her unmade bed and slept.

For the first time in weeks, she slept long enough to dream. She dreamed about Garda. More of a kind of nightmare, she was running down moonlit rooms screaming and covered in blood. She surfaced after a while but sank back into a confused sleep. She was swooping down to the jade green depths of Garda. Swimming figures around her were trying to catch her, but she slipped through their fingers. But sooner or later they would catch her. She would have liked to have wakened up, but somehow couldn't. Even the phone's insistent ringing didn't waken her.

In a rage, Sammy Plaister, at Malcesine, slammed the phone down.

And Emilia slept on.

Mother Agnes, at Toscolano, did without sleep, examining Pascal's diary.

She read accounts of masked balls, with details of costumes and sketches. She read snatches of pasted in love letters, and then accounts of huffs and quarrels. And through it all, sublime snatches of poems, which seemed to have nothing to do with the personality revealed in the diaries.

Her eyes swam and her head throbbed, but she kept on turning pages.

Then she came upon it, the thing she was looking for. An entry for a past summer.

"Emilia turned weird and nasty last night. I really think she is off her head. She nearly strangled Melly when she found Sam in his bed. And then pulled a knife. She cut Sam's hand badly when he took the knife off her. Now she's packing her cases and howling and sobbing. Poor cow! But she really makes me shudder when she gets into a state like this."

Mother Agnes felt a bolt of lightning strike her brain, and all the facts and the suspicions sorted themselves out in neat columns, and she felt she almost had the solution. Another diary page she opened at random further on brought confirmation.

"S. P. says he will let me inscribe one of the volumes to him."

There on the poetry leaflet posted to her last night was the dedication to Sammy Plaister!

So Sam was one of the investors of the Tontine. Pasternak was a *nom de plume*, as Frank had guessed. And Peppy's next door neighbour, Melly Whitbread, was the last signatory. The last piece fell into place when Agnes phoned Peppy back.

Yes, the next door neighbour was Mr. Melville Whitbread. The postcard from Sirmione said Poor Guy dead. Not poor guy. Guy Everard. And the signatory was Sam. The card had been posted three days before Guy's body had been dragged from the lake. When Sam Plaister could not have known he was dead, unless he himself had killed him.

Melville Whitbread was the only one to stand between Sammy and his inheritance. Sam was still in Italy, but his wife, Emilia, was perhaps poised to strike on his behalf.

"Listen, Peppy, keep an eye on your next door neighbour, will you? I mean seriously."

"But I always do, mother Agnes. I always ...." But Peppy's mobile had run out of steam.

On the plush banquette of the Cafe Greco in Rome, Angel was just beginning to yawn coyly, and say she felt sleepy, when Frank's cell phone sounded.

"*Si, Pronto! Io sonno Frank Childers.*"

Then, "Yes, Mother Agnes, of course you're not disturbing us!"

Then he listened in silence, just saying 'of course' and 'no problem' occasionally.

"What time did you say the flight was? Nine fifteen, Roman time. Rome Ciampino. Gotcha! To London

Stansted. No bother. Arrive midnight, London time, connecting to Glasgow at one twenty. Arrive two twenty five. That seems to be straightforward. And the tickets? Brilliant! They're in the name of the Convent of the Bleeding Heart. Ciao! Arrivederci!"

He turned to Angel, sitting dumb struck beside him. "Sorry, Angel. That was Mother Agnes. She thinks the old chap who lives next door to Peppy is in real danger. I'll have to get to Crimea Pass to save him. And maybe wrap up this whole crime scenario. No, I'll have to do it all by myself! Listen, I'm so sorry! I thought we might get in a little bit of practice, if you know what I mean? Sorry! Must dash!"

"No worries, Frankie! The notion is off me now!" said Angel, disconsolately.

16

Running Out Of Time

Dashing was putting it mildly. Frank had to use all his considerable charm to persuade the Rome restaurateur to summon his private car for Frank's use. Rome's taxis were fully booked getting the *glitterati* to late dinner dates, and getting the young to nightclubs. Childers insisted on dropping off Angel at the small hotel, where he grabbed his bag of necessities. When he explained as best he could the intricacies of the situation, and his need to desert her, and fly back to Glasgow, she began to get the picture. She had been so wrapped up in her own problems, outside events had not made much impression before that. And she didn't insist on seeing him off at the airport, which was a relief.

Swimming across town, in a sudden storm of rain which battered his loaned limousine, in the mini rush hour of concert goers and glitzy diners, Frank seemed to see the same famous landmarks appear and disappear repeatedly. He began to complain to the swarthy silent driver, when they were stewing round the Coliseum for the third time, it seemed, and surely in the wrong direction.

"Short Cutting!" was the only explanation he got.

Frank was anxious to reach the airport in time for check in. Punctuality was a fetish for him at the best of times. As it was, he had to flash his Detective Inspector's badge in order to be let through. And a pretty uniformed attendant ran before him, somehow managing, in her high heels, to outpace him. He was the last person to get on the plane before the steps were wheeled away. As the plane reared into the sky, Frank, still in his seatbelt, felt his thoughts jumble and his eyes close, for forty long winks.

In her messy farm cottage, Emilia Plaister stirred. The first thing she did was to put her landline on answer. Every now and then she checked the messages Sammy left at regular intervals. Increasingly irate messages. Emilia tittered to herself. First things first, she thought. She'd have to get rid of these grey roots before she went to visit that awful Melville Whitbread. He had always been so nasty and critical. Not just about the literary arts, which was after all had been his profession, but also about women in general. He had a spiteful eye for little feminine shortcomings that most men wouldn't notice. She recalled that time at Limone, when he'd purloined her padded bra, and paraded about in it, just to make a fool of her. For this interview, she'd look her best, if it took her all night.

Maybe not; she suddenly recalled Sammy was so fussed about the wretched Tontine. She'd better hurry up. Thank goodness she had her shampoo-in hair dye in the house.

At Stansted, Frank was on the phone to Mirkshields Police Station. There seemed to be some sort of conspiracy against him. It took him ages to get through from the main desk to his colleagues, and they insisted on thinking he was winding them up. Just as Frank thought he was making them understand this was a matter of life and death, that an old literary critic was about to be murdered by an angry poet's wife (perhaps that did sound a bit weird), Frank's flight was called and he had to disconnect.

Emilia Plaister, by this time, was nearly ready to set out on her journey to Crimea Pass. Her hair had turned out a treat, nut brown and curving into its usual bob. The only outfit that was clean was a rather shiny suit with bugle beads that had hung in her wardrobe since a silver wedding reception. She should have worn it before. She looked great in it. She realised when she was in the shooting brake, speeding towards town, that she still had on her slipper boots. But she'd heard boots were becoming fashionable again.

And some instinct made Emilia drive to the lane below Crimea Pass, and she got her car parked outside the garage there. She stumbled up the stone steps of Number Three and immediately saw Melville's name on the door, and a note pinned to it, 'Ring and Enter'. (Peppy having dropped the card in his door, Melly was inviting offers for the Art Posters.)

Emilia entered, but without ringing.

"Cooeee!" she called, approaching the ventriloquist's mannequin-like figure propped up in the hole-in-the-wall bed. Melville Whitbread gave a terrified squawk, and trembled.

"It's only me, Melly! Emilia Plaister-Pierce. Milly, you used to call me in the old days. Don't you recall, Melville? Milly-Molly-Mandy, you used to say. Sweet as sugar candy! Don't you remember? No? Well, maybe you were always more interested in Sammy than in me! That summer on Garda! Sammy and I were newlyweds then! But you were always a fascinating man. And quite handsome, too!" Emilia sat down uninvited on the chair beside the bed. She looked closely at Melville's cringing, drawn features.

He had shrunk down under the bed covers, in an instinct of self-preservation.

"Not as handsome as Sammy, though. That mane of raven black hair. Snowy now you'd call it. And a figure like Apollo. Now he has a little paunch! I often thought, Melly, you bad boy, that if you hadn't come on to Sammy when you did, he would have returned with me, and that might have been the time I'd have produced a child. You never know. There's a time for flowering, and if you miss it...." She broke off, to peek under the bedclothes impudently. "I see you've got your jimjams on underneath. Modest. Not like when you and the boys used to go skinny-dipping at Limone. I used to worry that Sammy would drown. He wasn't such a good swimmer as the rest. My heart used to be in my mouth. You all went so far out, where no-one could reach you. I used to watch from the terrace. I was never allowed to join in. Finally, I gave up and went home, didn't I, naughty Melly? I yielded you the field. I shouldn't have done. I won't again."

Emilia's eyes began to wander round the room. "Oh Melly! Sambuca! You've got it in especially for me! My tipple. I should really flame it. Have you a lighter? Never mind, Melly, I'll have a little glug just now, and find some matches later." She knocked some of the fiery liqueur back, straight from the bottle, before returning it to the thirties cocktail cabinet.

Emilia started to dance around the house, exclaiming in admiration at the lovely things.

"What beauties!" she cried "I adore Chryselephantine figures, oh what treasures!"

Melville emerged from under the covers, regaining his voice.

"Milly-Molly-Mandy!" he cried. "Listen, darling, I'll give you a figurine. To take away with you. Only I'm expecting some dealers any minute, for Sammy's posters." he explained.

"But, my dear man!" Emilia came to stand over him. She swaddled him to the neck in his silken covers. "Don't you know we don't need to sell them now! When the Tontine comes into force, when Sammy is the Last Man Standing, he won't need to sell them, will he?"

After all the rush to get there, Frank was stopped at Glasgow International Airport to have his Armani workbag checked. A Customs and Excise executive had been alerted by an eagle-eyed attendant at passport control. Frank's unusual travel patterns across Italy had aroused her suspicions. And a man travelling on his own, with only hand luggage. Classic!

"Follow me, Sir, please!" As Frank was led into a side room, all around had small pleased smiles on their officious faces. Bound to get a drug bust! Easy!

"But you don't understand!" Frank cried, but they'd heard it all before.

They'd even insisted on phoning Mirkshields Station to authenticate his badge.

In Crimea Pass, Emilia was becoming effusive. "And it's all thanks to you, Mr. Whitbread. You let Sammy in on the ground floor of the Tontine, when the Sally Garden came up for grabs! And now you're about to be paid back! Though not perhaps the way you expect!"

"But Milly, Emilia, if Sammy and I are both left standing on the Tontine date, we'll both fall due for the investments, shared equally between us. Isn't that enough, Milly?"

"Well, I don't know, I rather think Sammy might quite like it all, although he'd be the last one to admit it. Of course he's always been so fond of you. But nothing lasts forever, does it Melly? Youth goes! Beauty goes! Wealth comes and goes. Finally life goes. Nothing nice lasts forever. That's what you said, anyway, when you chucked me out of your villa. You said Sammy was finished with me. And I'll let you into a secret. I finished with Sammy's baby, in revenge! You could hardly blame me. And then he came back to me after all. But by then it was too late. And now he's involved with Dolores. He says she's done him a favour, and he'll have to marry her, to shut her mouth. So I'm thinking of doing him a favour, too! Anything she can do, I can do better, Big Stookie that she is! We'll buy her off easy!"

"Anyway!" She revealed the torn remains of the "Ring and Enter" note. "I've locked up! They won't be ringing and entering. Now my dear, what shall we play at? Oh, look!" Emilia had got her glinting eye on a marquetry chest inlaid with mother of pearl. "Your dressing up chest, when we used to play charades. I'll never forget you as Cleopatra, and Sammy as Anthony. I was the asp, I recall." She stalked round the room, huffily.

Then she grabbed the Sambuca and glugged again, choking and laughing.

"Here, Melly! You have some too!" She forced the bottle between his lips and giggled as the old man gagged and the sticky spirit spilled down his immaculate shirt front.

"Melly, dear! Your eyes have gone funny! Are you hiding something? What can it be? A postcard, from Garda? Well, now you must know that Sammy is rid of Guy for good! And that goes for big Donnie Donald too. Poor Pascal has yielded up the ghost, in idyllic circumstances, Sam says, so don't be too sorry for him. He had a nice peaceful end, more than Binkie Boyne had at the club! How do you feel, now that leaves only you, and Stanislaus Pasternak, aka the ever charming husband and lover, Sammy Plaister? You are all that stands between him owning the Sally Gardens. Which, by the way, Lord Donald has planning permission for razing to the ground and building blocks of pseudo Art Deco flats."

"But Melville, I see you looking concerned. Don't worry, though, Sammy Plaister won't. He'd rather lord it over all the members and make their lives a misery, pay back old scores. And that's the favour Dolores did for him, toppling Donald, I think. Did he fall or was he pushed? We'll never know! Are you shaking under your covers? But Sammy is in Garda, being so jolly with everyone. No-one will suspect him, if you were to suffer a wee accident too. Sammy is fond of you still, I won't deny that. He wishes he could have thought of a way to spare you! Can you, Melly? I can't! But then I was always dim. And none of my poems scan, as you so often remarked in your column. You kept your praises for Sammy. Do you remember, dear? And his homoerotic poems, some would say obscene jingles, under the *nom de plume* of Stanislaus Pasternak, you liked even more. How we all laughed! And I quote!"

"He was a good poet. His last collection 'Idylls of the Queen' makes him a great one!"

"Oh Melville, why don't you sit up properly, dear, and pay attention? What I'm saying is important. I've waited many years to say it. Are you looking for your mobile? Come now, you know you don't know how to work it, you old silly!" she said, kicking it under the bed.

"Melville! Why don't we play at Dressing Up, pet? Tell me what you would like to be."

Emilia ruffled through the Dressing Up box, getting out silken and satin garments, and glittering necklaces and bracelets, trying them against herself, along with ostrich and peacock feathers. She tried on a Midshipman's cap she found, doing a little hornpipe in her felt boots. She gave a little scream as she pulled out some iridescent drapes from the very bottom of the chest where playbills and press cuttings were stashed, yellowing and torn.

"Melville, darling! I do believe I've found your Cleopatra outfit!"

Meanwhile Frank Childers, released from the Interrogation Suite, was skidding out from the large recently fortified doors of Glasgow International Airport, to join the long taxi queue. His shiny Detective Inspector's badge did him no good at all with the stewards there.

17

Dressing Up

"Oh, Mr. Melville Whitbread, do you recall these costumes? *Commedia dell'Arte!* For your *Ballo* in Maschera! You, as I recall, were an Auguste. Sammy was gorgeous as Pierrot! Pierrot Lunaire! The night was moonlit. We were all moonstruck. I fell asleep in Sammy's arms. When I awoke, I followed the path the moonlight made through the villa. Into your room. Sammy lay naked, asleep in your arms. I decided then to leave. He decided to stay on."

"I don't blame Sammy. You were so rich. Rich as Croesus. Everything you touched turned to gold. And we, Sammy and I, were stony broke! Shall I read you a poem I wrote about it?"

Melville Whitbread had more or less given up hope. He had mentally abstracted himself from his present predicament as much as he could. He only wished the monster lady would hurry up and finish him off. He had stopped watching her, as she fiddled with his most precious possessions, re-arranging his cabinets, and chucking things about. What harm had he ever done her?

Apart, that is, from alienating the affections of her husband, revealing to him his latent homosexuality.

And showing up her performances in bed. He guessed they hadn't been up to much, even for a woman. She was obsessed by reproduction, by all accounts.

Emilia looked up wickedly from the Dressing Up Box where she was folding the costumes now, in a horribly housewifely way. "Well," she said, smiling brightly at him, "Want to hear it? It's part of a sequence called 'Rivers of Blood'. All about menstruation."

But Melville, from desperation, had gathered up his courage. He sat up.

"Mrs. Plaister!" he spat, "Madam! You have decided to do away with me. That is obvious. Your excuse is the wealth Sam stands to gain with my demise. I do not buy that. You merely want to pay me back for taking him from you. And for keeping him, I may say, at my beck and call, for so many years! But Sammy was always such a one for the ladies. He quite broke my heart!"

"More fool you! I was the love of his life. Not any of those tarts at the Sally Gardens! And I kept him for so long. He let himself be kept. Till I got to my present disgusting state. I didn't expect to keep him then. And I in return got his poems published for him. And limited editions of his erotic verse, under his pseudonym of Stanislaus Pasternak. You were always all for him, hardly an unbiased critic. Couldn't stand my work."

"The reason, madam, I never got your work published, was because it was tripe! Pure shite, I may say! So if you wish to slay me, madam, please go ahead. But I will not listen to one of your obnoxious, sentimental, and crude verses. In fact, if you don't shut up, I will strangle myself!"

Emilia was listening to him, fascinated, her hands clutched in front of her, in an almost pleading mode, and her eyes wide open in alarm. Melville took advantage of her sudden capitulation and went on.

"And, as a matter of fact, I do not believe Sammy was guilty of all the deaths ascribed to him." He swung his stick-like striped pyjamaed legs over the side of his bed, and shook his crooked gnarled finger at her. "If Guy Everard died other than accidentally, it was probably at the hands of one of the girlfriends he treated so brutally. Pascal died as he had lived, chasing pretty boys! Skelly-yed Donald fell down the steps of the Arena, you say. So what? He was always falling down. Never learned to go downstairs without holding on to the banister. Maybe Skinny Dolores shoved him, anyway. Who cares?"

"Now Sammy and I are left to inherit. When we do, we shall get on like a house on fire! Now do me in, or get the hell out!"

While he spoke, Emilia seemed to be having some kind of fit. Her eyes rolled in her head, and her mouth fell agape. Melville sneaked out of bed and crept to the door. But Emilia was instantly there behind him, with the strength of ten crazy ladies. She twisted a long silk scarf round his neck and threw him back onto the bed. He felt his shin bones crack against the cast iron bed frame.

Melville passed out, but came to again all too soon. She was still there. He looked down and saw with horror he was dressed in one of the Bakst costumes he had had reproduced for his Arabian Nights ball. His pathetically bony upper body was bare, except for a gold satin bustier linked with chains to a golden belt. Around his loins hung a pair of ballooning damson coloured silk pantaloons.

Emilia was shoving pointed golden slippers over his misshapen feet.

The Golden Slave. She had got him up in the costume of the Golden Slave, from the ballet Scheherazade. The slave who is killed by one blow of a scimitar, and proceeds to dance on his head! Melville wondered what death she had devised for him.

"Now then! The Piece de Resistance!" Emilia lifted his head and placed a swathed turban upon it, the bird of paradise feathers protruding from it all twisted and broken.

He opened his mouth to scream, but discovered she had tightened the scarf twisted round his neck and stuffed an end into his mouth as a gag. She pulled the other end tighter, even, round his throat and tied it to the iron bed head fitted into the bed recess.

He thought he would have already died from her rough handling. He thought his old heart would have given up. He struggled, but that just made the scarf bite tighter. (Emilia had learned all about knots for her tests in the Girl Guides. She had made it to Sixer, and had always been scrupulously fair, through strict, to the little wimpish girls under her.) Emilia smiled, remembering her girlhood successes, as she attended to the knots binding Melville's ankles together, and holding his hand above his head, in an absurd approximation of a Ballets Russes pose. He expected to die from fear, but his poor heart kept pounding on, and the pain shot through him from his hacked shins. Saliva soaked the gag in his mouth as it tightened with his struggles. He was slowly choking to death.

He blacked out again. And when he came to, horror of horrors, Emilia stood before him in the Columbine dress she had worn in her youth, her skinny vapid youth. Poor Sammy must have married her just because he was sorry for her.

"Sammy will kill you for this!" he wanted to tell her. "Do you think you will have pleased him? Even if he is desperate for the money, for all of the money. Even if he might have yielded to the temptation of giving you the okay, he'll still hate you for murdering me!"

But he could only moan and groan into the scarf that was choking him.

Emilia came to the bed, and officiously gave the scarf, now blood-stained from his mouth, a little tweak. For the first time he noticed that she had removed his false teeth, and they were grinning at him from his bedside cabinet.

She was looking around now for something, again. She couldn't find it, among the mess she had made of the flat.

And just then, there came the gentle rap from next door that showed that, keeping her word, Sister Mary of Perpetual Succour, when she returned home, was checking on him. Three little taps, a pause, three more little taps, a pause, three more. Unfortunately, his tormentor, Emilia, had sussed out the pattern, and returned the taps in the correct order. She smirked over at Melville as she did so. He groaned afresh, and Emilia switched on the retro Bakelite radio to mask the sound. Thereafter, excerpts from Swan Lake played quietly and seductively. Emilia sat in alert silence watching him, and waiting for Sister Peppy to fall asleep next door. At the violin solo, Melville's breathing slowed, and his brain clouded.

He dreamed he was back at Limone, climbing the hills among the lemon groves. He was gasping for breath, but felt excited too, as if he was going to meet a lover. When he wakened, she had fallen asleep, seated on his chair, and slumped over the end of his bed, crushing his already crushed toes. He was not going to be allowed even to die in peace. He saw then what she was maliciously up to, what had been her idea from the very start. She was staging his death as an auto-erotic accident, where strangulation was supposed to help the sexually impaired to gain a climax.

And she had scattered all his collection of retro pornography about, to shame him.

To add to his miseries, he saw he had wet his beautiful satin quilt. And the silken Bakst pantaloons were clinging round his loins, deflated and damp.

He tried to hang onto the scarf to tighten it and strangle himself. He did not wish to die of slow suffocation.

He had a moment of hope, when Peppy's phone rang next door, and he heard her answer. The radio had been switched off, and he thought he might attract Peppy's attention somehow. But the call had been from one of her homeless hostels. A young woman who had taken an overdose was hysterical, asking for her. She wanted Peppy to go and sit with her in the Accident and Emergency department of the Prince's Infirmary, and hold her hand when she was getting her stomach pumped out. Peppy was up and dressed and out her door ridiculously quickly. Melville heard heart-breakingly normal noises as Jimmy the mechanic from downstairs persuaded Peppy to let him give her a lift to the hospital. Melly's heart sank as the van roared off.

From then on, Sister Peppy's phone rang all the time. Then her mobile which she had left behind in her rush started playing *Sheep May Safely Graze* at regular intervals.

Emilia began to seem agitated. There was something else she had to do. She remembered, and poured another glass of Sambuca, and rubbing the rim with sugar, she lit it with the kitchen matches she had located in the corner cabinet drawer. She had one delicious sip. Then, as it flared up again, she tossed it on to the embroidered cushion on the bentwood chair. It began to smoulder instantly. Emilia was gratified. She had dealt with Sammy's last urgent request. To destroy the incriminating post card he had sent Melly from Garda. "Poor Guy Dead Sell Posters". How stupid Sammy had been, Emilia thought, admitting to knowing of Guy's death two days before the bloke's body was dredged up. And how could she find a postcard in this mass of memorabilia? The best thing was to burn the lot. She slipped out of the flat and skipped down to retrieve her car.

Mrs Emilia Plaister

"Thanks a million, Lady!" said Benjie, as Emilia chucked a ten-pence piece into his trilby hat.

She got into the Station Wagon and turned easily out of Crimea Place into the Saltmarket.

Meanwhile, Frank Childers was trying to get reception on his mobile, with not much luck.

"I really need your help! I am Detective Inspector Frank Childers, of Mirkshields Police Station. I'm on my way to Flat 2a, 3 Crimea Pass, from the Airport. But I fear I won't be in time. I think an elderly gentleman, Mr. Melville Whitbread, is in danger. Send me backup now!!"

There was garbled speech on the other end which he could not make out, but he didn't like the sound of it, or of the roars of laughter in the background. Police Stations were getting used to dealing with hoax calls. In Crimea Pass, the smoke was already beginning to curl into the stairwell.

Emilia smiled as she drove at speed into High Street, talking into her phone. A taxi was approaching on the opposite side of the road, as she manoeuvred round the ancient Tolbooth, the prison Tower beleaguered for decades amongst Glasgow Cross traffic.

The taxi had slowed down for the lights there. Emilia, caught up in the opposite stream, glanced towards the cab, then roared off at speed. She had recognised the cop, Frank Childers, from the Sally Gardens, sitting hunched in the back. She was turning round to look again when the wheel twisted from her grasp and she slammed into a police car reluctantly responding to Frank's panicky call. There was a horrible rending noise as the fortified police car ripped the side off Emilia's tatty station wagon. But Frank's taxi sped on unawares.

When Peppy returned from her errand of mercy, she was alarmed to find smoke drifting Into Crimea Pass from her close. And the stair head was full of smoke as she rushed up. And worse still, she could see a figure hammering on Melly's door, shoulder charging it and cursing.

"Chuck it or I won't answer for the consequences! I warn you, I am a registered nurse! You're only going to do in your shoulder! That only works on TV! Who are you, anyway?"

Frank chucked it, and wearily showing his ID card, he slid down the side of the door to collapse on the door mat, eyes streaming with exasperation, and irritation from the swirling smoke.

"You'd better leave it to me!!" Peppy ordered, bossily, "The door is steel lined! Wait here!"

What had that stupid nun meant? Was she going off to phone the police or to make a novena?

But Peppy materialized right beside him, and dragged him to his feet to make way for her pal Jim the mechanic, who had armed himself with wire cutters, a power drill and a crowbar. Frank took a back seat, spluttering and coughing, as the mechanic drilled out the steel encased door from its hinges, in a controlled and workmanlike way. All three stepped over it into the ravaged flat.

Frank got the old man changed into striped blue pyjamas and shoved the quilt in the washing machine. Melly's face was already turning black and blue. Frank had scooped up the pathetic pornography, and instead of throwing it out, had folded it and put it in a drawer, just as Peppy came back from mopping up the kitchen. She reported that it wasn't too bad in there.

"I was about to bathe this gentleman myself, but maybe you'd like to take over, Sister?"

"Just call me Peppy. And I'm really more of a social worker than a nurse." she mumbled. Peppy was sometimes unaccountably squeamish. She certainly didn't fancy washing Melly!

When the ambulance men arrived to take Melly away Peppy offered to travel with him, though she'd only just returned from the hospital. She was glad to leave Frank, who struck her as a wimp. Melly would rather have had Frank go with him, but Frank said he'd deal with the Fire Brigade (now to be heard arriving noisily outside). Frank said he'd lock up after them and keep the keys.

So Melly was strapped on to a stretcher, clutching an Art Nouveau lady in an erotic pose. Frank had saved her from the flames, after getting the old man released from the strangulating scarf, while Peppy and the mechanic had played fire extinguishers on the flames as if it was fun.

"What's your name, sonny?" Melville asked, reaching to kiss Frank's hand from his stretcher.

"Frank." answered the detective. "Frank Childers. I'm a cop. But don't hold that against me!"

"Just give me the chance, Frank! And I like cops. I knew a cop once who ..."

His reminiscences were interrupted as the medics angled him over the banister railings to get him down the narrow stairs. They were delighted their patient had recovered so well, being able to chat once he'd got his teeth back in. At first they'd thought he was a goner.

When Frank had at last got rid of the firemen who had stood around the remains of the fire contemptuously, with idle hoses – they'd thought it hardly worth charging their heavy hose pipes – he looked despairingly round the debris round Melly's bed, soaked and burned and trampled. Mother Mary Agnes had impressed on him the need to locate the postcard that Sammy Plaister had sent Melville Whitbread from Garda. The only hard evidence they had.

The little corner cabinet's door still swung open, from where Melly had grabbed his ivory figurine to take with him to hospital. It must be his favourite piece,

Frank thought. Odd that it seemed to be one of a pair. Why hadn't Melly taken the other? Frank examined the prancing figure. No damage there. He turned his attention to the base. Some new scratch marks. Was the base detachable? He twisted, and sure enough the pedestal came off. And fitting exactly into a rectangular hollow in the ebony base was the postcard. The incriminating postcard from Garda.

Squatting in the close mouth opposite Benjie, who was still strumming his guitar, Frank was phoning Angel. He was ready for a long affectionate conversation about how much he was missing his little wife, and how much she was missing him. And about him having against all the odds rescued the poor old man. But Angel had heard the guitar music and was suspicious.

"Where are you anyway'?" she asked. "Are you at a party? Whose party are you at?"

Frank, although dropping with fatigue, went back to Melly's flat, to help Jim, the young mechanic, to re-hang the door on its hinges and restore and realign the many locks and chains.

Poor Emilia had received summary punishment for her involvement, Frank was informed, when the team whose squad car she'd crashed into at last phoned to explain their non-arrival. Her body had been taken by ambulance to the Prince's. At a later post mortem, evidence was been discovered of a serious brain disorder and that the balance of her mind had been disturbed.

Before the tests had been done, it was kind of obvious anyway, to the young medics, from the crazy stained old silken clothing Emilia Plaister had been dressed up in.

18

Revelations

Towards morning, Tamara Tainsh, returning from being a Lady of the Night, strutting her stuff round Beechwood Square, recalled, as she was about to put her key in the lock of her flat on the lower level of Crimea Pass, that she was out of bread and milk. She shook her golden cascading curls in annoyance. It was just the time when late night shops were shut and early morning shops had yet to open. So she ran upstairs to Sister Peppy's flat. Sister Mary of Perpetual Succour, that is. Tammy knocked the door quietly.

Peppy could tell her door was being knocked in a hesitant way. But how can you knock a door quietly, she thought? You can either knock a door or leave it alone. Peppy was tired, after being at the Prince's with her addict, and then with Melly. But she recognised Tamara's intention, and she was grateful for it. As she opened her door, she was glad Tammy had not been shouting and singing rude songs, or even trying to kick the door down.

Sister Peppy reckoned she must have overdone her explanation for the last part of her name, the 'succour' part. Her new Crimea Pass friends must think she meant 'sucker'.

Anyway, Peppy, in her flower-printed dressing gown, pottered about making tea, and buttering her last two rolls for Tammy and herself. Just as if she hadn't been up all night. Tammy would need sustenance. When she got back to her flat, her mother, who looked after Tammy's baby, would usually head back to her own house. Which meant Tamara was left to mind her own baby till it was time for her to get dolled up for her 'Night Shift', sauntering around Beechwood Square, rain or shine. Talk about 'Working Girl', thought Peppy. You could say that again!

Try as she would, Peppy could not resist laughing at some of the stories Tammy told her about her clients, her punters. For a nun she gained an encyclopaedic knowledge of sexual *mores* among Glasgow low-lifes, such as some of them not wanting to take their raincoats off before indulging in sexual intimacies. Some of them were high-ups too. One had wanted to marry Tamara, but his temper had been so dodgy that Tammy preferred to stay 'on the game'.

Frank Childers, who, after helping to make the flat lock-fast, decided to stay on for a while to wait for the old gentleman, should he be discharged early, and sat down on the other bed, for a moment, the bed in the kitchen (the one that had not been soaked with various liquids). It had been made up as a show bed, never being slept on. The linen was edged with antique lace, over which a shantung silk embroidered coverlet was thrown. Frank slumped sideways putting his feet on the bedside chair. Ideas were racing around in his head. It looked as if Melville had hidden the postcard as a favour to Sammy. Or perhaps to blackmail him. So why had he taken the wrong figurine with him to hospital? He must have known where he had placed it. (The fact was, of course, that Emilia had been playing around with the china in his cabinets.) Now Frank had that card in the breast pocket of his cream linen jacket. He jumped up. It might be as well to hide it, for the moment.

Frank could hear the girlish giggles as he stood outside Peppy's door. He pushed the post card within an envelope through the letterbox, holding the lid carefully as the card floated silently onto the carpet. He had included a note.

"This card is extremely valuable. Guard it with your life till I reclaim it. Frank Childers."

Frank went back next door to wait for his colleagues to turn up. They'd no doubt be along any minute, he thought, bitterly, since it was all over bar the shouting. But if he had checked the texts on his mobile he would have seen that he shouldn't hold his breath, waiting for the cops. Since they had been involved in a fatal car crash their vehicle had been towed off for examination. And since it appeared that the incident, a small house fire caused by the occupier smoking in bed, had been dealt with by the Fire Service, that might not be for some time. A further text stated that since the occupant was in hospital, the emergency call had been cancelled.

Frank slipped off his shoes, and hanging his jacket over the chair, lay down on the bed, the best bed, with feather pillows, and fell asleep in a second, dreaming of Rome. Of the small hotel he and Angel had booked into, but hardly got the benefit of, in any pleasurable way. They'd certainly missed out on muffins. But he began to dream the sun was glaring into his eyes.

He awoke with a start, to find a figure leaning over him, shining a torch in his face. There was also a large filleting knife pointing at his throat. He stopped himself from sitting up.

The face above him wore a jolly smile, although the birdlike eyes glittered in malevolent amusement in the torchlight. The man's glossy black and white hair and his jade waistcoat made him look like a magpie about to scoff a blackbird egg, shell and all.

"Sammy!" Frank spoke through gritted teeth. "I wondered when you were going to turn up, mate." It was hard to sound gallus in his recumbent pose.

Frank could have kicked himself that he had given in to sleep. And he hadn't heard a thing as Sammy let himself in. Why had he not engaged the repaired security chains? Plaister rattled his enormous circlet of burglar's master-keys under Frank's nose, in provocation.

Then he gestured, with the tip of the knife, that Frank was allowed to sit up.

"How come you're here, young man?" Sam Plaister asked pleasantly, "Somebody clype?"

"Mother Agnes put me wise to you. I would have worked it out myself, in the long run. Listen, Sammy," Frank yawned, "before we start, I am arresting you on suspicion of, well, murder and attempted murder. You do not have to say anything. But if you do, Sam, what you say may be taken down and used in court, in evidence against you."

"Are you sure you've got that bit right? That's not how it usually sounds on television."

"But you know what I mean? Have you anything to say?"

"Yes, son, plenty." Sammy wiped his beak-like nose with his snow white hankie, his way of signifying emotion.

"For a start, are you kidding about arresting me? Which of us has the filleting knife? I used to use it on fishing trips, and now I don't like to be without it. And I don't particularly like your tone of voice, Frank, to be honest. I thought we were pals. Now you're coming the big time cop on me. You'd think you had something against me. And how are you going to remember what I say? And who will believe you?"

"No hard feelings, Sammy, it's just that, with all these people coming to sticky ends, well, I consider it kind of my job to sort it all out."

"Isn't it outwith your jurisdiction, as they say? If the Polizia, don't mind, why should you?"

"Apart from anything else, Mr. Plaister, I can't help being curious as to how you worked everything out. I take it the incidents had to look accidental, for the Tontine."

"Natural deaths or accidental deaths are a prerequisite of a Tontine agreement. I wonder if Melly will decide to gift me his share. Listen Frank, would you do me a favour, my boy? Get me my portfolio of posters out from under the bed. I'll dispose of them myself, now Melly's in the hospital. I was just leaving after identifying Emilia's poor body, when I saw him being bundled onto a trolley. They'd advised me of the car crash when I landed at Glasgow Airport. Did you hear if the car's a write off? I kept telling her she should check the brakes. But she'd got so absent-minded of late. Will the old chap recover? Hurry and get the portfolio out."

"Thanks, son! Sit down in the chair, will you? I'm going to have to tie you up. I must have a wee rest myself. You've gone a kind of funny colour, Frank. Don't worry! Relax!"

But the detective couldn't relax. As he scrabbled under the bed for the portfolio, his hands had brushed against Melville's high-tech mobile phone, which Emilia, in contempt, had kicked under the bed. He pressed a button or two, relying on touch, without daring to look at the dial. He hoped he'd switched it to Record. He shoved the phone under the lace of the pillow. He had to leave it there, as Sam Plaister climbed up to recline on the bed, his beaky head on the pillow, the glittering knife in his hand.

"I never would have believed it of you, Sammy! You seemed such a nice guy!"

"Yes, that was the beauty of it, Frankie! But, really, if you knew the full story, I'm not such a terrible villain as all that! "

"I'd give a lot to know your side of it, Sammy. And you'd be in no danger. Without any corroboration, in Scots Law, my evidence would be inadmissible."

"It would be corroborated if you were wearing a wire! You're up to something funny!"

"Do I look as if I was wearing a wire? It would spoil the line of my threads!"

"Okay, then! Strip down to your boxers, and prove it!"

"If you insist, but the trouble is, I'm not actually wearing boxers!"

Plaister simply gestured with the tip of his knife for Frank to get started. He watched him undress with a connoisseur's eye. He certainly was a fit young man, he thought, taking in the defined muscles of his lean, tanned, torso. "Hurry up!" he growled hoarsely, expecting total nudity. Then, "What on earth are those?" he said. "What is the police force coming to?"

"These are the latest! They're Bjorn Borg Fun Stretch Cotton Trunks!" Frank explained.

Grinning, Sammy Plaister had to admit Frank was not wearing a wire under the revealing stretchy long leg shorts. He began to talk about his exploits, enjoying the audience, waving the filleting knife around in the air, to make points. "By the way Frankie, you haven't seen a post card round the place? A post card from Garda? You haven't got it on your person I see."

"I can't understand," Frank tried to distract him, "why you pushed Lady Georgie into the lake."

"Of course I didn't push her. I pushed my old friend Pascal. He bumped into Roxanne. She bashed into Lady Georgie. Georgie was supposed to shove Lord Donald into the water, trying to save herself. Instead she saved Lord Donnie. Much good it did her. He came a proper cropper in the end, didn't he, Frankie boy? And no-one can link me to that. He'd run out of luck. He nearly killed himself in the library, trying to grab the Tontine agreement. Mother Agnes saved him then. Come to think of it, I owe her one for that. She can be somewhat annoying, that big lady! Don't you think, Frank? Unless, of course, you like her. Did she play the pander to you and the pretty nun? Did she get a kick out of it, herself? I must admit I was shocked when I saw what you were up to!"

Frank bit his lip, then asked, "But Dolores, did you ask her to finish off Professor Donald?"

Plaister took his time answering, as if anxious to tell the exact truth.

"I don't believe I ever did, exactly. But she saw the way the wind was blowing."

A smile of satisfaction playing round his lips, Plaister turned over, stretching himself out, and re-arranging the frilly pillows. Frank's heart nearly stopped beating. But Sammy turned back again, without the phone having been dislodged from its hiding place under the pillow.

"You're not sorry for our Donnie, are you? One of his deals went wrong, and he decided to make money by selling the Sally Gardens for modern flats. I couldn't have that. And the others in the Tontine would have agreed with him. They would have sold their shares to him, when we reached the Tontine date when all bets were off."

"And that's why you did in Guy Everard, Sammy? He was for selling?"

"Not only that. The man was a cad! He was after Dolores, like everybody else, including you."

Frank blushed right down to his Bjorn Borgs. So everybody knew about his affair.

"Guy was absolutely vile to Pascal, when Roxanne was making fun of him. He didn't stick up for him at all. And he wouldn't let Donnie go after him, either, when poor old Pascal ran off in the huff. If I hadn't been distracted, playing sandcastles with Lena, I'd have gone after him myself, probably."

"I heard you deliberately turned away. And that Dolores was the only one buried in sand."

"Well, it's not exactly a crime turning your head away, is it, when an old fool rushes off to do something he'll regret. By the way, don't worry about your phone, I've got it safe and sound. Talking of old fools, Frank, did you see Melly in his dressing up clothes? I never heard how that worked out. Emilia was phoning me about it, just before her crash, poor dear."

"Yes, I did see him, as it happened. He did look funny, but somehow I didn't feel much like laughing! How could you, Sammy? After all he's done for you?"

"But, my dear, I did nothing! I was just having a laugh with Emilia about the old days, the Fancy Dress balls in Limone. She just went a bit too far."

"I see what you mean, but what about Everard? It's not a capital offence, being a prick!"

"He treated Roxanne very badly too. He came on to her at the Lido, crudely, in front of everybody, so as to humiliate her. Then he told her he preferred Dolores, and told her to get lost. I was just arranging to have him float out to sea on the lilo, when Roxanne came back and nearly spoiled everything. She whipped his trousers and shorts off for a joke. Debagging, we used to call it at Cambridge. If he'd wakened up, I'm not sure that Roxanne, the poor tart, wouldn't have made it up with him again. If he'd wakened up. But after all the wine he'd had, he never bloody wakened up." Here Plaister couldn't contain his sniggers. "Okay, okay! He got a slight crick in his neck too, when he hit it against my fist." Sammy held out a powerful hand for Frank to admire. "Did you know I was into Karate? Maybe I'm not such a wimp after all!"

"But what about Pascal? I thought you two were buddies from way back! You must have known how vulnerable he was."

"You don't blame me for Pascal's aneurism? Really! How unfair! If he hadn't got himself all worked up, lusting after those Dutch boys, he might have lived to fight another day!"

"Would you let me get into bed with you, Sammy? I'm getting stiff and cold sitting here. You could warm me up!"

"Another time, Frankie. You see I am a bit of a fool, I agree, but I'm not a complete bloody nincompoop. I'm rather tired, too. And I don't feel too well. And I know you're only into women."

"Sorry, Sammy! No offence!"

"And none taken, my boy. And I've read your texts. The cops will not be coming, I'm afraid, or rather, I'm not afraid! I must just have a little nap."

Sammy collapsed into a deep sleep. Not dreamless, though. He dreamed someone was playing with him. Playing at Cowboys and Indians. He groaned aloud in his sleep, in delight. He was the Indian, and the Cowboy was tying him up with strong sure hands. Sammy Plaister moaned on an ascending scale, and was disappointed to be wakened up by ten uniformed policemen crowding round the bed, jostling to hold him down.

Maybe disappointed is the wrong word. The circumstances of his arrest would serve Sam Plaister as material for sexual fantasies for the long years of his later imprisonment.

Frank had made a better job of tying him up, than Sam had, in his amateurish way, made of tying up Frank. Emilia, with her Girl Guide experience, had done much better on poor Melly. And Frank had a recording of the whole interview with Sam Plaister. The only thing that Detective Inspector Childers hadn't quite managed to do, was to get back into his trousers, when the cops he summoned from Mirkshields Police Station finally arrived in full force, to try and take the credit.

This they might well have done, if the one missing element of a conviction had not been missing. The small, battered, highly coloured postcard from Garda.

"Detective Inspector, is there a reason for your state of undress?" Frank's boss, Doubleday, asked. "And the suspect here, whom you've arrested, and tied up with pulley rope, any evidence?"

"Just this recording taken from a mobile phone in which he admits to several charges."

"Dare I ask? Apart from that, anything else?"

"Well, I have a postcard from Garda in which he shows knowledge of the death of Guy Everard two days before the body was found. As per post mark. At least I had the card, but I can easily get it back, I'm sure."

Frank didn't get it back easily. Peppy denied all knowledge of the letter he had posted containing the card. Neither of them could think what had happened to it. Till Tamara Tainsh turned up, having gone to get her baby. She handed the baby to Peppy, and flung down the card on the kitchen table in front of them.

"Not worth a bean!" she said contemptuously, "I went to the Fence's to get it valued for you," she said to Peppy, blushing only slightly. "Pure rubbish, he said it was. Not antique at all, just digitally reprinted. Still if you like it, Sister Peppy, I suppose you'd better keep it!"

"Sorry, Frank!" said Peppy, handing the card back to him, "Would you like a wee cup of tea?"

19

Above Garda

"But who was Stanislaus Pasternak, again?" Sister Mary of the Angels wanted to know.

Angel sat at a window seat looking out at the cloud forms over Garda. She had all at once lost her fear of flying.

"He never existed, Angel! Haven't I explained often enough?"

"Sorry, Mother Agnes! I just don't have your kind of analytical mind. I could never do crossword puzzles either, you know. Pasternak?"

"A red herring. He was one and the same person as Sam Plaister. Who was given a share in the Tontine by poor old Pascal, his former lover."

"And the others in the Tontine." Angel counted on her fingers. "Professor Donald, Guy Everard, the poet Pascal Stone. All dead. Have I missed anybody?"

"Binky Boyne. Accidentally drowned in a tub of lethal herbal bath water, conveniently."

"Still one missing, Agnes."

"And Plaister himself, as Pasternak."

"Gotcha! No, there should be another one."

"That's Melville Whitbread, the poetry critic. The one who lives next door to Peppy."

"Right! He'll be Last Man Standing, and inherit the Sally Gardens."

"If you could call him that, considering he's been bedridden for the last twenty years, poor soul!" Agnes muttered, clutching her rosary beads.

The plane from Bergamo flattened its flight path over fabulous Lake Garda, before gathering itself to ascend to the cloud domains. Angel watched, amazed, as the peaks and valleys of cumulus stratus imitated the mountain ranges below. She peered down over the wing as the hidden steep slopes and valleys of the lake were glimpsed in colour coded changes from pearly aquamarine to deepest jade green and peacock blue. Old Benaco (the ancient liege lord of the lake and all the treasures therein) ruefully gave up a few of his secrets to curious sky travellers that day.

The ashes of Pascal Stone had been accepted into the bosom of Lady Garda just the day before, when Pascal's body had been released by the Polizia for burial. Jackie had insisted on cremation. That's what Pascal had wanted, he said, and he'd mentioned many times that he wished his ashes to be scattered over the lovely lake of Garda.

As for Guy Everard's bloated corpse, caught in a fishermen's net and hooked out after three days below water, an ex-wife had turned up to claim it for herself. Hysterical, and looking for scapegoats, she had joined with Detective Frank Childers in insisting that the death be considered as suspicious. The other ladies who had vied for Guy's stinted affections, even Roxanne, now considered she was welcome to it.

Dame Georgie had arranged to have Donald's large body flown home in a specially constructed huge lead lined coffin, in a freight transport plane, draped with the flags and emblems due to a Professor, property speculator, and benefactor to his native city of Glasgow and his adopted county of Inverclyde. She still blamed herself for letting him out of her sight, stupid big galoot that he was.

Dolores Kant seemed to have disappeared into thin air, in spite of all Roxanne Renton's efforts to trace her. The Milan detectives held as evidence one of a pair of crimson Jimmy Choos to support the charge of maliciously causing Donald Donald to tumble down the stone steps of the Arena, although it might just as easily have backed her defence. The spiky heel was horribly injured, nearly broken in two, and it was scraped and scuffed where it had grazed a sharp ancient slab as she had fallen up the stairs. She might have broken and scuffed it in an unsuccessful attempt to save Donald Donald. Roxanne was sure she had, and poor Dame Georgie was equally sure she hadn't, that Dolores had tripped and kicked him.

Dame Georgie had reluctantly agreed, though, that Donnie had regularly fallen downstairs because of his sight impairment, ever since he was a silly little plump lad in Primary School, and tiny Georgie his only playground friend.

Georgie's tears had been enough to persuade the lady police officer to release Donnie's body to her, after taking a sole print of the shoe, and DNA from blood splashes on the toe. There was no suspicion of Sam Plaister's involvement. If Sammy himself had not suggested his complicity to Frank Childers, the Arena di Verona would have kept one more bloody secret.

Sam's murder of Guy Everard came down to the postcard from Garda for authentication. The fact, uncovered by Mother Agnes, that Plaister had written a card showing knowledge of Guy's death before the body had been discovered.

There was also Sam's taped and cynically Rabelaisian confession by voice message. The cops were shocked by that, and Roxanne had not backed up his allegations as to Guy's behaviour. The Italian pathologist had discovered an injury to Guy's cervical vertebrae, probably caused by a blow. So Guy had not simply been floated out onto the lake on his lilo. Roxanne, the only other suspect, had such tiny plump hands, and all her pearl pointed fingernails were intact, that she could not have administered the blow. Detective Superintendent Doubleday had agreed as pretty Roxanne held out her dainty fleshy fists for his inspection.

Mother Agnes, having requested an interview, had asked the Italian lady police officer on the cases if it was not unusual that one group should have suffered three such fatalities.

"Do not distress yourself, Mother Agnes!" she had answered, cool in her spotless beige uniform, a pistol slung at her slim waist. "If the old gentlefolk had not deceased this summer, then perhaps decease next. What matter?"

"I'm sure it mattered to the deceased gentlefolk!" Agnes had said. "And Guy Everard wasn't so old. You couldn't tell after three days in the lake."

At least Melville Whitbread had survived, Agnes thought, rescued just in time by Frank, from a death by slow strangulation. She and Angel had been the last to leave Italy, Angel having had to hang around in Rome to be officially released from her vows. So her pregnancy was now a month further advanced and confirmed in other ways than by the first scary test (amazingly, if not scandalously close to the first morning Angel had tumbled out of the little narrow bed, in the attic in Verona).

But Angel had not yet started to experience morning sickness. She was unrealistically euphoric, Agnes thought. (Agnes who had had some experience of midwifery in her Dublin hospital as a young nurse, before taking a different kind of veil). Angel was always wondering aloud about why women made such a meal of morning sickness.

Lena Wallace had flown back soon after Sammy had sneaked aboard a flight for Glasgow, ahead of the pursuing authorities. She still felt grateful to Sammy, for all he had done for her, for her baby Joel in particular. She had even asked if she might bring little Joel to see him in Barlinnie. She was pleased that Sam had already started a major work, 'The Ballad of Bar El', in the style of Oscar Wilde. She hoped it would see him through the years ahead till he could get parole.

Mother Agnes was sitting next to Angel, in club class, with plenty of room around them. Their airline had been most accommodating getting the package trip party home after the tragic events. The members of the holiday trip had been booked in separately for the return journey, depending on when the Polizia wanted to interview them. The lawyers had been sent home with a rugby team group doing a stag week, and had been so unaffected by the events as to join in the bawdy songs as their aircraft cleared the peaks round Garda.

Agnes had some cobwebby white knitting in her hands, with which she was embarrassing Angel (now Angela Childers, but always Angel to her and to Frank). She had been laboriously trying to explain all the criminal activities that had been going on all around her while the young woman had been wrapped up in her own feelings and her unlooked-for romance, and her still-more-unlooked-for pregnancy.

"But did Professor Donald Donald fall, or was he pushed?" Angel asked crudely.

"Let's give Dolores the benefit of the doubt. She led the man into a dangerous situation. Dangerous for Donnie, that is, because of his vertigo and his monocularism, which changed his perception of depths. She was then unable to save him. Or did not save him, even if, as it might be, she did not actually trip him up. Maybe she was just the ultimate silly bitch."

"But why should we give her the benefit of the doubt?"

"Because we all need the benefit of the doubt sometimes, Angel. Maybe even you!"

Agnes took a minute to count her stitches. "Certainly myself!" she declared.

"I can't see that, Mother Agnes. How do you work that out?"

" 'If each of us got his deserts, which of us would 'scape whipping?' Shakespeare asked."

"Then you'll never be whipped! Everyone knows you're a saint. A very annoying saint!"

"But I whip myself, if no-one else will! You don't know, Angel, you don't know!"

"Is that why you went to confession on Limone? To the priest who spoke no English?"

"It turned out his second degree was from Edinburgh, and I kept my worst sin to myself."

Angel turned towards her companion, puzzled, her eyes still flooded with the skies she had been watching, and her own happy reflections. "I suppose you could try telling me, Mother Agnes, and I could try not telling anyone later, not even Peppy."

"I'm as likely to swim the length of Lake Garda as you to keep a secret from Peppy!"

"No, but really, Mother Agnes, cross my heart and hope to die!" Angel spat on her finger and crossed her heart, over her new blue striped summer dress.

"Oh, Angel, you'd think you'd be ashamed, making such a great oath, forbidden by the teachings of our Holy Mother Church, not that you'll have to bother so much now!"

"Well, the thing is, Sister Angel, since you force me to tell you, in a nutshell, the fact is, I think I killed a man. A man I loved, and to whom I wouldn't give the benefit of the doubt!"

"A crime of passion, Mother, I'm sure no jury would convict." said Angel, shocked.

"No jury got the chance, thanks to your boyfriend, Frank. He covered up for me. But he knew the truth fine well. It hasn't preyed on his mind."

Mother Agnes turned her head to the window, but her view, screened by a shade, was merely a reflection of her own troubled face.

Angel, who all the time, had been expecting some minor crisis of conscience, or even a satisfactory explanation for some serious sin, sat aghast. Then she reached over to put her arms round the older woman's neck.

"At least there's no death penalty now, Agnes!" she whispered quite seriously. "That would have been awful. Frank and I will always love you, anyway. You should try giving yourself the benefit of the doubt. How do you know what happened? He might well have died anyway. It might not have been you who finished him off!"

"But you don't understand, Angel. I still want it to have been me who finished him off. I would do it again today! Part of me still delights in it! And that is the reason none of my Confessions are valid, I made none with a sincere purpose of amendment. And every single time I take Holy Communion, I commit the gravest sin, the sin of sacrilege!"

"Well, all I can say, Agnes, is that I, too, might have killed anyone who hurt you or Frank! And if anyone ever laid a finger on Thingy, when it's born, I would kill them in the most horrible way I could think of. I would have to get a weapon, maybe a poker or a saw-tooth dagger. I wonder which one would hurt more? I would choose the one that would hurt more. Would you send me to the electric chair for that, Mother Agnes, if we had one? Or force me to do penance my whole life long, and never to give in to any happiness? If it was me?"

"If it was you, Angel, no!"

"So are you better than me, that you can't forgive yourself?"

"No, not exactly, no, of course not. It's just that ..."

"It's just that you are an idiot. You can't believe everything your conscience tells you. Be strict with your conscience. I am with mine, Mother Agnes, you may have noticed. And who was it secretly gave me the go ahead to you know what with Frankie? Admit it!"

Agnes blushed rosy red. "I don't know how you can say that, Angel, all I did was present you with the facts and lay your options before you."

"And another thing, Mother Agnes, if you don't stop this conscience nonsense, I won't let you be Godmother to little Thingy, and I won't call her Agnes after you. As a matter of fact, I don't much like the name Agnes, so would Oonagh be alright, the Irish version?"

"And if Thingy is a boy?"

"I'm going to call him Romeo, after Romeo Beckham, and to remind me of Verona!"

"So you should call little girl Thingy Juliet!"

"Brilliant idea! Oonagh Juliet? Juliet Oonagh? Which do you think?"

After that, Mother Agnes gave up her knitting and packed it away. The rest of the flight she prayed for the souls of the departed, the wicked perpetrators themselves done down, and innocent or wicked victims cut off in the pure flower, or the rank weed of their lives. Kaddish, she had heard Jewish people called prayers for the dead. She thought the church should try more of their ways. She wondered if a Rabbi would hear her Confession. It wasn't likely. But she had taken the first step then, in educating her troublesome conscience. Angel saw that as they were coming in for landing, struggling with seat belts.

"Now you're alright, Agnes", she said. "I myself will give you absolution. *Ego to absolvo!* That feels better, doesn't it? You'll be alright if we crash land. Straight in the pearly gates!"

Mother Agnes, though, didn't laugh, as she stood, seatbelt still unfastened, as the warning lights came on, towering over the young woman.

The smile faded from Angel's face.

"Never say anything like that again! Do you hear me, Angel?"

"Yes, Mother Agnes!" Angel bit her lip. "I didn't mean ... I was only..."

Agnes sat down and got the seat belt to fasten round her bulk.

"My crisis of conscience is no laughing matter, my dear. But it's my fault, anyway ... Don't cry! I should never have burdened you with the knowledge of my crime, young and foolish and headstrong as you are. And you must never ever reveal to Frank that you know the truth. Even he does not know the exact depth of my villainy!"

"Oh Mother Agnes, I ... I'm afraid I'm going to be horribly sick!"

"Holy saints in heaven, Child! Take this paper bag. That's what it's for! Sure you've chosen a fine time to find out the hazards of pregnancy!"

"You mean morning sickness? But it can't be! I don't believe in morning sickness!"

"Really? All finished now? Well, perhaps it is only air sickness. Let me wipe your face. Well, I suppose later on you could try not believing in labour pains."

20

Thin Air

Dolores Kant had disappeared into thin air, or into the luxurious moist air that floated over the Garda resorts, one night. Roxanne and Aldo had been as good as their words, and searched all the glamorous bars and bistros that Dolores would be likely to favour.

Or else her friends were just unlucky, or too absorbed in themselves. Perhaps just not paying enough attention to what was under their noses. They might well have struck lucky the very first night of their search, when, on an impulse they had got the ferry to Limone, and sat down at a cafe overlooking the lake, whose scarlet awnings looked like red sails. Aldo could vouch for it being one of Dolores's favourite places. He ordered two Camparis, for old times' sake. Dolores had held the pink liquor up to the brilliant red reflected light. It was the first time, Aldo recalled, that Dolores had admitted she was mad about him.

Sensing his melancholy thoughts, Roxanne stretched across the pink linen cloth and took his long brown hand in her pale plump paw. Aldo squeezed it and stared into her eyes, only to be interrupted as the *cammariere* whisked away their supper dishes and loaded them on the dumb waiter, lowering them into the basement kitchens.

If, instead of resenting the diversion, the couple had followed the dishes downstairs, they would have been incredibly lucky. They would have found the needle in the haystack that the Milan Polizia could not.

Because Dolores, fleeing on bare feet from the Arena in blind panic, had, as she calmed down, reflected that she had better go on fleeing. She had used lots of her cash hiring a surly cab driver to take her to the nearest ferry port.

After that, she criss-crossed the lake all day long, never getting off the ferry boat, in fact falling asleep on out of the way hard varnished benches now and then. The hoarse cries of the boatmen as they announced landing places mingled with her dreams delightfully. Finally she came wide awake as they approached Limone, her favourite resort.

By that time, Dolores was ravenous. She who boasted about never having a proper appetite. Who survived on a delicately planned diet high in protein and low in fat and carbs. But starvation was different. She began to crave food, to look enviously at passing children eating ice creams as they ran about. Aromas of roasting meat led her to the Limone hillside bistro that she favoured, and she swung elegantly through its bead-curtained door.

Waiters, recognising her, rushed to serve her, advising her about the specials on the menu. She effected an amazing job of repairing the damages to her appearance that her long lake voyages had cost, making the most of the facilities of the damask-curtained gleaming ladies' room, with its pink linen towels. She pinned her hair severely up in her everyday style, and sprayed it with the glossy lacquer the bistro laid on for lady customers. Then she scooshed herself with their perfumes, redoing her make-up from her small make-up bag. Luckily for her, the crushed velvet opera-going dress she wore hardly looked more crushed.

She ordered a feast with her usual discrimination, appreciated by the maître d'hôtel. She even asked to see the chef to congratulate him on his cuisine and thank him. Then she emptied all the money she had, in Euros, one traveller's cheque and pound coins onto the pink cloth, and divided the hoard (which would have been totally inadequate in settling her bill) among the staff. Then she explained to the chef, in whose eye she had caught a gleam of appreciation, that she had no remaining funds available.

The chef, a corpulent man, but with delicate sensibilities, led her discreetly below stairs to his domain, and handed her a long pristine white apron and a pair of household gloves. Dolores, without turning a newly arranged hair, got stuck into the piles of greasy dishes steeping in the sink. Rinsing them off, she disposed them in the huge dishwasher with such efficiency that the domestics brought the waiters in to watch through the doorway.

And it was at this point that Roxanne might have caught up with her pal and delivered her over to the authorities, had she not chosen to hustle Aldo out the door.

When the dishes were washed and stacked, and most of the clients gone from upstairs, Dolores removed the apron and gloves, and stood stoically waiting to see what other humiliations would be wreaked on her by the owner, should the chef summon him. But the chef himself turned out to be the owner, and not only of that bistro, but of several around the lakes. And he had an eye for a beautiful woman, should one cross his path. He sat Dolores down at the scrubbed kitchen table with a coffee and a Cointreau. Kissing her well-manicured hand, he made her a proposition she couldn't refuse.

"And they say the age of chivalry is dead!" Dolores muttered, settling down for the night on the waterbed in the Hotel du Lac, where her new lover had ensconced her. Now she just had to wait till everyone had forgotten her.

One person, though, had not forgotten about Dolores. Detective Frank Childers was morally certain she had deliberately catapulted Professor Donald to his death. It seemed however, extremely unlikely that anything would ever be proved. But Frank began to have suspicions about the death of Bryn K. Boyne.

The cleaners at the Sally Gardens were so slovenly that there were still traces of the bathwater left in the big tub (since no-one had fancied bathing there again). There were even traces of the little bouquets, dried up and gone to seed. Frank had arranged to have all the slime and grit and dust analysed. The reports showed high levels of chemical toxicity.

Binkie's big body had been cremated with the utmost speed. So Frank's suspicions were merely conjectures based on the tales of the strange indigo colour of the corpse that had been manhandled out of the club at dead of night. Even Frank had to give up, eventually, trying to pin anything on Dolores.

Dolores certainly had always had a way with herbs and flowers, growing cottage garden style in the mossy plot of ground at the back of the clubhouse of the Ancient Society of Scriveners and Limners – that is, Sally Gardens – club. She always had a way of making displays with wild flowers and weeds. Hollyhocks, black bryony, Solomon's seal, and other plants known for their medicinal properties. She had been much admired for the arrangements she made for the Sally Gardens, even strange, small but powerful ones for the bathrooms. Dolores smiled her secret smile, breathing in the thin scented air that rose at dawn from the lake below. As she toyed with her long glossy hair and stared out over Lake Garda in the mornings, from her hotel room balcony. A half smile that had in the past had alarmed all three of her former husbands.

And back in the Sally Gardens, spores and microbes and bacteria were fulminating behind plasterboard alcoves and locked doors that no-one could bear to open. And deep down, way below the cracking foundations, seams of coal were exploding in underground streams. Meanwhile the surviving members of the trip to Garda scanned the pin-holed notice boards to see if there was anything good on that week that looked like fun.

21

Declining And Falling

It turned out that Melville Whitbread, of all the people who didn't need it, fell heir to the Sally Gardens club house, the stylish premises of the Ancient Society of Scriveners and Limners. He neither needed it nor wanted it, having the title deeds of other, better, properties secure in his safe, built into the space above his two bed recesses in his period flat. And Melville was nobody's fool. He knew the property had had little attention over the years, so the first thing he did (when he had recovered from the bruises and distress caused by the crazy Emilia Plaister-Pierce) was to call in his surveyor to give it the once over with his harsh beady eye. The surveyor had gone about ripping chipboard false walls away, and crashing through attic floors on purpose, while the bemused club members were still having birthday parties and poetry readings in the dusty premises.

Samuel Plaister had done the sensible thing and held his hands up, when he discovered that, notwithstanding his extreme precautions, his confessions had been recorded on Melly's state-of-the-art mobile phone, so casually kicked under the bed by the deranged Emilia. He had even managed a sarcastic smirk, as he held out his hands to be handcuffed by one of the eleven officers who had answered Frank's summons to Crimea Pass. He couldn't help being amused by the fact that Mirkshields Police Station thought it required so many of their finest to arrest a frail chap with prostate trouble. Especially since the aforementioned chap was already effectively enough bound and tied to Melville Whitbread's recessed bed. It had been his declining health, he explained later, to a jury of his peers, when he had sacked his counsel and decided to go it alone, that had made him embark on his criminal crusade to retain the Sally Gardens. Sammy enjoyed his last shaft of limelight. It was like giving a poetry reading, only better, and he had picked up a lot of pseudo-legal jargon.

The Sally Gardens wasn't such a windfall as Sammy had imagined. The sharp-nosed surveyor pronounced that in the next strong wind it might fall down on its own, saving the cost of demolition. It became obvious why the vacant feus the original builder had snapped up, had remained vacant. It was discovered a maverick seam rich in coal ran right across them. Professor Sir Donald Donald, maligned, misunderstood, and largely un-mourned, had in fact been quite justified in his master plan. His ultimately charitable plan had been to do away with the historical building, lovely but shoogly as an old Beauty in the last throes of delirium tremens. He had then intended to sell the vacant plots to a consortium with the clout to get the gardens excavated and concreted over to some depths, to render the old coal workings stable. (This in particular was what his wife Lady Georgie had objected to. She adored the gardens of the club house, and the wildlife that eked out an existence there, in the heart of town). With the cash from that, he had meant to rebuild the club, with as much period detail as was feasible. (Dame Georgie had hated this idea too. She had got above herself, and forgotten she had Donald's cash to thank for buying her an Honour, when her musical career had declined. She took the side of the artists and poets, who actually liked dust and decay.)

The building had been declared unsafe, and to avoid a compulsory purchase order Melville Whitbread sold it to the very consortium previously organised by the erstwhile trustee, Professor Sir Donald MacDonald Donald of that Ilk.

The dismemberment and evisceration of the body of the old building took a tortuously long time, as it lay in the centre of a built up area. Blokes in hard-hats practically lived in the portakabins there, feeding the feral cats that still scampered round the overgrown gardens.

So Melville Whitbread finally got his hands on all the contents of the Ancient Society of Scriveners and Limners premises. You could say he had devoted a large part of his career as a fence to clearing out the excess of works of art and objects of virtue which had at one time cluttered up the club, and threatened to overflow the store rooms, causing fire hazards. He had always been fair in the prices he had given for the stray artworks which had been lying around tarnished and untended, more or less doing nothing, destined to be purloined from time to time by hard-up club members. And he had always found the figurines, the bronze busts and the ornate fitments good homes, never selling them to be cast into a 'Lump' of metal in some shady shop. The jewellery shop in Crimea Pass, too, although not averse to receiving stolen goods, also went out of their way to sell on to respectable traders or to give a good bargain to lovers of fine things.

But even Melly's entrepreneurial instincts and organisational abilities had deserted him when he was confronted with the embarrassment of riches contained in the Sally Gardens. One day he had sprung from his bed and dressed in his best checked tweed suit (a little too large for his diminishing frame). He had summoned Jimmy, the mechanic from down the lane. Jimmy had given his white van a good clean with a power hose, and, himself showered and in clean overalls, had reported for chauffeur duty. Melly had determined to find out the worst for himself, before he was a day older and more decrepit.

Melville had steeled himself for what he might find. Still, the reality came as a shock. All the pieces were of such a high standard, it would be a crime to shove them into an undifferentiated auction sale. They should be catalogued for specialist sales. He would have to take on staff, but whom could he trust? He had asked Frank, but Frank was loath to leave his steady job, now he was married. Frank suggested Lena Wallace, which turned out to be a great idea. It took her mind off the loss of her lover Sammy, and her guilt at dumping him for her new boyfriend Enzio (divorced but not yet separated from his wife).

Dame Georgie Donald felt guilty too, for all the nasty things she had said to Donnie that awful day at Bergamo airport. She had still been screaming at him in passport control there, when Dolores Kant had come rushing up, and made an impassioned plea for him to stay on with her. Who had she been kidding? (Well, Donnie, obviously.) Georgie reckoned though, he was probably going through the male menopause, and she should have understood. Then he had plummeted to his death down those death-trap stairs at the Arena. Dolores had not understood what a big baby Donnie was. How much help he always required from her, even just to get up and down stairs, with his funny eyesight. Or maybe she did!

Frank Childers, even yet, maintained his suspicions about Dolores having tripped up Professor Donald on purpose. But yet he began to wonder if his eyes, blinded by the pyrotechnics of Norma being immolated on stage, had not deceived him into thinking Dolores was guilty.

Melville Whitbread came back one day, when all the mountains of paintings and drawings and lithographs and statuary and bibelots had been cleared away, by an army of beige-coated workmen, strong and knowledgeable, of whom Lena Wallace was the stern but fair General. Lena was the only person, apart from Melly himself, who was prepared to forgive Sammy for his multiple murders. She had offered to take Melly to Barlinnie prison in Glasgow, where Plaister was housed, in order to cheer him up. Melville wasn't quite sure about that. He wondered if Sammy would ever forgive him for the way things had turned out. When he hadn't managed to conceal the incriminating postcard Sammy had sent to him from Garda. And also the fact that the art posters had been deemed to be still the property of the Sally Gardens, and henceforward owned by Melville, along with everything else of value.

While Lena, in fluorescent overalls, was supervising the packaging of several bits of masonry salvaged from the clubhouse, and due to be incorporated in the new building, Jim the mechanic helped Melly round, after placing a cashmere overcoat carefully round his boss's shoulders, since the weather had turned wintry again. The old man pointed his swan-headed stick at various forgotten pieces still lurking in corners, and Jim retrieved them.

The roof was still being dismantled, as carefully as possible. The slates were being saved and the carved finials to rhone-pipes and chimney heads were being cut out with power drills, to be built into the new

"Empire" flats that were about to go up when the site was cleared. Just as Sammy himself would have done, Lena Wallace comforted herself. He was always such a stickler for detail. And a decent man too, except when it really mattered.

Melville bravely got himself down to the basement in the one lift that still worked in the half-dismantled building. The service lift that the club servants used to employ to get the trolley loads of food upstairs for ceremonial dinners. Jimmy had to help him into it, as it did not stop exactly at the landing sill any more. Lena Wallace had used the lower floors, the basement and sub-basement to stack articles that she thought might have a sentimental value to club members, but as yet only Melville had turned up to look them over. Melville was glad he had, and grateful to Lena for her finer feelings.

The first thing Melville saw when Jimmy had set him on his feet on the cold stone-floored, tile-walled, basement room, was a little rosewood card table. The lid was quartered on the diagonal and opened to a baize topped table which swung aside to reveal a secret, deep, compartment. Melly gasped. The table at which he and Sammy had played bridge all those years ago, with Pascal and whoever had been Pascal's boyfriend at the time. There was a photograph album of a squad of fit guys which it took him a while to realise comprised himself, Pascal and a young Sam, in various resorts on Lake Garda. The rest of the secret drawer was filled with unpublished poems by old poets. Melville's eyes grew dreamy.

"Oh, Jimmy!" Melville looked up at his young helper with brimming eyes. "What happy times we all had! Sammy and I, Pascal and Jackie and the old crowd, before money got so scarce and so many people went into a decline. I wonder if I might visit Sammy in Barlinnie after all. What a brutal place to put him, beside thieves and murderers. I'm sure Sam didn't do half the things they said. Or at least didn't mean to do. Poets have fragile natures."

Melville wiped a tear from his rheumy eye as he paused outside the upright, still intact, front door, with its recessed carved entrance way. He paused for a moment to look up at the façade, now looking like a ruined castle. He meant to come back and scrabble through the remaining stuff in the basements. But as a power drill started to chisel out the remaining stone willow branches encasing a rhone pipe, a corner of the chimney head juddered, rocked and fell down, exploding as it landed just behind the old man's feet. Jim leapt to pull him aside, and Melly collapsed into his arms.

It would be better not to push his luck, he thought, returning to this scary place. And as Jimmy drove him home in the passenger seat of the white van, cosily wrapped in a tartan travel rug, Melville thought again about leaving Jim an inheritance, as he had intended. He would grant him an annuity instead, for the rest of his, Melly's, life. And he might make Sammy Plaister a similar allowance too. To make up for losing the Tontine. There was no point in tempting fate. Inheritances did funny things to people. Especially to poets, who have a different way of looking at things. Their art is everything to them. Their muse comes first. He wondered if Sammy would get parole.

The Glasgow Art Club, just round the corner from the Sally Gardens, offered the dispossessed members of the collapsing club a good deal. They would extend to the artists members of the Scriveners and Limners a similar artist membership there, without having to stand for election, which might have been a bit embarrassing (not every member having retained the standard of merit that had got them elected). The lay members they offered a reduced fee for the first year.

But not many former members of the Sally Gardens took them up on it. They turned up their noses at the club house, because it did not have a garden, the fine gallery there having been built on the garden grounds. And the Glasgow Art Club ethic was more painterly than poetic, although poets had always been welcomed there. But the Scriveners thought the painters ruled the roost at the Glasgow Art Club. And some of the Limners thought those painters were of the kind who stood yards back from the canvas and used long-handled brushes, like Whistler, and that they could never measure up to that even if they tried. Even if they felt like trying.

Two poet members decided to join. Detective Inspector Frank Childers was one. After a swift look round, he had offered to inventory the bronzes, and catalogue the first editions. Angela Childers (Angel as was) joined too, in the hope of being asked to give poetry readings. And Lena Wallace was another new member from the Ancient Scriveners and Limners. She did much better at her new club, as no-one knew what an outsider she had been at the old one, and how shockingly she had been treated by some members there. Some of those insolent members had suffered horribly brutal deaths afterwards, but no-one could blame Lena for that, of course. Even though she had on several occasions made nice little dollies out of wax and paper, and stuck some very decorative hat pins into them when she was feeling upset. So Lena wondered why, then, did she still feel a little bit guilty at what had come to be known as the Tontine murders. She had of course administered a teensy weensy sleeping draught to the noxious Guy Everard, as a little jape, before he fell asleep on his lilo, never to waken up.

As the demolition continued at the Sally Gardens, workmen discovered dry rot in hidden spaces, that had been secretly eating the heart out of the old building. And had always caused that funny smell that no scented candle could mask.

The rubble from the Sally Gardens was used as landfill for the new flats. And occasionally yuppies, tending their tiny plots, would turn up the odd squeezed out tube of burnt umber or flake white, which had pushed its way to the surface. Along with ineradicable dark spotted foxgloves and the black bryony, and the fierce yellow henbane, from the old Sally Gardens. As well as the quixotic multi-coloured wild poppies as immortalised by so many poems in the Hunterian Gallery archive of the august Ancient Society of Scriveners and Limners.

22

Aftermath

Frank Childers couldn't keep his wife Angel away from the Sally Gardens garden grounds. An old wash house still stood leaning against the back brick wall. Because the lean-to shack was in a no-man's-land of disputed ownership, it had escaped demolition. The grass and wild flowers had grown up around it, making it the last relic of the ancient feus. It even had a little willow tree spreading over it, and a rusty iron bench stood outside. A thin little tabby had managed to give birth there and nurse her brood of multi-patterned kittens. Angel, herself hugely pregnant, had got obsessed with the survival of the litter. Especially when the very last of the masons packed up his tool bag to go. He had offered to take the mother cat back on the bus to his home in Drumchapel, but he said he wouldn't risk the kittens there.

So Angel had made Frank, sweating and sneezing, pack the cat and her kittens into a cat travel basket. She waved to the workman as they drove off. The Convent of the Bleeding Heart was the first place she'd thought of taking them. And she still hadn't come up with a better idea. Mother Agnes would look after them, she knew, since Frank had made such a fuss about being allergic to even the nicest of the kittens, the ginger one she particularly liked. Angel felt quite worn out after running around to capture the quick little creature.

Mother Agnes was not quite as pleased to see the kittens as Angel had expected.

"Oh, thanks loads, Angel," she said, putting down her prayer book as Angel waddled unannounced into the parlour. "Just what I needed! As if I hadn't enough silly wee creatures on my hands to look after."

Mother Agnes was feeling the weight of being in virtual charge of the Convent of the Bleeding Heart, since Mother Benigna rarely left her cell these days. She hardly got a minute to say her Office. But she saw Angel's face go a bit wan.

"So a few more won't make any difference!" Agnes said, changing her tune, "Watch that wee ginger devil there! He's working his way out!" and Mother Agnes smiled a little wearily.

But the ginger kitten had already escaped from the basket and made for the door, and Angel dived after him. She gave a sharp scream, and clutched her lower abdomen, as her waters broke, and a flood spread round her. As she crouched in agony on the floor, she began to whimper.

"Jesus, Mary and Joseph, Angel!" shouted Agnes, jumping to her feet, "It looks like you've gone into labour, you silly girl! You'll be after me to lend a hand, I suppose! Now stop that noise! Just breathe slow and shallow from the diaphragm. Slowly! Say a decade or two of the holy Rosary, Angel. Wait now, till I see is the wee head descended, or if we've time to call an ambulance. Now don't you be worrying, Angel. Sure I have plenty of recent experience! With silly wee sheep and donkeys! But I expect you'll be hardly different!"

"Now don't push till I tell you! I said don't push!"

23

Crimea Passes On

The quality of visitors to Crimea Pass became outlandishly superior. So much income was generated by the judicious sale of the Sally Garden heirlooms, and by the sale of most of the garden grounds in such an urban area, that Melville Whitbread indulged in spectacular flourishes of charitable acts.

A stream of religious superiors made the pilgrimage to Gallowgate. A Papal *Nuncio* in glittering white and violet came to bless Peppy and her 'Girls' (largely beneficed by Melville), and they made a pretty chorus line, learning to curtsey nicely for the occasion.

The Head Rabbi came too, disappointingly wearing a hat and coat.

The Moderator of the Church of Scotland came in jabot and knee britches.

The Lord Lieutenant of Glasgow visited in lacier frills and weirder knee britches.

All these, Melville Whitbread entertained in his Single End, like the mythical urban saint he was fast becoming. He retained the custom of dressing formally above the comfortable striped pyjamas he had grown accustomed to. And he sat stoically bolt upright, either in bed, or on his bedside bentwood chair, accepting thanks and congratulations.

"Congratulations for not getting bumped off!" he thought, smiling on only one side of his face.

But when Cardinal McCreish paid an impromptu visit with his secretary and caddy, Tito, during a golfing trip to Scotland, he did not receive a warm welcome. Perhaps Melly thought the Cardinal's plus fours and Fair Isle jersey were in doubtful taste. Or perhaps the cleric's good name had been tarnished by Angel during one of her long chats with Mr. Whitbread, when they scoffed fish and chips, and glugged champagne. In fact, Cardinal McCreish had been barred from entrance by the brawniest of Melly's home helps, and sent on his way with a flea in his ear.

He did not go far, however, just next door to Peppy's flat, which he'd heard about, and been scandalised by. It happened that day that Mother Agnes was visiting, with Angel and dainty little baby Oonagh Giullietta. Peppy was tickling the baby as she lay on the patchwork quilt in the cosy hole in the wall bed recess in the kitchen. The door had been left on the latch as they expected some of Sister Peppy's young ladies to pay a visit later.

At first the Cardinal was struck dumb, but when he recovered the power of speech, he laid into Mother Agnes as if she were responsible for everything, including the existence of baby Oonagh. He especially went on about late returns for VAT and tax. (Admittedly, Mother Agnes had got into rather a muddle about that, since Peppy had left, and Angel was absorbed in looking after the baby.)

"I could have you shut down like that!" McCreish cried, snapping his nicotine stained fingers, "And what's this I see on your website? 'Mother Agnes, Agony Aunt'! And you're not even charging for the service! You're not a bloody charity, you know!"

"But, your Eminence," Sister Peppy reproached him, "We are a bloody charity, registered as the Democratic

Convent of the Bleeding Heart. We get loads of donations."

At this, the Cardinal's secretary, Tito, whipped out a notepad and started making entries.

"Just watch your tongue!" the Cardinal advised, "or I'll have you Sisters out of that fancy gear and into twinsets and pleated skirts. And as for you, Mother Agnes. I'll send your donkeys to the knackers' yard, and throttle your parrots and budgies and ducks. And you, Sister Mary of the Angels, or whatever you call yourself now, get that infant to stop crying or I'll strangle it, too!"

"Have you written all that down, Brother Tito?" the Cardinal asked as he was storming off down the tenement's curving worn down steps, "We'll see what the Holy See has to say!"

Unfortunately for the cleric, at that moment he bumped into Tamara, the prettiest of the young Ladies of the Night that Peppy had made it her mission to help. Since he was leaping down several steps at a time, in temper, he might well have sent Tamara tumbling backwards downstairs, if she had not grabbed on to the Cardinal's Fair Isle jersey. Tito, skipping down after his boss, had been sent sprawling, and he and Tamara and the Cardinal all had to struggle to extricate themselves from each other.

At this unlucky moment, a posse of pressmen exited from Melly Whitbread's flat, just as McCreish was roaring "Get off of me, you tart! Can you not see I am one of God's Holy Anointed?"

Telling the tale later to Melly Whitbread, Tamara pointed out how unfair that was, since the Cardinal had worn only the smallest insignia of his status, a small clerical collar, mostly covered up by his Fair Isle jersey. Repeating her story to the journalists later, Tamara was eager to point out that she would never knowingly have caused embarrassment to a Cardinal, she was always the soul of discretion when dealing with priests.

The cache of precious unpublished poems Melville had found in the rosewood table from the Sally Gardens (which he had brought to his tiny flat) led to him starting 'Crimea Press' in the back premises of the garage below. Jimmy the mechanic had it up and running in a few months.

Wherever there is a new printing press you'll find lots of poets old and new, young and old, trying to get in on the ground floor, where it happened that this press was actually located. The poets offered money and favours to Jimmy to slip them between the covers of his poetic sheets. Jimmy, though, was loyal to Melville, and always consulted him about the poetry and poets on offer. But he did organise poetry readings in the local pub, The Inkerman's Head, for the poets he had been forced for the moment to turn down. The Inky Heid in consequence became very genteel, although even the most willowy poets put on rough working class accents there. And all the poor winos and druggies were forced to go away out London Road to pubs further afield, to cash their giros. They were afraid of losing touch with Sister Peppy. They liked the great wee tea parties she gave in her single end, where they drank loads of elderberry wine and sat on the bed, singing hymns (real hymns, too, from their childhood, not daft hymns some wee nun had made up on her own) and eating bacon rolls. So they had to trudge back in a group along Gallowgate, sometimes nearly getting killed, spilling over into the roadway. They still came running to Peppy if the Dole stopped their benefits for doing a wee obligement, as opposed to a paid job of work.

And Tamara Tainsh and the other little tarts, though embarrassed at always meeting posh people visiting Mr. Whitbread when they wanted to see Sister Peppy in a hurry (maybe wanting to dump their squalling babies on her, so they could get a couple of hours sleep), never stopped coming to appeal to her if their pimps were being pure unreasonable about working hours.

Frank Childers often called in to see Melville. Since he had saved the old man's life, he felt bound to him, in a way. And Melly, in gratitude to him, had offered to publish a slim volume by Sister Mary of the Angels, the nom de plume of Frank's lovely wife, Angela Childers.

The collection is called 'Postcards from Garda', and was based on Sister Mary of the Angel's experiences on her life changing visit to the lake, and is published here by special arrangement with Crimea Press.

24

Poems from Garda

Sister Mary of the Angels
(Angela Childers)

POSTCARDS FROM GARDA 1

It's not the painting that's hard
For the artist arrived on Garda
Although of course you must deconstruct
Postcard vistas to constituent parts
Which I suppose are slivers of light
Finally if you are plucky or lucky
Slotting them together the right way up
In a scheme aesthetically viable
And still identifiable
With the legendary views before you
No, the difficulty on Garda is crowd control
Unless you like Madonna have bodyguards
You're more or less at the mercy of strangers
Being asked how you do it
And where do you get the patience
Then there's the danger that the Spirits of Place
Will rise from the lake and go for your throat
And your paintings will all blow away off the boat
In sudden inclement weather
Or worse still stick together

LIMONE 2

Shy Sly Limone
Prettiest of her sisters
Lies clinging to her hillside
Hiding her greatest treasures
From frazzled prying Turisti
Rooting in boutiques for keepsakes
Taking a turn along promenades
Averting their gazes
From vistas too dazzling
Too burning for sore eyes
Strangers leave the frantic village
Stagger up the romantic hillside
Surprise Limone where she lies
Sighing in her scented groves
Closing her weary blue eyes
On the teeming bay below
Go to the lovely musky chapel
San Rocco the saint of hopeful travel
Blesses us stoically from above
Quaint as the day he was painted
Stay there, Pilgrims
Till the ferries whisk the Stranieri away
Wait comrades till the dusk drops
Over the range of mountain tops
Gaze at the vistas nearly out of sight
Glazed in indigo and violet light
Now Limone will peek out girlishly
In spite of her venerable years
Chic in her evening gear
Nearer and sweeter than ever before

But take care now Pilgrims
Not to stay on too late
Waiting for someone or other
Gazing out over the lake
For suddenly Garda's huge moon rises
And beautiful Limone appears
In her purest of guises
Serious and serene in monochrome
Perfumed in jasmine and oleander
Travellers you might never go home!

Austere among her sisters
Mistress guarding the Garda peninsula
She was not always as prudish
 As good as now she may seem
The rude asymmetry of her ruins
Approached by land
Speaks of a handsome warrior matron
Genutrix of fortifications
Refuge of passionate warrior nations
And poets gone out of fashion
But the siren had soft spots for shady boys
Catullus sent to her to be chastised
Referred to her as his Lady
And rushed from afar to her bed
"Enjoy your Lord!" he said
And see here she is described
"A beautiful woman lying on her side
Offering herself softly to the waves
To be whipped and then caressed
By the divine impudent tide"
Exiled from Rome
At his luxurious home in Sirmione
Catullus wrote uxorious poems to Lesbia
And lines to her wee dead bird
Through the ages poets have conned his pages
And taken him at his word
Even the obscure like me
As well as the infamous and the famous
"Vivamus Lesbia Mea
Atque amemus!"

GARDONE AND HER SISTER   4

Signora Gardone is a sophisticate
Most glamorous of her sisters
We speculate how she was funded
But the money has lasted long enough
To keep her looking great to date
A heart breaker just past her prime
The Belle Époque was her fabulous time
Since most of her assets are intact
She doesn't waste her mornings looking back
Her salons cater for every poetic fad
Her casinos have vistas of mirrors
Like Last Year in Marienbad
The lovely little sister Gardone ignores
Is Isola del Garda right next door
Floating like a mirage just across the lake
Partly manmade ravishingly fake
Secret hidden sometimes veiled in mist
Languishing in her gardens
Waiting to be kissed

MALCESINE

Malcesine warrior maiden
There's no getting over the fact
You're distinctly lacking in tact
Your demure lake sisters know for sure
That you're usually spoiling for a fight
Though your name means "Bosom of Honey"
I'd put my money on you
In any hair pulling night club altercation
And fortification is so your thing
Kings and Princes occasionally enslave you
After all you're almost human
But Nymph you're still your own woman
Arrayed in fancy dress armour
You prowl your castle ramparts
Staring with narrowed eyes far over Garda
Or glaring at the skies summoning thunder
Where bombers came one day
To strafe Malcesine Bay
So okay we hear what you say
Besieged by foes over the centuries
Yanks Austrians Scalligeri and Guelph
But Malcesine darling daring and charming
Why don't you lay down your iron age arms
And try to get over yourself

TOSCOLANO MADERNO

Toscolano and Maderno modest twin sisters
Not identical but unlike most siblings
Getting on so well
Hosting luncheon parties
Telling each other secrets
Talking in pretty whispers
Holding hands over flowery bridges
Martha and Mary of resorts
One sorting artefacts in factories
One minding kids in tiny lidos
Putting up with tourists' snash
Hush! They know what lies below
The chancy waters of Garda
Just where you're standing my friend
On the fine landing stage wine glass in hand
They see the marble ruins of old Benaco
Glittering fathoms down
Drowned by antique earthquakes
Here where the lake meets the town
It would take just a second the Sybil sisters guess
To make a fearful mess - mere ballrooms for fishes
Of all this precious gear and hard won riches

RAINY DAY AT MADERNO

Rainy day at Maderno
Distant views no longer exist
Misty Naiads dally in the shallows
Twitch the chains of craft at anchor
The rain torrents down cobbled lanes
And Iris throws rainbow arches
From Sant'Andrea and back again
Close up we inspect nude statues
Of Art Nouveau reclining muses
Stretch out lunch all day
Then climb to the Convent of Stella Mans
Mid scented verbena and clematis
Drenched and drooping still
As rain slides down the hill
After we dine we sip digestifs
As the mist lifts
We drift round freshly laundered streets
The moon lays out her white sheets line by line
The Sisters said tomorrow would be fine

IN AT THE DEEP END   **8**

The lake is an aquarelle
Dashed in by a master
Nile green to ultramarine
A few specks of unmixed pigment
A figment of the shimmering glare
Or a daring distant swimmer
 Skimming innocent and sweet
Fins of lake fishes brushing his feet
In the deepest of the deep blue
Sweetheart I'm sure it's you
From my shady terrace over the lake
I'm shaking in my shoes for you
In at the deep end as usual

Lovely ports passed by with barely a sigh
Cassone Porta di Brenzone
Then Casteletto then Pai
Siren names cried husky and high
When do we choose to dash off the boat
Leaving companions alone to float
On their own to the next resort?
Riva del Garda San Zeno di Montana
San Felice del Benaco Salo
Called out satiric and low
Why do we choose not to give them a go?
How can we sit still as hills rise to meet us
Send silver showers to greet us
Wait dabbling pale feet in the lake?
The Siren Bays look amazed
Spirits of place turn cold shoulders
Green mountain terrain and black boulders
As we hard heartedly power away
Feigning disdain but wounded I think
Sinking to one rain smudged line
Never to be seen again never to be found
This time around

ABOVE GARDA

They say from future space stations
Seas and lakes will become transparent
Showing traces of ancient civilisations
Drowned cities and submarines
Flying home low over Garda
In peaks of cumulus stratus
Fit playground for Pegasus
Violet and pink and white
As sun on the Dolomites
Cloud valleys slip away
And the lake is revealed instantly
Glistening below a wing
Shown deep as the peaks are lofty
Dense cobalt and antique green
Not frothy surface aquamarine
Not caring for human losses
For storm tossed ships
Or unknowing last kisses
On the lips of star crossed lovers
Two faced old Neptune gives nothing away
Garda's keeping her secrets today
Keeping her sins unconfessed
As clouds congress above her
To cover her traces

"Sangue! Sangue! Guerra! Guerra!"
Is Norma for or against war?
Ice cream vendors cry their wares
As Norma tears her heart out
Invasion fire and flood and desecration
The decline of an Imperial civilisation
So what's new and what's old news?
In the Arena on cold stone pews
As Norma on her pyre ends this vendetta
Tourists are still chewing their bruschetta

OLD POETS

I saw a posy of old poets
Pale complicated and sweet
A Fantin-Latour of fine faces
Open and completely
Unworldly other worldly it's true
What they say about poets
Not like me and you
The old poets were dispatched into taxis
In assorted picturesque batches
Translucent muses on silver wings
Singing indecipherable hymns
Hovered hopefully for a while
Then retired shyly to cloud cover there
High over leafy Beechwood Square
Leaving in the deserted gallery
The scent of Chanel Patchouli and Versace
Cheroots and Sobrani cigarettes
Like the incense of last kisses
Or the Mystics' odour of sanctity
Starburst lilies pressed in dusty books
With hand tinted postcards from Garda

Lightning Source UK Ltd.
Milton Keynes UK
UKOW02f0639140415

249598UK00004B/115/P